Marcia Willett's early life was devoted to the ballet, but her dreams of becoming a ballerina ended when she grew out of the classical proportions then required. She had always loved books, and a family crisis made her take up a new career as a novelist – a decision she has never regretted. She lives in a beautiful and wild part of Devon with her husband, where she loves to be visited by her son and his young family.

For more information on Marcia Willett
and her books, see her website at
www.devonwriters.co.uk/marcia.htm

04371175

Also by Marcia Willett

FORGOTTEN LAUGHTER
A WEEK IN WINTER
WINNING THROUGH
HOLDING ON
LOOKING FORWARD
SECOND TIME AROUND
STARTING OVER
HATTIE'S MILL
THE COURTYARD
THEA'S PARROT
THOSE WHO SERVE
THE DIPPER
THE BIRDCAGE
THE CHILDREN'S HOUR
THE GOLDEN CUP
ECHOES OF THE DANCE

MEMORIES OF THE STORM

MARCIA WILLETT

CORGI BOOKS

TRANSWORLD PUBLISHERS
61–63 Uxbridge Road, London W5 5SA
A Random House Group Company
www.rbooks.co.uk

MEMORIES OF THE STORM
A CORGI BOOK: 9780552155236

First published in Great Britain
in 2007 by Bantam Press
a division of Transworld Publishers
Corgi edition published 2008

Addresses for Random House Group Ltd companies outside the UK
can be found at: www.randomhouse.co.uk
The Random House Group Ltd Reg. No. 954009

The Random House Group Limited supports The Forest Stewardship
Council® (FSC®), the leading international forest-certification organisation.
Our books carrying the FSC label are printed on FSC®-certified paper.
FSC is the only forest-certification scheme supported by the leading
environmental organisations, including Greenpeace. Our
paper procurement policy can be found at
www.randomhouse.co.uk/environment

Typeset in 11½/15½pt New Baskerville by
Kestrel Data, Exeter, Devon.
Printed and bound in Great Britain by Clays Ltd, St Ives plc

To Father Keith and the Sisters at Tymawr

MEMORIES OF THE STORM

PART ONE

PART ONE

CHAPTER ONE

All day she'd been waiting. A gust of wind, lifting the bedroom curtain so that it cracked and billowed like a sail, had shaken her from a troubled sleep just after dawn. The corner of the curtain caught a photograph standing on the rosewood chest and tumbled it to the floor. She struggled up, the ragged fragments of her dream still wheeling in her head like a cloud of bats, and pushed back the quilt murmuring, 'Oh, no. Oh, no,' as if some terrible calamity had taken place. The glass was smashed: one shard remaining, long and jagged and curving upward, which seemed to cut the photograph in two, separating the four figures. Holding it in her hand she stared down at it, frowning in the half-light from the window. She and Edward smiled out with all the strong confidence of youth whilst the two other boys appeared dimmer by comparison, still imprisoned beneath the glass.

On reflection, this image was appropriate. She and Edward, the younger daughter and the eldest of the boys, had formed a natural alliance based on their mutual love of poetry and music that had set them a little apart from the two middle boys, who were athletic, strong and vigorous, and from the oldest of all the siblings: the gentle, domestic, sweet-tempered Patricia. How proud their mother had been of her sons; how disregarding of her two daughters.

Hester tilted the frame, looking for herself in the old, faded photograph. Is that how she'd been in that last summer before the war: chin tilted, with an almost heart-breaking look of fearless expectation? Edward, much taller – cheerful and careless in an open-necked shirt – had his hand on her shoulder. Their cousin and Edward's contemporary, Blaise, must have been behind the camera.

Abruptly she laid the photograph face downwards on the chest. The breaking of the glass had caused some kind of parallel rupture in her memory, cracking open the concealing layers of forgetfulness. She was seized by a sudden, formless panic – as if the break presaged bad luck. That was connected with mirrors, not ordinary glass, she told herself firmly. Yet tremulous anticipation, speeding her heartbeat and sharpening her hearing, pulsed into her fingertips and made her clumsy as she collected together the sharp fragments.

Downstairs, wrapped in her warm, faded shawl, she placed the larger pieces of glass on the draining board and bent down to take the dustpan and brush from the cupboard under the sink. Watched by an enormous, long-haired tortoiseshell cat, disturbed from his slumbers by the Aga, she put the kettle to boil on the hotplate, found a torch and went upstairs again to sweep up the remaining pieces of glass. The torch's beam picked out tiny shining specks scattered across the polished boards and the silky faded rug as, painstakingly on her knees, she swept up each one.

Later, after breakfast, she went out through the French windows and stood on the paved terrace above the river. The shining, tumbling water, shouldering its turbulent way between grassy banks, was silvered and glossed by the sun, which glinted through the naked canopy of the overarching trees. The strong south-westerly wind roistered in the highest branches of the tall beeches, plucking at the few remaining leaves and whirling them down in showers of gold. They floated away downstream, past the open meadowland where sunlight and water fused and dazzled, until they were lost to sight.

Hester rested her hands lightly on the stone wall. There had been heavy rain up on the Chains during the night and the boulders below the terrace were covered by the weight of water flowing down the Barle, but she could see their smooth, rounded shapes. It was here, just here, that Edward had fallen – no wall, back then, to break his headlong crash onto the boulders beneath – and she, held back by the urgent hands of her sister-in-law, had been prevented from trying to reach him.

Along with the vivid memory of the scene – Edward entering unexpectedly through the French doors from the dark rain-swept terrace to see his wife in the arms of his oldest, closest friend – came the familiar sense that something was not quite right. In Hester's mental picture of the drawing-room that evening there was always an unexpected flash of colour, a shape that eluded her but which she knew was out of place: mysterious shadowy corners, golden pools of lamplight spilling across polished wood, bright reflections in the mirror above the fireplace where blue and orange tongues of flame licked hungrily at the wood in the grate. A newspaper, casually flung down, was sliding from the chintz-covered cushions of the long sofa under the window, where damson-coloured damask curtains had been pulled against the wild night, and it was there, from just behind the sofa, that something pale but bright flickered suddenly out into the firelight – and just as suddenly disappeared.

A noise distracted her. Opening her eyes, glancing down, Hester saw a party of mallard being borne rapidly along on the bosom of the river. Quacking enthusiastically, they paddled furiously into the quieter waters beneath the trees and came splashing up the bank and onto the lawn. Hester turned back into the house, picked up the end of a loaf from the table as she passed through the kitchen, and went out across the grass to meet them. She laughed aloud to see their comic waddling as they rolled from one flat splayed foot to the other whilst the females still made their hoarse insistent cry as they approached. She forgot her premonition whilst enjoying the antics of the ducks but, once their daily ration was finished and they'd plunged back into the river, she was immediately prey again to a formless anxiety.

It was almost a relief when she heard the telephone bell as she was finishing an after-lunch cup of coffee. Willing herself to be calm, she recited her number clearly into the mouthpiece and was almost shocked to hear her god-daughter's voice.

Whatever she'd been expecting she hadn't imagined it to have anything to do with Clio.

'Listen, Hes. The weirdest thing. I've met someone here called Jonah Faringdon whose mother stayed with you at Bridge House during the war after her own mother was killed in a raid. She was called Lucy Scott. Mean anything to you?'

Lucy. Little Lucy. Hester took a deep breath.

'Yes. Yes, indeed it does. She was a small child, of course.'

'I was wondering if I could bring Jonah back with me this evening? Give him some supper and have a chat and then I could drive him back to Michaelgarth or . . .' A slight hesitation.

Hester found that she was responding automatically to the unspoken request.

'He could stay the night here. You won't want to be turning out again. If he's agreeable to it and he's not expected back.'

'That would be great. We'll both have to be back here tomorrow morning anyway. He's a playwright, by the way. It's all shaping up very well and there's a real buzz already. I'm so glad I offered to help Lizzie out. We'll tell you everything later on. Can't quite say when we'll be home but sometime early evening. I'll do the supper and make up his bed. OK?'

'Quite OK.'

'Sure, Hes? You sound the least bit muted. It's just such a fantastic coincidence, isn't it?'

'Yes. Oh, yes, it is. Extraordinary. I can hardly believe it.'

'It's really weird. He can't wait to see the house where his mother stayed. And you, of course.'

'Of course. And I shall look forward to meeting Jonah.'

When she picked up her cup again the coffee tasted cold and bitter, so she set the cup back in its saucer. Her hands trembled very slightly and she covered them with the folds of her shawl. Little Lucy: so many memories crowding in, some happy, some poignant – and bringing with them a tiny twist of guilt. She'd always regretted that she'd never said goodbye to Lucy. Her departure had been so unexpected, so precipitate, and Hester had had other, more desperate demands to which she'd had to attend. It was too late when she'd realized that she hadn't said goodbye to the child; too late when she'd begun to wonder if she should have made certain that Lucy was safe.

Deliberately she turned her mind to happier recollections. For just over a year Lucy had lived with them at Bridge House and the whole family had loved her and taken her to its heart. Out of all the memories, one shone more clearly than the others, and Hester smiled a little, remembering.

Every morning before breakfast, Hester and Lucy go together to feed the chickens. Each carrying her pail of mash – Lucy's is a small red plastic seaside bucket – they cross the lawn and pass through the gate into the little meadow. Since the early years of the war most of the grass has been dug up so as to grow vegetables to feed the family, but part of it has been fenced off and here the fat red hens have their house: a rather ramshackle wooden building with a good strong door to shut against the fox. Hester knows how Lucy likes to go inside the little, low-roofed house, to put her hand into the prickly straw-lined laying boxes and feel the smooth eggs waiting. As the hens squawk and scuttle around the feeder, Hester waits whilst Lucy fills her empty, food-encrusted pail with the precious eggs. Nor does she neglect to examine the grassy margins of Hester's well-dug vegetable patch: the hens are allowed free range and there is sometimes treasure to be found in a clump of grass or a patch of nettles.

Hester watches, tenderly amused by the spectacle of the little girl – her long brown hair falling over flushed cheeks, her small careful hands parting the long grasses – and she enters into the excitement, new every morning, at the discovery of an egg laid secretly away from the little wooden house by a wayward hen. She bends to peer into the pail, held triumphantly aloft – 'Oh, well done, Lucy. Won't Nanny be pleased!' – and smoothes back the long hair, retying Lucy's ribbon. Lucy's brown eyes sparkle with delight and she takes Hester's hand as they go back to the house.

Hester realized that she was holding her hands tightly together within the folds of the shawl, as if she were clutching at something long since vanished. Sitting back in her chair she made a conscious effort to relax. It would be several hours yet before Clio would be home.

Because of the storm the journey from Michael-garth was full of natural drama. It was nearly dark when they set out and rain beat relentlessly upon the windscreen of Clio's little car. In the tunnel of light made by the headlamps Jonah watched the trees bending in the wind, their twiggy fingers lashing the car's sides. He was feeling rather apprehensive. It was one thing to come down to the country home of the actress Lizzie Blake to talk through ideas for the film event she was planning; quite another to be speeding through the countryside with this rather dynamic girl who'd picked him up yesterday from the train at Tiverton Parkway.

As they drove away from Michaelgarth, Jonah had the oddest sensation that the whole matter was out of his control; that events were being just as efficiently stage-managed as one of his own plays. The difficulty was that he couldn't quite decide whom, in this instance, the producer or the director might be.

'I have the feeling that meeting Hester is important to you,' Clio was saying, changing gears, glancing to the right before turning into another narrow lane. 'Not just an idle enquiry but something more than that.'

He remained silent for a few seconds, surprised by her prescience, remembering his mother's unexpected response when he'd phoned a few days earlier.

'I shall be on Exmoor for the weekend,' he'd told her. 'Lizzie Blake has this idea of running a film event in the grounds of her country place and linking it up with the Porlock Arts Festival. She's persuaded a West Country television company to show a thirty-minute drama all written, filmed, acted and produced by sixth-form students, as long as it's up to a reasonable standard. I'm one of a

20

group of professionals who has to show them how it's done. Rather fun, by the sound of it. Lizzie was Margery Kempe in my play *The Pilgrim*. Do you remember meeting her and Piers when we brought it to the Festival Theatre?'

'Of course I remember them both,' Lucy had answered. 'This is so strange, Jonah. I was thinking about Exmoor only last night, being there in the war at Bridge House.' He heard her give a huge sigh. 'I wonder if they are still there, the Mallorys.'

'I could ask around.' He'd tried not to sound too eager. 'Bridge House. That's the one in the photograph, isn't it?'

'It's all so long ago.' She'd retreated hastily, as if she'd been caught with her guard down and was regretting it. 'Nobody will remember.'

'They might. Piers' family has lived on Exmoor for ever. I'll ask him if he knows the Mallorys at Bridge House.'

And so he had, with astonishing results.

'To tell the truth,' Jonah admitted now, in answer to Clio's question, 'it's as if something's happening that I've always been half expecting ever since I first saw a photograph of my mother as a little girl in the garden at Bridge House.' He hesitated, not yet ready to discuss his mother's reluctance to talk about that period of her history. It seemed disloyal, somehow, to try to describe her reaction of fear and denial to a girl that he'd known for such a short time. 'When I was a small boy it was so strange, to see my own mother as a child, even younger than I was. She lost both her parents as a result of the war and generally she doesn't talk about it so I was rather surprised when she mentioned Miss Mallory.'

'Doctor,' Clio corrected him. 'Hes was the Professor of Nineteenth-Century English Literature at Lincoln University. She's been retired for a while now.'

'I see.' Jonah wanted to ask lots of questions but suddenly felt rather shy of this practical, quick-witted girl. 'It's very kind of her to ask me to stay. After all, she doesn't know me.'

A particularly savage blast of wind battered the car and he recoiled in his seat. Clio seemed unmoved, driving with speed and efficiency.

'You're not quite a stranger,' she said. 'She knew your mother and she's known Piers and his family for ages.'

'Even so . . .' Jonah was beginning to be aware of a heightening of tension, of some approaching calamity. The headlights of a wide, high vehicle travelling in the opposite direction blinded them so that the car swerved a little as the lorry rocked and splashed past them.

'Sorry about that.' Clio's laugh was a little shaky. 'He seemed to need rather a lot of road. Not far now. This is Winsford.'

Twinkling lights shone comfortingly through the rain-streamed windows; cottages clustered in around them and then fell away behind as Clio changed gear and the car began to climb. They seemed to be on open moorland now and, so great was the wind's force, it was as if some giant fist were pressing down upon them. Suddenly there was the rattle of a cattle-grid beneath their wheels and then they were plunging downhill again through a great avenue of trees; drifts of sodden beech leaves gleamed wetly at the sides of the road. Gradually Jonah became aware of another sound beyond the howling of the gale and the hiss of rain and the rhythmic swish of the wipers: a growling, roaring, restless voice that seemed to be travelling with them.

'Can you hear the river?' cried Clio. She seemed almost elated by the wildness.

A stone wall loomed up in the headlights' beam and the car began to slow.

As they turned onto the narrow bridge, Jonah saw a figure of a man leap out of the darkness: he was signalling them to stop, his mouth wide open as if crying for help. It seemed that Clio would drive right over him and Jonah shouted and caught at her arm, trying to wrench the wheel.

'What is it?' Her voice was high and frightened. 'For God's sake . . . !'

He felt the juddering of metal on stone as she slammed on the brakes and the car scraped the wall but he was already undoing his seatbelt and fumbling with the door catch. The rain beat down on him, plastering his clothes to his back, as he ran back over the bridge. His voice was caught and flung away on the wind, drowned by the insistent roaring of the water, but there was no sign of any man. Clio was beside him, grasping his arm.

'What was it? What did you see?'

'There was a man. You must have seen him.'

'No, there was nobody. The headlights must have played some trick with the shadows. There's nobody here. Come on, we're drenched. Let's get inside.' And, still holding his arm, she led him across the bridge and into the house where Hester was waiting.

CHAPTER TWO

Later, upstairs in her room at the end of the house, Clio sat on the tapestry stool and stared at her reflection in the ancient spotted looking-glass. It creaked and protested in its mahogany stand as she tilted it a little, before picking up her brush. She was still shaken by Jonah's violent reaction and by the jarring physical shock of the car hitting the bridge. No real harm had been done but she was confused, not only by Jonah's insistence that he'd seen someone but also by Hester's behaviour. Instead of reassuring him by telling him that there could have been no man on the bridge, she'd watched him with a kind of anxious compassion that had made Clio feel quite angry, possibly because of her own fright.

'The bridge leads only to the house and the garden,' she'd said, sounding cross in her attempt to rally Jonah. 'It doesn't go anywhere else. It's private. Hester's already told us that she's been alone all day. Why should anyone hide on the bridge in this weather just to jump out at us and run away?'

She'd looked at Hester, seeking confirmation, but Hester's eyes had been fixed on Jonah's face.

'I saw him,' he'd repeated stubbornly.

'I think we need a drink,' Hester had said – much to Clio's relief – and Jonah had swallowed two fingers of Scotch and begun to pull himself together. At this point Clio had left them, coming upstairs to make up his bed.

Now, as she brushed her hair, Clio's attention was caught by the glimmer of a white envelope propped against one of the pretty hand-painted glass candlesticks. Because this small room, with its one electric socket, was difficult to light adequately, Clio had placed candle-holders in every possible place: two shallow pottery bowls on the high, narrow mantelshelf above the tiny Victorian grate, one tall brass serpent on the small bamboo table beside the bed, and four in different styles of glass on the polished Edwardian washstand that served as a dressing-table. She'd lit them all as soon as she'd come into the room and immediately had grown more calm, soothed by the familiar pattern of objects and the sense of security this little room always projected.

Putting down her brush, Clio reached for the envelope and studied the impatient, curling writing. Oh, how well she could imagine him, crouched at his desk, fielding interruptions, dashing down the words. Quickly she tore open the envelope and unfolded the sheet, her whole attention fixed on his message to her.

Honestly, darling, I can't believe that I ever agreed to let you go. Not even for a whole wilderness of godmothers who have had hip replacements. I simply can't do without you a moment longer. I know that these four weeks are part of your holiday but the place is in chaos; nobody understands how I *work* and no quiet sanctuary to flee to at the end of the day.

Can we meet somewhere? *Please!* Bristol? Exeter? I suppose you couldn't escape to London for a few hours? Please, Clio, give your mind to a meeting next week, however brief, or you won't have a job to come back to because the agency will simply have ceased to exist. You are essential to it and to me.

His signature was unreadable. Clio pressed the paper to her face, hunched on the stool, longing for him. Falling in love with him had ruined everything: all her well-laid plans, her sensible goals for the future, smashed by her absolute need – and his.

'This is Peter Strong,' her boss had said, introducing them. 'This is Clio Taverner, Peter. Clio runs the place actually, but don't tell the MD I said so. I wish I could take her to Boston with me, but there we are.'

'We can't talk here,' he said – and took her out to lunch, bombarding her with questions about the advertising agency, her PA work, herself. To begin with she was mesmerized by the sheer force of his personality but as she grew accustomed to him – and with the assistance of a large glass of Sauvignon Blanc – she began to enjoy herself: responding and expanding under the warmth and intensity of his concentration.

She was so sure, so joyful in this new and overwhelming love that possessed her, that when she heard about his wife and his brood of children she was certain that there must be some mistake: not just for the obvious reason – that she did not want to see him as a philanderer – but because he was so *not* the ordinary sort of man who had those kind of dependants. His character was an interesting mix: single-minded toughness and a brilliant flair for words combined with minute attention to detail and an amazing memory for small sweet things. He never avoided mentioning his family if the subject were relevant but he talked about them as if they existed in a different sphere that was quite remote from his work and his relationship with Clio. He separated his life into watertight compartments and, because this was perfectly natural to him, she seemed able to accept it too. When she tried to rationalize this to herself she realized that his sense of urgency, of immediacy, made anything other than the present dimension unreal. When he was at the agency his work was of paramount importance; when he was alone with her *she* was all he saw or heard or wanted, and she found it impossible – almost foolish – to worry about anything beyond her delight in his company. She'd never been so con-centrated on before and she was bewitched by it. His attitude seemed all the more reasonable because his family lived in Hampshire, where his wife ran a livery stable, and Peter stayed in London four nights each week. It underpinned the ability to compartmentalize that came so readily to him.

He liked Clio's tiny slice of a house – three rooms on three floors – much better than his rather bleak apartment though he always returned to it each night, however late.

Before too long reality asserted itself. She became accustomed to weekends without him, outings put off at the last moment, the unexpected arrival of one or other of his family at the flat; and yet the sheer quality of the time they had together cancelled out the loneliness. She kept up with her friends, went skating, to Pilates, to aerobics classes, knowing that she would see him each weekday morning and that his eyes would light with a kind of relief and joy.

'Aaah,' he'd say – as if she were a long, cold refreshing drink. '*There* you are.'

Clio put the paper back into its envelope and resumed the hair-brushing but her thoughts were busy. For the first few weeks after the operation, Hester had been looked after professionally. It was Clio who'd suggested that she could take four weeks of her holiday time to be with her until she was strong and self-sufficient again. Peter had agreed to it, and there was only one more week to go, but it would be heaven to see him briefly. How could they meet – and where? An idea so simple that it took her by surprise suggested itself. Why not invite him here, to Bridge House? It would be interesting to see Peter and Hester together: Peter so vital and intense; Hester so intelligent and detached. Clio laughed aloud at the prospect, and wondered how her godmother was getting on with Jonah. She hoped they were having a good heart-to-heart about the war. Remembering that she was supposed to be making up his bed, she went out onto the landing and along to the airing cupboard to find some sheets.

'I remember your mother very well,' Hester was saying. 'Such a pretty little girl. We were all very fond of her.'

She realized that she was making an effort quite as much to raise her own spirits as to distract Jonah from his preoccupation. She knew, too, that she could not take him into the drawing-room. After her day-long premonition had culminated with such violence in his experience on the bridge, her usual detachment and common sense had deserted her: the drawing-room held other vibrations to which, in his present state, he might respond. Instead, she poured him another Scotch and led the way out of the large square hall, with its inglenook fireplace and comfortable chairs, into the book-room where she had been sitting earlier, beside a small wood fire.

'Mum never talks about the war,' he answered, looking around him appreciatively, taking in the book-lined walls, the small revolving table beside

31

the wing-chair, the chaise longue under the window. 'She's got a thing about it. I suppose that losing both her parents gave her a horror of it all. I knew the name of your house from some photos we have at home of my mother when she was little. She's made a bit of a mystery of it all, to tell you the truth, and when she mentioned your name I felt as if an opportunity I'd been waiting for had suddenly come. And then that thing happened on the bridge.' He glanced at Hester apologetically. 'I'm behaving like an idiot but it was very real, you know. I *saw* him . . . Sorry. This is an amazing room.'

She acknowledged his attempt to pull himself together and gestured to the other armchair.

'Sit down,' she said. 'This was my mother's favourite room. She said that it was the only room in the house where you couldn't hear the river.'

Jonah sat down and stretched out his legs towards the fire. 'Didn't she like the noise of water?'

'She found it rather relentless. There are moments, you know, when you want to turn it off, just for a moment; to shout at it to be quiet. Especially at this time of the year.'

'I wondered what it was,' he told her. 'When we were in the car, I mean. I could hear it in the background, like some growling, angry voice. Rather menacing. I can understand how your mother must have felt about it. It must be rather frightening sometimes.'

'Towards the end she found it so. Especially at night. She seemed to hear voices in its roaring.' She fell silent, sipped at her Scotch, trying to see her way ahead.

'Voices?' His own voice was reflective as if he were imagining it. 'Particular voices, d'you mean, or what?'

Hester hesitated. 'She wasn't quite herself at the end. My two brothers were killed early on in the war and the eldest, Edward, was in Singapore in 1942 and taken prisoner by the Japanese. She adored her sons and the shock of losing them weakened her. She was never particularly strong and she just seemed to lose interest in living. Worse than that, she had no desire to live in a world where such appalling things were happening. Edward's capture was the last straw. She couldn't co-exist with the thought of his imprisonment. She died in the autumn of 1942. Sixty years ago.' She nearly added, 'This very night,' but felt that this would simply add to the emotional tension.

'How terrible for you to lose your brothers and your mother within such a short time.' His horror was genuine. 'You must have been terribly young. Was my mother here then? Was she evacuated?'

'She arrived later in the war.' She responded instinctively to his sympathy, abandoning some of her caution. 'Your grandfather Michael and my brother Edward were at Cambridge together. They were very good friends and, when your grandmother was killed, Michael asked if he could bring Lucy to us.'

'So you knew him? You actually knew my grandfather. He came here to this house. How amazing! So you really do remember my mother?'

Hester hesitated again for a brief moment, then reached into her pocket and drew out a small snapshot. 'I thought this might interest you.'

Jonah bent over it eagerly: two figures posing just outside French windows opening on to a sunny lawn. The bigger girl with short dark hair was kneeling beside a small child. One arm was round the little girl, the other gesturing towards the camera as if to fix her attention. 'Look,' she might be saying. 'Look, Lucy. Smile.' On the back in fading ink were the words: 'Hester with Lucy in the garden at Bridge House. June 1945.'

As he looked, a memory, whole and complete, slid into his mind. He was standing at the door of the small attic room watching his mother searching for something in a chest. The musty scent of old clothes and books was in his nostrils and the unshaded bulb glimmered weakly, lighting pieces of broken, dusty furniture but leaving cobwebby corners unlit and rather menacing. His mother wrestled with the drawer, tugging at it sharply so that it slid out suddenly and a big envelope with old snapshots came spilling to the floor.

He ran forward and caught at one of the snapshots, peering at the small figures before turning it over to see the names written on the back: 'Lucy with Robin and Jack at Bridge House. August 1944.'

'Who are these children?' he asked his mother curiously. 'Lucy. That's you, isn't it? But who are these little boys?'

'I don't know.' She took the photograph from him quickly and put it back into the envelope, shoving it into the drawer and closing it. 'It's all too long ago to remember.'

An atmosphere of fear and distress alerted him, young though he was, and later he crept back to look at the snapshot again: the three children captured in the grainy texture of the past, beaming at the camera, and the name typed on the big buff envelope: 'Major Michael Scott', his grandfather's name.

Now Hester watched him as he turned the snap-shot over and he glanced at her almost unseeingly and shook his head.

'This is extraordinary,' he said at last. 'This reminds me of the one we have at home except that, in that one, it's my mother with two little boys. Jack and Robin. Their names are written on the back of the snapshot just like this.'

'That would have been my nephews. My sister, Patricia's, two little boys,' said Hester. 'Jack and Lucy were very close friends.'

'The photograph always fascinated me but she simply refuses to talk about it. Can you imagine why that should be?'

'It was a very painful time for her,' Hester replied cautiously. 'Tell me, how is Lucy? Where does she live?'

'In Chichester.' Jonah was reluctantly diverted. 'My parents have lived there all their married lives. My father was a science teacher but he's got this ghastly disease called lupus. Have you heard of it? The body's immune system goes into overdrive and attacks itself. It's pretty grim.'

'I am so sorry.' It was Hester's turn to be horri-fied. 'How frightful for him. And for poor Lucy.'

'She'll be amazed when she knows I've actually been here. I hope she won't be upset. How long was she here with you? I didn't realize that you were all friends. I assumed it was just a normal evacuation thing.' Jonah settled more comfortably in his chair, ready for confidences. 'It must have been wonderful for her to come here to you all, having just lost her mother. Did my grandfather bring her down?'

Before Hester could answer, the door opened and Clio put her head round it.

'I thought you'd be in the drawing-room,' she said. 'Supper's ready and Jonah's bed's made up. Come and eat.'

The breakfast-room was connected to the kitchen by an archway through which the working area could be glimpsed. The paraphernalia of cooking, pots and pans and utensils hastily cast aside, was prevented from intruding on the comfortable simplicity of the room by the simple mechanism of an amber-coloured velvet curtain twitched across the archway after the last plate had been carried through. Coming in from the small, cosy book-room, Jonah was struck by the light, uncluttered space: honeysuckle-coloured walls, a stripped wood floor with several blue rugs making deep pools of colour, a square table covered with a cream oilcloth patterned with tiny, dark green ivy leaves.

Clio appeared to have recovered from her fright

on the bridge. A smile of suppressed excitement was pressed upon her upward-curving lips and she was wrapped in a large apron that had 'Kiss the Cook' printed across it. An enormous tortoiseshell cat – so large that Jonah doubted he was real – was curled in a basket chair.

'That's St Francis,' said Hester. 'He was called Billy to begin with but his unusually philanthropic attitude towards birds and rodents required some kind of public recognition.'

'It doesn't matter what you call him,' said Clio, noting Jonah's doubtful expression. 'He'll ignore you anyway. I call him Frank.'

Jonah put out a cautious hand and stroked the soft warm animal rather gingerly. St Francis stirred, licked his left flank once or twice and resumed slumber without acknowledging Jonah's caress.

'Told you so,' said Clio with some satisfaction. 'Come and sit down. I've made a mushroom omelette and then there's a casserole.'

During supper it was easy for Hester to divert the conversation away from the war to Jonah's work: the scripts he'd written and the novel he was presently adapting for television. Clio had seen one of his plays, which they discussed at length, and he entertained them with stories about productions and famous actors. He was a witty raconteur,

making them laugh and encouraging their questions, so that it was much later, when Clio was
stacking the dishwasher in the kitchen and Jonah
and Hester were still at the table drinking coffee,
that tension crept back to chill the cheerful atmosphere.

'It's stopped raining,' Clio called through the
archway, 'though there's a terrific gale blowing.
Listen to the river.'

She leaned across the sink and opened the
window so that the restless voice that had distantly
accompanied their supper was suddenly borne in
upon them on a wild rush of wind, clamouring now
with a renewed violence.

'Can we go out and see it?' asked Jonah. 'The
river must be pretty impressive after all that rain.'

To Clio's surprise, Hester rose and took him
out through the kitchen into the yard rather than
on to the terrace outside the drawing-room where
visitors were usually shown the river. A light outside the door illuminated the courtyard and he
passed Clio's car and went on to the bridge. Hester
watched him from the doorway, Clio at her
shoulder. The noise of the water was overwhelming:
brawling, brutal, black and oily-looking in the darkness, its sheer force was breathtaking. Branches
and other detritus swirled upon its swollen breast,

smashing against the stone piers of the bridge and vanishing beneath the arch, and all the while the river roared and thundered as it raced between its imprisoning banks.

Jonah came back to them slowly, his face clenched painfully as though his head hurt; his eyes looked at them unseeingly. He staggered slightly as the wind gusted even more strongly, and Clio put out her hand and drew him into the warm shelter of the house.

'I'll show you your room,' she said, concerned by his expression. 'Let's get your bag. I left it in the hall.'

They went upstairs together and Hester returned thoughtfully to the kitchen to finish the clearing up. When they reappeared about ten minutes later, both looked equally strained.

'I'm sorry we didn't get round to talking properly about Mum and the war,' Jonah said rather awkwardly to Hester. 'I'd like to know more. It's odd but I feel strangely affected by this place.' He grimaced, as if embarrassed by his admission. 'Probably overwork. I think I'll turn in.'

Hester, who was not given to endearments or shows of affection, touched him lightly on the shoulder. 'We *will* talk, I promise. When the moment is right. Sleep well, Jonah.'

He went away from them, up the stairs, and Clio gave a little shiver. It was obvious that Jonah's reaction had renewed her earlier anxiety and convinced her that something mysterious was happening. She came up close to her godmother, looking seriously into her face, and Hester took a deep, steadying breath.

'Who was it that he saw?' asked Clio. Her natural poise had deserted her and she seemed vulnerable, even frightened. Nevertheless, Hester decided that this time she must answer truthfully.

'He saw his grandfather,' she said.

CHAPTER THREE

It was with an unexpected light-heartedness that Hester woke next morning. The gale had roared away to the east, leaving a freshly rinsed, clear blue sky, and the air was cool and still. The weight of premonition and anxiety that had arrived so suddenly with the wild south-westerly wind had now swept off with it, leaving Hester with an unfamiliar sense of anticipation. This morning the bright sunshine that glittered on the dripping trees and gleamed over the rain-drenched garden mocked at the fears and terrors of the night and dispelled the shadows.

Hester, congenitally uncommunicative until after her second cup of coffee, was relieved to discover that Jonah was not inclined to early morning conversation. He smiled at the two women, accepted some coffee and picked up a section of the newspaper. Clio, recognizing the familiar signs, shrugged mentally and ate her toast in silence. Jonah ate nothing, drank his cup of black coffee and then went away to pack his overnight bag, which gave Clio the opportunity of proposing her plan to invite Peter down.

'Of course,' said Hester, pausing in her daily battle with the crossword. 'It was so kind of him to let you have the time off to look after me. By all means invite him to stay. I should very much like to meet him.'

She was aware of the sharp look Clio shot at her but pretended to be absorbed again in her crossword. She suspected that Clio was trying to decide whether she should speak openly about her relationship with Peter – about the personal aspect of it – and Hester knew that such a disclosure would require explanations, justifications, even advice. She would prefer to wait until she'd met this man with whom Clio had fallen so much in love before she revealed her own fears. She'd been in love, long years ago, with a married man: a university lecturer with whom she'd had a brief but passionate affair. The remembrance of it made it difficult for her to criticize Clio's relationship with Peter, especially as she had no idea how he felt about his wife, although her instincts told her that it would be Clio who would suffer most.

43

Hester had long been hoping that Clio would open her heart, thus giving them both the opportunity to speak truthfully but, with Jonah likely to burst in at any time, this was certainly not the moment.

Meanwhile her god-daughter dithered uncharacteristically at the end of the table, holding her plate in one hand and the marmalade pot in the other, and they were both relieved when Jonah reappeared, bag in hand, and paused to speak to St Francis, who was washing himself in a slanting puddle of sunlight in his favourite chair.

'My parents have a dog,' he said. 'She's a pretty Sussex spaniel, very sweet, but I rather like this enormous fellow.'

'I'm a dog person,' Clio told him over her shoulder, removing her breakfast things and picking up her car keys. 'But I can't justify having one in London. Maybe, one day . . .'

'It's a pity you won't be here for Lizzie's event,' said Jonah. 'I think it's going to be fun. Any chance of getting more time off next spring?'

Clio grinned. 'Lizzie asked me the same question. I don't think Peter is quite that philanthropic.'

'Peter?'

'Peter's my boss,' answered Clio. Her voice was proud, defiant and tender, all at once, and Jonah's eyebrows flicked upwards as if he'd made a rather disappointing discovery.

Hester noted his expression.

'Come back again, Jonah. Come and stay,' she said to him as they wandered out to the courtyard. 'You must speak to Lucy first to make sure she's happy about it, and then come and stay and we'll talk.'

'I'd really like that. It's taking time for me to get my head round it all. That my grandfather was actually here with my mother, I mean, and that they were friends with your family.'

'Watch it, Hes. He'll be making up a story about it if you're not careful.' Clio was standing by the car with the door open, watching them with affection. 'He's a dramatist, remember.'

Hester gave a final wave as the car turned onto the road, smiling a little. St Francis had strolled out behind her and was now sitting on the bridge with his tail hanging down, and she smoothed his hard head. There would be no need for Jonah to invent a story: the truth was more than enough to satisfy his creative need. And how like his grandfather he was: not very tall but neat and strong-looking. As he and Clio had come in through the door last night, his black hair plastered to his skull, his dark eyes shocked and wide, her heart had somersaulted in recognition. Just so had Michael looked all those years ago, coming back into the house from the dark, wild evening, with Eleanor's arm protectively about his shoulders, soaked with the rain and dazed with horror.

Leaning on the bridge beside St Francis, Hester was uncomfortably aware that the memory of her sister-in-law was still able to trigger a reaction of animosity. From the very beginning, when Edward had brought her home to meet his family, Hester had disliked Eleanor. Standing in the sun, stroking the cat's soft warm back, Hester wondered just how much she would tell Jonah. Where would the story begin? With the return to the family's fishing lodge by the river Barle when their father died in 1936 and she was just eight years old? She could remember the preparations for the long journey to the West from Cambridge, one or two of her father's colleagues from the university coming to the station to bid them farewell: her mother, silent with grief, and attended anxiously by her two older children, Edward and Patricia, whilst their nanny kept the three younger ones entertained.

She could remember, too, the terrible emptiness and anguish in her own small heart. It was because of the sudden death of her adored father that she'd transferred her love wholesale to Edward, who most resembled him, and why, five years later, she had so resented Eleanor. Perhaps that was the beginning: Eleanor's arrival at Bridge House with Edward.

St Francis was purring with a kind of rumbling growl, pulsating gently beneath her caressing hand, and Hester chuckled suddenly with a swooping uplift of the spirits. The prospect of revisiting the past, exorcising the ghosts, filled her with an odd kind of pleasure. It would bring release to relive it. After all, there was nobody left to be hurt by the story that she would tell Jonah: surely not even Lucy could suffer now. Last night she'd been fearful, infected by Jonah's reaction on the bridge and anxious lest she might reveal secrets that his mother had deliberately kept private. This morning she wondered if she'd been foolish. If Lucy gave her blessing to it then she would gladly tell Jonah their story. Already her mind was fingering the past as one might peruse an old book, turning the pages and looking upon long-forgotten scenes.

She leaned on the sun-warmed stones beside the cat and gave herself up to the luxury of remembering.

In the car the atmosphere was oddly strained. Without Hester and her calm acceptance of the previous evening's events, Jonah and Clio were both suddenly rather shy.

'How different it looks this morning,' Jonah was saying, clearly determined to play the part of an appreciative guest. 'It's an extraordinary landscape.'

They were travelling beneath a canopy of bare branches, the high wooded hill rising precipitously to the right of the road; the misshapen woody roots of massive trees grasped the mossy banks like prehensile toes digging deep into a rich black mulch of wet leaves and earth. Beyond the river to his left, Jonah glimpsed bright, jewel-green meadows fringing the further bank but, as the road climbed steadily round the side of the combe, the noisy torrent was left behind. Peering from his window, Jonah could still see the glint of a small stream far below as it curled and twisted along the valley floor to join the Barle at Marsh Bridge.

Clio was wondering what to say to him that would distract him from the unexpected drama of their arrival. This morning, in the bright sharp sunlight, the idea of an apparition seemed an impossible one. Yet Hester had been firm: something from the past had reached out to touch Jonah; that much was clear.

'He saw his grandfather,' she'd said. 'Something

happened here that might well have left some kind of emotional vibration' – and had been unwilling to say anything else beyond expressing a hope that she and Jonah would have a long talk together.

After that, Clio had taken refuge in thinking about Peter and planning his visit. She'd decided that the elemental wildness of the storm had heightened reactions, normal feelings were clearly out of control, and hoped that things would look different in the morning. And so they did, yet it was still difficult to think of just the right conversational opener. As they passed over the cattle-grid onto the open spaces of Winsford Common, Jonah solved the problem for her.

'I'm sorry you won't be here for Lizzie's event,' he said. 'Have you been taking a sabbatical from work?'

'It's my holiday, actually. Hester's had a hip replacement and though she was looked after by the Social Services for the first few weeks, I thought she might like someone with her until she could drive again. Peter let me take my holiday in one go.'

'Lucky for Hester. How did she come to be your godmother? Do you mind me asking?'

'Not a bit. My mother was one of Hester's students and my father was reading History at

49

Lincoln at the same time. Hester and my mother developed one of those real bonds that occasionally spring up between student and tutor and they stayed closely in touch after Mummy graduated. Daddy was doing his Ph.D. at Bristol when they got married. He'd just heard that he'd got his MA when I appeared on the scene. Hence the name: Clio was the muse of history but not many people know that these days. It's spelled with an "i" not an "e". Anyway, Mummy asked Hester to be my godmother and when I was little we usually spent part of the long vac with her and other members of the family at Bridge House. She always keeps my room for me. My parents moved about rather a lot when I was growing up, they're a peripatetic pair, and Hester has been a constant in my life. It's been important and special to have her there.'

'I envy you.'

Clio had the feeling that, although Jonah was staring out over the sunlit spaces of gorse and heather to the distant hills in the west, he was seeing something else: a child arriving at Bridge House, perhaps, and running up the stairs to make sure that her little room was just the same.

'Jonah's brilliant,' Lizzie had said to her. 'He's amazingly visual; so quick to see a scene or pick up a nuance.'

Now, Clio believed that he was doing exactly that. Glancing sideways at him, she saw that his face was intent and his whole body tensed as if he were watching a little scene of his personal devising and hearing voices other than their own. His expression reminded her of Peter's when he was thinking through a new advertising campaign. She knew better than to interrupt someone who was working, and turned right at Spire Cross without further comment, but she knew exactly the moment when he returned to her, his attention once more focused with them inside the car, and she smiled.

'You'll see Winsford properly this morning. It's a lovely little village.'

They were descending between high banks and tall trees, down a narrow lane running between whitewashed cottages and stone houses into the village.

'It's great. Oh, and look! The river's come back,' he said cheerfully as they sped away again up towards the valley road to the moor. 'Fantastic!'

'Only it's not the same river,' she said. 'This is the River Exe. *Our* river is the Barle.'

He laughed at that, as she had meant him to. 'Nice to have your very own river as well as your very own room,' he commented. 'I rather envy you

Hester as well. My godparents have never shown much interest in me. I like Hester. She has that self-contained serenity of the true academic or, perhaps, a nun.'

'How odd that you should say that.' Clio sounded startled. 'Hester wanted to be a nun when she was young, but somehow it didn't work out.'

'Really?' He was intrigued. 'I wonder why not.'

'I've no idea. She has a cousin, Blaise, who is a chaplain to a convent of contemplative nuns in the north of England. She adores him and I have to say he is utter heaven. Anyway, after the war, when Blaise took Holy Orders, I think that Hester decided to try the contemplative life for herself but she gave it all up before she'd finished her novitiate and went to university instead.'

'And that worked for her?'

'Oh, yes. Her father was a Cambridge don and her brother Edward and Blaise were at Cambridge so you might say that academia was in the genes. The whole family had a passion – well, Hester still does – for the poetry of John Clare. She wrote quite an important book about him back in the seventies when he was still very underrated. There's been a resurgence since, so I understand, but old Hes was a real mover and shaker of her time.'

'Was she in love with Blaise?'

Clio glanced at him, almost shocked. 'I've no idea. Why do you ask?'

'I don't know.' He hunched slightly in his seat, as if thinking something through. 'It's just odd that she should suddenly want to go into a convent, I suppose, unless it was because he was unavailable.'

'She might have had a vocation.' Clio sounded faintly defensive.

'But she didn't, did she? Or she'd have stayed. I'm sorry if I sound inquisitive or rude. It's just that I'm really hooked by all of it, I don't know why.'

Clio shook her head. 'I think you can see a play coming out of it. Or a treatment. Or whatever you call it.'

Jonah grinned, seized by the mysterious, magical excitement of a new creation revealing itself to him. 'You could be right,' he answered, and then leaned forward in his seat as the car turned off the lane and into the drive, which wound across the wild open heath.

Michaelgarth stood high above them, strong and invulnerable on the bracken-covered slopes, looking beyond Porlock Common to the sea.

'It's wonderful, isn't it?' asked Clio, following his gaze.

He nodded. 'We were all rather surprised when Lizzie decided to move to Exmoor,' he told her. 'A lot of people split their lives between town and country, of course, but Lizzie seemed so settled in her little house in Bristol. I believe she still uses it when she's working but it came as a shock to hear that she was going to marry a man who lived and worked on Exmoor and was planning to spend all her spare time there. Now I can understand why she loves it here so much. It's not just the house, is it? The whole place is just magic.'

'I quite agree but we mustn't forget that Piers has something to do with it too,' said Clio mischievously.

She drove through the archway into the old garth and parked the car in the open-fronted barn. Michaelgarth had been built on the ruins of an old priory. High walls connected the house to the stables and barns so that the ancient cobbles were enclosed and the whole was possessed by a sense of peace and timelessness. Climbing out of the car, Clio and Jonah crossed the garth and went together into the house.

CHAPTER FOUR

As soon as she had deposited Jonah safely with Lizzie and her other guests, Clio asked if she could make a telephone call. She knew that Peter would be at the London flat, his habit being to stop there for coffee and what he called a 'Russian five minutes', after travelling up from the country. He was rarely in the office before ten o'clock but when he did arrive he was utterly focused on the day ahead; his family life carefully filed away into another, separate compartment.

He answered on the second ring, his voice sounding rather flat.

'It's Clio,' she said. She no longer said 'It's me' ever since he'd once mistaken her voice for that of his eldest daughter and she'd never forgotten the tiny shock of hearing the unfamiliar tone of protective tenderness with which he'd spoken to her, thinking she was Sarah.

'Darling,' he cried now, as if he were drowning and she were a lifeline flung to him unexpectedly. 'Where are you? Did you get my letter?'

'Yes. Yes, I did. Listen, I'm at a friend's house so I can't be long. I had this idea about us meeting up. Why don't you come down here for a couple of days? Down one day and back the next. I could pick you up from Tiverton Parkway. Hester's less than half an hour away.'

'Hester? Your godmother?' He sounded baffled. 'Are you actually suggesting that I should meet your godmother, sweetie?'

'Why not? I've asked her if you could stay with us and she says she'd love to meet you. It would be fun.'

'Would it?' He sounded frankly sceptical. 'Are you serious, Clio? I think I'd feel just a tad nervous under an old biddy's beady eye.' He chuckled, inviting her to share the joke. 'Can't you just see it? I'm a bit old for creaking floorboards and being sized up by an elderly matriarch.'

Clio was taken aback, almost affronted by his assumptions about Hester. She'd given him credit for a more imaginative attitude. She realized with a pang of horror that he'd disappointed her but she refused to accept his stereotypical viewpoint simply for the sake of harmony between them.

'Hester's not a bit like that,' she said stiffly. 'You've got quite the wrong idea about it all. I hoped you'd see it as a visit to someone who is very special to me. Her age isn't relevant. Hester isn't the judgemental type – and there's absolutely nothing maternal about her.'

'Sorry. Sorry, Clio.' He backed off at once. 'If you think it'll work, then I'll fix it up when I get into the office. I'm missing you terribly and there's a panic on about the Harrison account. Twenty-four hours with you would suit me splendidly.'

She was touched as always by his readiness to retract from a position gracefully, though her confidence was slightly shaken.

'I really think it will work, Peter.'

'Of course it will. Take no notice of me. I've only just got in and I haven't made the transition yet. To tell the truth I'm having a bit of a domestic crisis.'

'Oh.' She was alert, fear speeding her heart. She could never decide how much Louise knew about Peter's London life. 'Nothing too serious?'

'We'll see. Anyway, nothing for you to worry about.'

Clio could tell that he was regretting the slip: he must be rattled to let his carefully segregated lives collide so casually.

'That's OK then.' She knew better than to

question him further. 'Will you let me know when you can get down? Any day this week will be fine for us.'

'Sure. Down tomorrow back on Wednesday would be the best bet, but I'll have to check the diary.'

'It seems odd, doesn't it, that I don't know what your engagements are?'

'Oh, my darling, it's just such a total desert without you around.'

'Good,' she said cheerfully. 'Just don't get used to it.'

'No chance of that. Look, I'll leave a message on your mobile as usual, shall I? I know you can't get a signal at Hester's but you can pick it up later on.'

'That's best. I'll be taking some people back to the station later this morning and I'll check for messages on the way home. There's no signal here either.'

'It sounds rather medieval,' he said. A twinge of doubt returned to colour his voice. 'Are you sure I shall like it?'

'Quite sure.' Her confidence had resurfaced. 'You can trust me.'

'Don't I know it, sweetie.' He was laughing again. 'Can't wait to see you. Bye.'

Sitting on the seat in the cloistered way outside the hall, which had once been the chapel, Clio thought about Peter. A few late roses still bloomed on the high stone walls; Lion, Piers' golden retriever, lay somnolent on the cobbles. Clio relaxed. The murmur of conversation and occasional bursts of laughter, Lizzie's voice reciting something and then breaking off short – all seemed to come from a great distance away. Much more real to her was the idea of Peter: his crisp fair hair standing up like an animal's fur as he came out from the shower; his long strong legs and broad brown hands with the nails always clean and pink as if they'd just been scrubbed. She could imagine his arm along her shoulders as he sat beside her, his breath against her cheek, the smell of his skin, and the other million scents and images and sounds that meant Peter to her.

The shutter in her mind, behind which all thoughts of Louise and the children were locked, lifted a fraction. She heard Louise's confident drawl and the higher, fluting voices of his children. She remembered them arriving unexpectedly at the office, during a trip to London to buy school uniforms, and how surprising it had been to see him so natural and easy, joking and letting his small son twirl in the big leather chair, before he whisked them all off to tea without a glance in her direction. Louise, darkly glamorous, had nodded to the members of Peter's staff with all the pleasant indifference of one brought up with servants, seeing them as so many useful appendages, rather on the level of the computers and the telephones: necessary but uninteresting. He'd made no mention of it afterwards – and neither had Clio.

A door opened, the voices came closer; the meeting was breaking up. Clio sat forward on her bench, checking automatically for her car keys and glancing at her watch: plenty of time for the train. She took a breath and straightened her shoulders. Perhaps tomorrow Peter would be on his way to see her.

'I hope you'll be around when I come down to see Hester again,' Jonah said, as they waited on the platform for the train from Plymouth.

'So you'll definitely be back?'

'Of course. I'm hoping that I'll be able to persuade my mother to talk about the war. I think that Dad being ill has changed certain perspectives for her and I know that sometimes she's a bit lonely. It's not easy being a carer. Unlike your parents, mine have been very sedentary: living in one place for all their married lives, very dependent on each other and a few close friends. I think Mum's feeling vulnerable and she might be more ready to talk about the past. Perhaps it's time: she wouldn't have mentioned Hester otherwise. I feel it is.'

'I hope you will come back,' said Clio impulsively, 'but perhaps we can meet up in London sometime.'

He looked pleasantly surprised. 'I thought you were . . . uh, you know?'

'I still spend time with my friends,' she answered rather crisply. 'Shall I give you my mobile number?'

He dug in his pocket for his mobile, tapped in her number with a pen and said, 'Ah, here's the train.'

His travelling companions joined them, bags were collected and farewells were said.

'Thanks for taking me to meet Hester,' Jonah said, leaning from the window for a moment. 'It's meant a lot.'

Walking back to the car, Clio checked her mobile for voice mail. Peter's message was short but clear.

'Catching the nine fifteen from Paddington. Will be arriving at Tiverton Parkway at eleven o'clock. Returning to London late afternoon Wednesday.'

She made a note of the train times, telephoned Hester to tell her that Peter would be with them in twenty-four hours and got into the car.

As she drove up the dual carriageway past Tiverton, she was already making plans for the next day: pick Peter up and take him home to lunch at Bridge House, then perhaps a trip over the moor to the sea and back in time for tea. In the evening it might be a good idea to go out to dinner, just the two of them, to Woods. Peter would like Woods, with its bistro atmosphere and delicious food – assuming, of course, that she could book a table . . .

Clio applied the brakes sharply as a pheasant careered into the road, racing dementedly in front of the car's wheels before launching itself into a wild steep flight upwards into the beech hedge.

'Crazy bird,' she muttered, startled out of her preoccupations. 'You were nearly lunch.'

Letting in the clutch, speeding off again, she tried to visualize the contents of Hester's freezer, wondering if there might be something good for tomorrow's lunch; Peter loved his food. Perhaps, just to be on the safe side, she'd stop off in Dulverton and go into Woods to ask Will, the bar manager, about booking a table. Then she could see what the delicatessen could provide: or perhaps she might buy a rack of lamb from the butcher? She drove over Barle Bridge, along the High Street, veered left into Fore Street and parked in an empty space outside the library.

*　　*　　*

When Clio arrived home she found Hester seated at the table in the breakfast-room with several large photograph albums in front of her. Clio dropped her parcels at the other side of the table and went to peer curiously over Hester's shoulder. The small black-and-white snapshots had faded writing beneath them and Clio bent closer to read the words.

'When you telephoned to tell me about Jonah, I remembered that these were in the cupboard in the book-room,' Hester told her. 'I hadn't looked at them for years. It's odd to see them again after all this time. How poignant old photographs are, aren't they? I can hardly believe that I was once the person I see here; I've been looking at me, wondering who I was and how I felt. It's the same in reverse, of course. When we are young we know that one day we will be old but it seems quite unreal. The old woman you see ahead of you, way down the road, is a stranger who could never be connected with how you feel now, at this moment: invincible, immortal.'

'That's true,' admitted Clio, thinking it over. 'I know that one day I shall be old but at the same time I feel that old age will be happening to a different Clio. It's not really anything to do with the me who is here now, today.' And suddenly she thought of Peter, and of making love with him, and knew that she needed him quite terribly, here and now, as a warm, vital talisman to ward off that cold, unimaginable future.

'Blaise was the keenest photographer of the family, and after he went away to the war Patricia took on his mantle.' Hester's calm voice acted as a remedy against Clio's sense of panic, rather like a cool hand on a hot brow. 'This one might interest you.'

She turned over the stiff grey pages and pointed to an outdoor photograph of three young men standing together rather self-consciously but smiling good-naturedly at the camera. Their hands were stuck casually in the pockets of their flannel trousers and two of them wore Fair Isle pullovers in that oddly shrunken style that seemed so much part of the pre-war age.

'"Edward, Blaise and Michael."' Clio read the caption aloud. '"Summer 1938 at Bridge House." Who's Michael? He looks faintly familiar.'

'He's Jonah's grandfather,' answered Hester, smiling to herself. 'Alike, aren't they?'

'Good grief!' Clio bent even closer, scanning the face more closely. 'So you actually knew him? Really knew him?'

'He was at Cambridge with Edward and Blaise, though Blaise was older. They were all great friends. Michael married first, though we never met his wife. By then the war had started and he didn't come here again until he brought Lucy down in 1944. By then, Edward was married too.'

'And Blaise?' Remembering Jonah's theory Clio watched Hester's face. 'He didn't want to get married?'

Hester seemed to withdraw: she didn't move but her expression fell into aloof, almost severe lines.

'No, Blaise didn't want to marry. At least, not in the conventional way. He fell in love very early in his life and he never wavered from it.'

'Fell in love? With whom?'

'With God and with the whole of the human race.' Hester looked both bleak and envious. 'That's why he took Holy Orders. You know all this, Clio.'

'I don't,' she protested. 'Well, I know bits of it, of course, but none of it properly. Obviously I know Blaise became a priest after the war but that's not to say that he might have married. I just wondered, that's all.'

'Wondered?'

'It was just seeing them together like that. It made me wonder. Blaise is so human, isn't he? He isn't all sanctimonious and distant. Actually, looking at this, he must have been pretty hot stuff when he was young.'

Hester chuckled. 'Oh, he was,' she agreed. 'Pretty hot stuff, as you say.'

'Well, then.' Clio breathed more freely, relieved to see Hester smiling. 'That's all I meant.'

'There was a moment,' said Hester, after a little hesitation, 'when I wondered if he might manage both God and a wife but it came to nothing.'

Clio looked away from the expression of puzzled pain on her godmother's face: it was both moving and discomforting. She could think of nothing to say and was grateful to St Francis, who chose to leap suddenly upon the table all amongst the books, scattering the loose snapshots.

'Gosh, look at the time,' Clio said. 'Frank's hungry and so am I. I'll get some lunch. If you clear the books away, I can lay the table.'

She carried the shopping into the kitchen but when she glanced back through the archway she saw that Hester continued to sit unmoving before the albums. She stared straight ahead, as though at some distant scene, and her hands were placed very lightly around the great animal as if she were warming them at a fire.

CHAPTER FIVE

All through breakfast the next morning, Hester was aware of Clio's tension. She looked slightly different today. Her gold-brown hair was held back with pretty combs, rather than twisted casually back with a piece of silk, her lips were touched with a slick of bright gloss and she wore caramel-coloured suede trousers instead of jeans.

Catching Hester's rather quizzical appraisal she said, 'He'll have to have Jonah's sheets,' as though to indicate a proper degree of indifference to Peter's visit, lest Hester was jumping to conclusions about the combs and the suede trousers. 'After all,' she added, 'it was only for one night. Peter wouldn't care anyway.'

Hester made no comment. She wasn't interested in Peter's praise or condemnation of the house-keeping arrangements since it would never have occurred to her that she or Clio might be judged accordingly. She was trying to assess whether Clio was merely excited at Peter's imminent arrival or if her god-daughter imagined some kind of emotional test might be involved in this visit.

'You look delightful,' she said – and Clio flushed brightly.

'Do I?' she asked carelessly.

Hester smiled at her, touched as always by Clio's unexpected moments of vulnerability.

'It always comes as a surprise that women look much older when they dress up. Have you noticed that?'

'No.' Clio was momentarily distracted from thoughts of Peter by this odd idea. 'Do they?' She frowned, trying to picture her friends in both casual and smart modes of dress, but failed to manage a comparison.

'Oh, yes.' Hester was adamant. 'They look more elegant, of course, but older. Take a fifteen-year-old girl out of her school uniform and, with make-up and a sophisticated outfit, she can look twenty-five. There is something rather poignant about it, rather like a small child dressing up in her mother's clothes. In the fifties, when clothes were so much more formal, all young women looked like their mothers; most unfortunate for them, poor darlings. Oh dear! Those frightful permanent waves, just like corrugated iron, and great gashes of dark red lipstick that made them look as if they'd been hit with a hatchet. So unflattering.'

Clio chuckled. 'And what did you wear in the fifties, Hes?' She looked at the petite upright figure sitting at the table: Hester wore jeans, a black roll-neck jersey and an old suede waistcoat. Her soft white hair was piled up into a wispy, untidy knot and her small square face was as wrinkled and brown as an autumn leaf. 'I bet you didn't dress like your mother.'

'Well, I didn't,' agreed Hester. 'But then, you have to remember, I had no role model. I went up to Cambridge in the early fifties when I was in my middle twenties, rather old by the other students' standards, but I'd had an unconventional up-bringing and had no difficulty in adapting to university life. Sartorially, I was probably what you'd describe as café society. Of course, slacks had become acceptable during the war and I had no shocked mama to gasp and roll her eyes at me.' She smiled reminiscently. 'The other students were very sweet to me. To begin with I think they thought I might be motherly – you know the kind of thing? Listen to their woes and teach them how to cook nourishing meals on a pittance. They soon realized that I didn't do maternal.'

'I bet they did.' Clio was amused by the idea. 'Anyway, at least it can't have been too strange. Almost like going home. Everyone must have remembered your family.'

'Oh, not strange at all. I was very happy.'

'And did you have lots of boyfriends?' Clio could easily imagine that the young Hester must have been rather fun.

Hester's eyes glinted at her across the table. 'Lovers,' she corrected mischievously. 'I never did things by halves.'

'I believe you.' Suddenly, with a little clutch of apprehension and excitement, Clio remembered Peter. 'And so you think I look older today?'

Hester studied her. 'A little. More sophisticated and therefore older. I suppose this is how Peter knows you best?'

Clio looked at her with sudden dismay. Hester's innocent question unexpectedly encapsulated the utter separateness of her life with Peter. Not for them the ordinary intimacy of daily life: no unadorned early morning face or scruffy weekend clothes; no meetings with friends at the pub or family get-togethers. Even after they'd made love, and he'd showered and was buttoning himself back into his city clothes, there was a formality about Peter, as if he were also shrugging himself back into

70

that other, separate life, and pulling on a different persona with his Thomas Pink shirt.

'I suppose it is,' she answered. 'It's a relationship based on work. It's not that we don't relax and have fun together, of course. We always have lots to talk about . . .'

Her voice tailed off uncertainly but Hester nodded understandingly.

'Talking about work can be a relaxation if it's what really matters to you both. You must have a very close bond.'

'Oh, we do,' cried Clio. 'It's just difficult to explain it.'

Hester got up from the table. 'You don't have to explain it. It's nobody's business but yours and Peter's. I can't tell you how much I'm looking forward to meeting him, though. It's so hard having this kind of conversation when you don't know the person involved. I'm going to feed the ducks. St Francis can come and watch. He finds them very amusing and they've long since ceased to be nervous of him.'

'I'm not surprised. He's about as scary as Bag-puss.'

Hester pulled her shawl around her shoulders, took up her stick and the daily ration of bread, and left the kitchen with St Francis stalking at her heels.

Clio began to clear the table, still thinking about Hester's comments. She felt uncharacteristically nervous. Peter's response to her invitation coupled with Hester's reaction to her appearance had shadowed her confidence with doubt and made a tiny crack in the fragile shield with which she protected her relationship with Peter. Presently she went into the little cloakroom next to the kitchen and stared at herself in the glass over the basin. She took out the combs and shook her hair free. Then, taking the narrow silk scarf from around her neck, she twisted her hair back and looked at herself again. She tore off a piece of loo paper and blotted her lips carefully, then flung the red-stained tissue down the lavatory and flushed it away. Studying herself she suspected that she did look younger: younger and more vulnerable. Would Peter notice any difference, she wondered.

Of course, it was just possible that he too might be feeling nervous. This thought comforted her and she was seized afresh by love for him.

The ducks fed, Hester wandered along the river path. St Francis pottered in her wake, pouncing on a leaf that trembled in the soft air as it drifted silently to the ground, before pausing to sit and wash his face with a velvet-padded paw. Hester moved slowly between the trees, noting the evidence of the river's passing. Twigs and stones and trailing tresses of weed cast high upon the muddy path showed where it had overflowed its banks during the storm. In the lower branches of the overhanging trees the detritus of the flood still clung. Traces of the water's immense force were everywhere, yet this morning the river chuckled and murmured softly, running smooth and sinuous in its winding bed, tame and sweet-tempered in the sunlight.

Hester had ceased to think about Clio and was wondering why she hadn't simply asked Jonah for Lucy's address – or her telephone number. What, after all, could be more natural than to speak to her? The fifty-odd years that had passed since their last contact must surely have done away with any awkwardness or pain, yet it had seemed right to allow Lucy the next move.

She'd been such a beautiful child: fearful on her arrival at Bridge House, holding tight to her father's hand lest he too be taken away from her for ever. Hester, remembering her own desolation when her father had died, had gone down on one knee so as to be on the same level saying, 'Hello, Lucy.' She could recall how the dark brown eyes had regarded her so gravely but presently the child had loosened her grip on Michael's hand and shown Hester the grey plush rabbit she'd carried. Patricia's boys – warned that Lucy had lost her mother in a bombing raid – had been sweet with her, taking her away to meet Nanny and to show her where she would sleep.

'I can't tell you how grateful I am,' Michael had said to Hester. 'I know she'll be safe with you . . .' And then Eleanor had come in, graceful and poised until her eyes fell upon Michael, and after a tiny, telling pause she'd said, 'Well, isn't anyone going to introduce us?'

Is that where it had all begun, this story that she would tell to Jonah? Hester knew that each of them – Eleanor, Michael, Edward – would have told it differently, each from his or her own deeply personal perspective, and she wondered if it were possible to tell it fairly and without prejudice. It had been a mystery as to why such a worldly woman should have fallen in love first with Edward and then – so disastrously – with Michael. Edward's love for her was easier to understand. He'd been so pleased with himself, so proud to have won this beautiful woman – even though she'd admitted to never opening a book if she could help it and whose only reading was, apparently, the *Tatler*. He'd been passionately in love, in thrall to

Eleanor's physical beauty, and, with all the romanticism inherent in his nature, had mentally endowed her with perfection of character too.

Their mother, privately dismayed, hoped that Eleanor would quickly cease to flourish in the rarefied atmosphere of Edward's love. It was clear that she needed a tough, physical response to her needs, and Edward's gentle diffidence and clever mind would never be enough. How would a poet – even a soldier-poet – satisfy such an unimaginative woman as Eleanor? And Edward was determined that one day he would be a published poet.

Sometime during his first year at Cambridge, Edward had quoted Hester some lines from one of John Clare's sonnets:

> Poets love nature and themselves are love,
> The scorn of fools and mock of idle pride.

'That's me,' he'd told her. 'And Mike too. Not that I can call myself a poet. Not yet. But just you wait.'

Their mother had encouraged them. John Clare was a link between Edward and his late father, who had been working on a biography of the poet when he died, and she strengthened the bond as much as she could. It was she who wrote to him at Cambridge, inspiring him to go on weekend pilgrimages to Helpstone to see Clare's cottage, and to seek out such places as Emmonsales Heath, where Clare had wandered as a child, hoping to find the end of the world, and the remains of the old Roman quarry at Swordy Well. Edward had infected Michael with his enthusiasm, dragging him along on these excursions, and soon they'd begun to incorporate Clare's language into their speech: 'proggling' for poking, 'soodling' for idly sauntering, 'blea' for exposed and 'haynish' for awkward.

'Rather blea,' Edward might say on a winter's afternoon up on Dunkery Beacon. 'Shall we soodle on down to Porlock for tea?'

Hester had picked up this language with delight and they had drawn her into their company, young though she was. She loved the bird poems – read to her by her father – and knew many of them by heart, rejoicing in the wonder, even amazement, that Clare showed over the tiny miracles of nature and his intimate manner of writing that seemed to involve her personally in his own delight.

Well, in my many walks I rarely found
A place less likely for a bird to form
Its nest . . .
. . . and you and I

Had surely passed it in our walk today
Had chance not led us by it . . .
. . . Stop, here's the bird – that woodman at
   the gap
Hath frit it from the hedge – 'tis olive green –
Well, I declare, it is the pettichap!
Not bigger than the wren and seldom seen . . .

Edward had brought Michael home to meet them all and soon he'd become as dear to their mother as her own children and Blaise, their cousin. What plans they'd made – oh, the glories to which they'd aspired. Then the war had come – and Eleanor with it.

A sudden scuffle of dead leaves beside the path and a robin flew up in a scatter of leaf-mould to preen himself in a holly tree where berries glowed a rich, bright crimson. Hester watched him for a moment, listening to the delicate sweetness of his song, and then turned to retrace her path through the wood.

There was no sign of Clio – perhaps she'd already left to fetch Peter from the train – but Hester was still thinking about the past and had temporarily put them both from her mind. With the true scholar's detachment she'd decided that if she were to be able to tell Jonah the story accurately then she needed to make notes; to try for some chronological order and to see if there were any old snapshots or letters that might bear out her memories.

She kicked off her boots in the scullery, passed through the kitchen and went into the dining-room which, since the recent building of the breakfast-room, had become a study. A specially designed table, built against one wall of the room, held a computer, a printer and a filing tray. Clio's laptop lived on a smaller desk that stood at right angles underneath the window. Each desk had its own padded swivel chair and Anglepoise lamp.

'It's only fair,' Hester had said to Clio, 'that if you're going to be looking after me, you have the space to work.'

Her own work – reviewing, writing articles, assisting her ex-pupils in their research – was still a very important part of her life.

Now, as she waited for her computer to boot up, she took a notebook from a drawer and a pencil from a black ceramic jar that had once held cheese. She began to make headings, to jot down names and dates, and was absorbed with her work when the study door opened.

'Oh, Clio.' She turned quickly, glancing at the clock. 'Are you back already?'

Clio stood in the doorway: her lips were pressed together, her chin tilted, and Hester got up at once.

'What is it?' she asked. 'Not an accident?'

'No, not an accident.' Clio's voice was brittle as glass. 'I picked up a message on my mobile on the way to the station. Peter can't come. He says that something's come up and he can't get away.'

She repeated his words with a deliberately inflected irony and, watching her, Hester could see that Clio was torn between an automatic desire to defend him and a very real need to submit to her disappointment. It interested her to see that, at some level, Clio clearly did not believe in Peter's reason for cancelling his visit, though it might be considered a quite reasonable one. The brittle voice, the flush on her cheekbones were the outward and visible signs of an inner resentment and humiliation. Hester wondered how best she might help her without trespassing.

'Of course, you did say that the agency was having difficulty with a client's account.' She offered it as a kind of stepping-stone out of the shoal waters of indiscretion and back to the more solid ground of Clio's self-esteem. 'You'd know all about that.'

'Oh, yes. I know all about that and I don't believe it.'

Hester was silenced for a moment by this flat

statement. Yet there was an air of unhappiness –
even fear – beneath Clio's angry reaction that
forced Hester into a more open approach.

'You think it was for personal reasons?'

Clio glanced at her, as if assessing Hester's
motives, and looked away again. 'Yes I do. I think
he's got problems at home and he chickened out.'

'Well, asking him down here was a very signifi-
cant step,' said Hester thoughtfully.

'Was it?'

Clio sounded so anxious that Hester was seized
with compunction. 'It was a reasonable request, but
think about it, Clio. You were asking him to leave
the safe, neutral ground of your relationship and
come to meet your family. Think how it must have
seemed to him.'

'But I didn't mean it like that. He wanted to see
me and I thought, Why not here? I thought you'd
get on well together. There was no way you were
going to ask him his intentions or embarrass him.'

'But did *he* know that?'

Clio, remembering her conversation with Peter,
bit her lip. 'I told him you weren't in the least
that kind of person. I thought he'd be able to
handle it. He's very good at keeping his relationships separate. Why make a big deal over a trip
down here? He comes to my flat.'

'But does he meet your friends there? Or family?'

'I don't have any family besides you, do I? Mum and Dad can never be persuaded to leave their olive grove in Greece and I hardly know my cousins. Not much risk of running into family.'

'So this was his first opportunity.'

Hester hadn't meant her remark to sound so brutal but Clio flushed and turned away.

'I'll go and organize some lunch,' she said. 'And I hope you're up for dinner at Woods tonight, Hes. I'm damned if I shall cancel the table.'

CHAPTER SIX

Lucy Faringdon was eating chocolate cake in St Martin's Tea Room. The atmosphere of the café, with its cheerful log fire and low-beamed ceiling and the busy traffic of people in the narrow lane beyond the window, all added to her enjoyment of the rich, sweet cake. The true, deep-down source of her happiness, however, lay in her sense of freedom. This morning a very good friend, who had worked with Jerry for the last twenty years at Chichester College, had come to see him and she'd been able to leave them contentedly together and come out into the town.

She sipped at her latte and then sat for a moment, simply relaxing gratefully into this moment of respite. Here, sitting by the fire, she felt an irresponsible light-heartedness that she knew from experience would be very short-lived. Nevertheless, she set herself to extract every moment of present pleasure – the melting texture of the cake on her tongue, the taste of the coffee – whilst also dwelling on the future promise of some shopping: nothing necessary or dull, just a few little treats. Deliberately putting away from her all the usual anxieties relating to Jerry's deteriorating health, she continued to plan her happy morning, thinking about the walk she would have with Tess, the Sussex spaniel, who was waiting patiently in the car. Maybe they would drive down to Bosham and walk by the sea, or go inland, perhaps . . .

'Lucy, my dear, how are you?' Someone bent over her, swinging between her and the window, and she gave a tiny cry of alarm – quickly stifled.

'Jennifer! How nice to see you. No, of course you didn't startle me. Not really. I was miles away, that's all.'

'You looked it. Nobody with you?' Jennifer Bryce, who had once taught Jonah at school, indicated the empty chair. 'May I join you?'

'Of course.' Lucy's smile hid her sense of disappointment: her lovely moment of peace was shattered. Now she must be polite, answer Jennifer's questions. Quite incapable of snubbing her or simply making some excuse to hurry away, she sat quite still as the older woman ordered coffee, refused cake, and then turned her large, pale, inquisitive eyes on Lucy. It seemed to her as if Jennifer was reading her expression eagerly, checking it out for weakness or despair. Deliberately Lucy schooled her face into a mask of polite nothingness, remembering how patiently and unwaveringly Jonah had disliked Jennifer Bryce through five long years of geography classes.

'And how is poor Jerry?' Her voice was thick with a treacly sympathy: a special hushed voice. 'The last time I saw you – goodness, it must be months ago – he'd fractured his back again and had been re-admitted to hospital.'

'It's all to do with this ghastly lupus. Poor Jerry. He's been on so much medication – steroids, warfarin, morphine, you name it – and he reacts so badly to some of them. Then, when he has to come off them, he has terrible withdrawal symptoms.'

Lucy tried to speak lightly, unable to bring herself to describe to this inquisitive woman the real humiliation and anguish of Jerry's ongoing pain – the swelling joints, constant fatigue, ulcers and the terrible breathlessness – nor the agony of watching someone she loved suffering so bravely.

'However do you manage, Lucy?'

Before she could answer, the waitress arrived and Jennifer leaned back in her chair to allow her coffee to be placed in front of her. Her square ugly hands opened her bag and reached for her tube of sweeteners. She dripped one into the liquid and began to stir the coffee whilst Lucy watched her.

However do I manage? she asked herself silently. How do I manage when I lie beside Jerry at night and I wake with a shock because quite suddenly he stops breathing and begins to gasp wildly for air? And each time I think, Is this it? Sleep apnoea, they call it. It's frightening and exhausting. His lungs are shrinking. We hold on tightly to each other and make silly jokes. 'You're through, Commander Air.' However do I manage? How does he?

'I'm not sure, to tell you the truth,' she said aloud. 'How does anyone?' She suddenly saw Jennifer as a gaping, ghoulish tourist, visiting her life with Jerry, staring in at it with avid interest but no true wish to understand. This image gave Lucy the courage to resist her. 'Look, Tess is in the car and I've already been far too long. It's lovely to see you but I must dash.'

'Oh, well, if you must . . .'

Lucy willed down guilt – her natural response to someone's disappointment or reproach – and smiled firmly.

'I really must. Poor old Tess will be crossing her legs.'

And now, she told herself as she went out into St Martin's Street and headed for the car park, I shan't be able to have a lovely browse in Between the Lines, just in case she comes out and sees me. And I wanted to get some cards and some candles. Damn, damn, damn.

Tess was waiting, nose against the glass, her tail wagging, and Lucy couldn't resist opening the hatch for a moment and burying her face against the soft warm dome of her head.

'What should I do without you, Tesskins?' she murmured. 'Where shall we go?'

Briefly she felt that she was in flight: from Jennifer, from her own responsibilities, from herself even. Where could she go to recapture that brief sense of freedom that she'd experienced earlier?

Suddenly she knew the place: a bridle path where Tess could run between pale, chalky fields, following the scent of a fox or putting up a pheasant with a whirr of its indignant incandescent wings. Tess's bright, rust-gold coat would be a clear note of colour amongst the dun-coloured countryside: bright as the honeysuckle's berries and the blood-red rosehips.

*   *   *

The damp air was cool and soft. Behind smoke-grey cloud the pale gold disc of the sun showed faintly, hard-edged as a metal coin. Cobwebs as big as tea plates, slung between twigs and branches in the straggling hedge, caught and reflected back the luminous shimmering light. Their hump-backed occupants crouched watchfully, racing out at the lightest vibration of a silvery filament to capture their unwary prey. Hands in pockets, Lucy followed in Tess's excited wake, looking for treasures that she might take back for Jerry. His painful joints, coupled with a severe reaction to insect bites, had begun to make country walks an anxiety rather than a pleasure but he liked to enjoy them second-hand, and she was learning to make a little excitement out of them for him rather than feeling guilty that she was still fit and free.

Guilt and fear: all her life she had wrestled with these demons yet, though she had never conquered them, she refused to abandon the struggle. Lately, as Jerry tried to come to terms with his illness, so she had begun to analyse her own character in the hope of becoming stronger through understanding rather than simply condemning herself for her failures. The shock of finding that she must be the carer and that Jerry – who had always taken control and been her refuge – should now look to her for mental and physical assistance had been terrifying. In attempting to deal with this role reversal she was making a greater effort to combat her own weaknesses.

Just lately, during those wakeful nights lying beside Jerry and willing him to breathe peacefully, she'd begun to look back at that part of her life she had so carefully concealed, searching for clues. Now, she was trying for a more positive approach. She'd started to realize that her own negative reactions to her fear – 'Oh, why are you always such a fool!' or 'Why don't you grow up!' – merely served to diminish her already low self-esteem. Against her will, instinct was forcing her back into her past as if the answers might be somewhere there. Cautiously, as if bracing herself for what she might see, she'd allowed tiny glimpses to show themselves. She could believe, at least, that it was partly due to her mother's influence that she'd grown up to become a superstitious child.

At first it is a silly game, hopping across the London pavement, holding Mummy's hand: 'Don't walk on the lines, darling, or the bears will get you.' 'See the magpie, Lucy? Only one. "One for sorrow." Oh, quick. Look for another one.' 'Touch wood . . .' Her mother never goes anywhere without her little carved bird mascot, kissing her daughter three times for luck, and, though she makes these little rituals into a game, deep down there is a hint of something else: fear. When she dies, killed by a bomb whilst playing at a lunchtime recital, Lucy's first terrified thought is that some good-luck formula must have been neglected. Nobody ever finds the little mascot and the small Lucy makes the inevitable connection. So it begins – that first insidious need to feel protected from an unseen adversary.

Her father is strong, and she clings to him, yet even he is not powerful enough to protect himself and, in the end, succumbs to the invisible power of evil: blown to pieces whilst attempting to defuse an unexploded bomb. After that, as indelible as pokerwork, three things remain burned into her memory.

The first, a whisper – a woman's voice, urgent and needy: 'It's because of Lucy, isn't it? If it weren't for her we could get away. You're a fool, Michael. Something terrible is going to happen and it will be because of Lucy . . .'

The second, Jack showing her the Midsummer Cushion: 'But you must never, never touch it, Lucy. It's very old and precious and Nanny says if we touch it something really bad will happen.'

Her first reaction is disappointment. It is not a cushion at all but a tapestry, framed and hanging on the wall in Hester's bedroom. Her initial surprise, however, is swiftly replaced with delight.

The Midsummer Cushion – oh, how beautiful; how magical to the eyes of a small child. A tapestry of every imaginable wild flower – ox-eye daisies, scarlet field poppies, yellow rattle and golden buttercups, eyebright and purple self-heal, all threaded through with long green grasses – lovingly traced in silk. Beneath the protecting glass, dried flowers have been gently placed beside the silken ones so that the whole effect is of a hayfield in June. She is drawn back to it again and again, creeping into Hester's bedroom to gaze enraptured at the pretty thing in its golden frame. One wild autumn evening she climbs onto the little stool and, on tiptoe, leans to look more closely at the tapestry. Losing her balance, she puts out a hand to save herself, catching at the edge of the frame. It comes crashing down, glass splinters all over the rug and the polished floorboards, the dried flowers crumbling instantly to dust. She has broken the Midsummer Cushion and retribution will surely follow swiftly. When the third thing happens, guilt and fear fuse into a single terrified reaction.

'Something terrible is going to happen and it will be because of Lucy.'

'If we touch it something really bad will happen.'

The voices have prophesied truly: murder happens and, in its wake, betrayal and loss of trust.

Lucy stood watching a flock of seagulls wheeling above the new-ploughed field. Against the soft grey sky the white under-feathers shone with a startling purity. Then, all in a moment as they dipped and turned, they were invisible, grey on grey. The voices had ceased to haunt her, though she could still recall the tense atmosphere and the little tingle of terror that had accompanied them. She'd long since realized that the first was the voice of a manipulating and determined woman, pleading with her reluctant lover, and the second was simply the repetition, by a little boy, of something he'd been told many times. Yet they'd had their effect on her, reinforcing the superstitious tendencies inherited from her mother. Even after all these years she felt the twist of guilt, the clutch of fear, when things went wrong or people weren't happy. It was an instinctive response, due to an odd kind of early conditioning involving both nurture and nature: because of her, or something she'd done, someone had died and lives had been wrecked.

Yet much worse even than the breaking of the Midsummer Cushion had been the loss of faith in the two people she'd loved and trusted most: her father and Hester.

Lucy reached up to pick a late-flowering crown of pale honeysuckle and a spray of rosehips. Added to a twig of golden birch leaves they looked charming. She'd put them into a vase for Jerry and tell him about the gulls whilst she made their lunch.

CHAPTER SEVEN

Hester was enjoying herself. Accustomed to a scholarly approach to work, she'd begun her little history for Jonah with a properly set out table of names and dates: her own family tree to begin with, just to give him something to work from, followed by the stark facts. She'd put in too much information to begin with, distracting herself with odd memories that could be of no interest to Jonah. For instance, stories of the two younger boys could have no relevance here. Killed so early in the war, they were simply two more names to confuse him. They were there on the family tree, of course, but nothing else relating to their lives would be recorded. Only those people who related in some way to Jonah's family would be mentioned. Some of her notes were made from memory, others from the diaries their mother had kept until her death in the autumn of 1942. She transferred the

cryptic entries, making her own observations along-
side.

1939

July 27th. All the boys home for the holidays and
Michael with them. Made a summer pudding.
(M's D)

September 1st. War has been declared. (M's D)

I remember that we all listened to the wireless
and I still recall the feeling of fear. I could see
that Mother felt the same way. Only the younger
boys were excited. Blaise and Edward were very
quiet.

1940

January 15th. A letter from Michael to tell us
that he is married. A small registry office affair.
Her name is Susan. Just like Michael's parents,
her father was killed in the Great War and her
mother died whilst she was still at school. So they
are both orphans. I can hardly take it in that
Michael is married and a soldier. (M's D)

I can remember her saying, 'Oh, how different
it is from everything we imagined for them,' and
she was very low for the rest of the day. Michael
sent a wedding photograph with a very sweet

note from Susan saying how much she was looking forward to meeting Michael's 'family'. It cheered Mother up no end. She was a musician – the violin, I think – but she never managed the journey to Bridge House.

1941
March 16th. Patricia and the children arriving with Nanny for the duration. (M's D)

Her husband, Rob, was at sea and Plymouth was being bombed. Mother was very relieved because it meant that the house would now be too full for us to take in evacuees.

March 21st. The first day of spring. Edward bringing Eleanor to meet us. (M's D)

We were all nervous, I remember. Patricia was afraid that Jack and Robin would be noisy and play up.

April 18th. Edward and Eleanor are married. A registry office wedding just like Michael's. Oh, this war! (M's D)

Edward telephoned from Ludlow where he was stationed and Mother spoke to them both. She pretended to be thrilled, though disappointed that it had happened so suddenly, but agreed with them that the war changed everything.

Afterwards she was very quiet and we all felt rather low. Michael, and now Edward, married and with none of the fun and excitement that we'd once visualized.

November 12th. Edward sent out to the Far East. (M's D)

They'd been living in a hiring near Ludlow and Mother offered Eleanor a home with us. She replied that she would stay on for a little longer with friends. I can remember how relieved we all were!

December 17th. Eleanor arriving for Christmas. (M's D)

I never knew quite why she came to us. Perhaps she had nowhere else to go.

1942
February 15th. Singapore has surrendered to the Japanese. (M's D)

Here her diaries end.

It seemed to Hester, as she worked, that her mother's diaries were unlocking the past for her. Other memories were triggered by these brief entries and though she continued to document them, her thoughts returned again and again to one particular event: Eleanor's first visit to Bridge House. Presently, she stopped writing and gave herself up to remembering.

On this wild spring day in 1941, the wind is so strong and gusts so fitfully that it seems to the assembled family in the big square hall that Eleanor is whirled in upon it, laughing helplessly, her hands to her hair. Edward, tall and elegant at her side, is clearly besotted by his companion and cannot imagine even for a second that his family won't adore her as he does. He takes her foolish little hat from her hands and leads her forward to introduce her. His face blazes with pride and he can barely take his eyes from her.

In the first moment when Hester sees that look on her eldest brother's face her heart sinks. From her position on the fender beside the fire she notes the confident look in Eleanor's eyes, the wide smile on her vividly painted lips and the pretty gestures with which she greets Edward's mother and Patricia, the eldest of all the siblings. Both of Edward's younger brothers are at sea but Patricia's two small boys are at hand, waiting to be introduced.

The eldest, three-year-old Jack, shakes Eleanor's

hand, staring up at her curiously, but small Robin is overwhelmed by this tall dark woman who bends over him. He begins to cry. Patricia gathers him to her, comforting but mildly reproving, as though she fears that their guest might in some way be offended. Eleanor simply laughs, takes a sweet from her bag and pops it into his mouth.

As if he is a dog, thinks Hester, to be silenced with a biscuit. Quickly she catches herself up: she must make an effort to be friends with Eleanor, though some deep instinct warns her against this elegant, self-possessed woman.

'And this is Hester.' Edward's thin sensitive face is alight with pleasure at the prospect of his favourite sister meeting his bride-to-be.

Eleanor's hand is warm; her look manages to be both critical and amused.

'Hello, Hester,' she says – and each is immediately aware of the other's antagonism. Eleanor makes some casual, laughing remark about Hester's letters to Edward – 'How do you manage to think of so much to say? Pages of them! I'm always *so* impressed, but then I can hardly think of enough to cover a single sheet, especially to a brother.' Within the compliment there is a little barb, something that implies that it's all rather pathetic – surely Hester has better things to do with her time than write screeds to her big brother? Hester refuses both the compliment and the jibe, simply smiling politely and saying nothing. Eleanor stares at her for a moment; then, with a tiny shrug and a little moue of the lips, which says that if Hester chooses to be unfriendly that's her problem, she turns away to join Edward who is now speaking to his mother.

Nevertheless, Hester is suddenly conscious of her old flannel skirt and unflattering jersey, and she is relieved when Robin comes to her on unsteady feet so that she can resume her seat on the fender and take him onto her lap.

And then Edward is perching beside her, still with that excited expression, saying, 'What do you think of her, Hes? Isn't she sensational?'

'Oh, yes,' she says obediently, staring at his flushed cheeks and the over-bright eyes that are still fixed on Eleanor as if he cannot bear to lose a minute of her. 'Yes, she's very beautiful.'

'It's like he has a fever,' she says to Patricia later. They are sharing a bedroom, just as they did when they were children, because Eleanor has been given Patricia's bigger room. Patricia is using the other single bed that is usually covered with piles of books. Hester has put them back into the bookcase, and she has allotted part of a drawer in the old painted chest for Patricia's needs. The wind rattles the windows and the river roars tumultuously.

'He has,' says Patricia, bending to peer into the spotted looking-glass, turning away rather despairingly from her pretty but rather indeterminate reflection. She too feels inadequate beside Eleanor's dark, highly polished brilliance. 'He's in love. That's how it takes you if you're lucky.'

'Lucky?' Hester makes a face. 'I wouldn't want to be like that, burning up with something that makes you different and . . . silly.'

She sits up straight against her pillow – arms folded, legs stuck straight down beneath the blankets – hating Edward's new silliness and resenting Eleanor for making her beloved brother look foolish; lovesick.

'It's not his fault,' says Patricia wisely, folding her clothes on the small chair and climbing into the narrow bed. 'You'll see one day.'

'I knew you were going to say that,' says Hester furiously. 'Honestly, you're so predictable, Pat. It's always the same thing: I don't know anything because I'm too young. I'm not that young. I'm thirteen, remember. I know how to feel things,' she adds rather grandly.

'But not being in love,' says Patricia. 'Not yet. It's

like a kind of madness, really. A fever, like you said just now.'

'Rob isn't like that with you,' protests Hester. 'He doesn't follow you about like a sick spaniel.'

'No,' says Patricia rather sadly, switching out the light and settling down to sleep. 'No, Rob's rather down-to-earth, I'm afraid.'

'I like Rob,' says Hester. She's rather shocked by Patricia's reaction. How could she respect someone who behaved so pathetically? 'He's . . . sensible.'

'Oh, yes,' agrees Patricia with a little sigh. 'Rob's sensible.'

And now Hester can remember that, three or four years ago when she was first married, Patricia used to have that same expression when she looked at Rob; that blind, worshipping look of adoration.

She stares into the darkness, listening to the river's voice. How frightening it must be to feel so strongly and lose all sense of self; how dangerous to expose one's vulnerability.

'I shall never fall in love,' she exclaims vehemently.

'Oh, shut up, Hes, and go to sleep,' mutters Patricia. 'You know how early the boys wake up, and Nanny has so much to do. I need some sleep even if you don't.'

Hester wriggles down, pulling up the blankets to

keep out the draughts. The river's voice can still be heard, singing its endless murmuring song, and she lies still, reciting Clare's poetry to herself:

Here the steep bank, as dropping headlong
    down,
While glides the stream, a silver streak between
As glide the shaded clouds along the sky . . .

And at last the words and the river's music blend together into a dreamless sleep.

She could still hear the river, louder again now, and with it the sounds of activity somewhere. Hester realized that Clio must have returned from her walk and was probably making some tea. She tidied her notes, saved her computer work and went out to find her.

CHAPTER EIGHT

'I've been thinking, Hes.' Clio took down the battered red Jackson's of Piccadilly tea caddy and peered inside. 'You can have Lemon Burst, Raspberry and Echinacea or Camomile. I really ought to go back to London on Sunday.'

'Raspberry, please. Well, why not? I'm perfectly fit now and I'm sure they must be missing you at the agency.'

Clio poured boiling water into two mugs. 'I think that there's a bit of a panic on. Peter never actually insisted on a cut-off date, only that you must be able to manage on your own again after the operation, but I feel I'm needed more there now.'

'It was very kind of him and I've loved having you here but, apart from anything else, I expect you're rather looking forward to getting back to your work and your friends.'

Clio put a spoonful of honey into her mug of Lemon Burst and threw the teabag into the bin. Hester took her own mug and went to sit at the table. Clio's expression was a familiar one, though she hadn't seen it for many years. It was her 'going back to school' face: a rather touching mixture of hopefulness and trepidation.

'Peter will be glad to have you back again.' Hester continued to be positive. 'I know you arranged a very reliable replacement but when you've worked so closely with someone, as Peter has with you – how long is it now? Nearly a year? – it must be difficult to adapt to someone new.'

Clio sat down opposite and St Francis leaped up to sit at the end of the table as if presiding at a meeting.

'I shall miss you,' said Clio. She looked faintly puzzled, almost irritated, at this discovery. 'I haven't spent so long here since school holidays when Mum and Dad were off on some expedition or research trip or whatever. It's been rather like a holiday, this last few weeks.'

'We've had some fun, haven't we? And then, of course, there was Lizzie. You've been quite busy at Michaelgarth, helping her with ideas and fetching and carrying people.'

'I think that's part of it,' said Clio. 'I love my job,

really I do, but it's a bit deskbound. I've enjoyed dashing about meeting Lizzie's theatre and film friends and doing my own thing.'

And Peter's knocked your confidence, added Hester silently, and you've had the opportunity to stand back and evaluate your relationship.

'Well, you could stay,' she said aloud. 'We could turn the clock back fifty years and you could be my companion and do the flowers.'

She smiled across the table at her god-daughter, who grinned back at her.

'I'm almost tempted,' Clio said.

Hester laughed derisively. 'You'd die of boredom in a week. If Lizzie hadn't wanted help you'd have been biting the carpet long since. You need someone to organize.'

Clio made a face. 'I could organize you.'

'No you couldn't,' replied Hester calmly. 'Not now that I can walk and drive again. You know how irritating I am to live with.'

'Well, of course I know that. I can't imagine how Frank copes with you. I suppose it's because you're both so detached and self-contained—' She broke off, thinking of Jonah, and Hester raised her eyebrows interrogatively. 'Jonah said that about you. That you were as detached and serene as a nun.' Clio hesitated. 'I said you'd nearly been one.

What happened, Hes? Why didn't you take the veil or whatever you call it?'

There was a short silence.

'I couldn't deal with community life,' said Hester at last. 'I was too arrogant: too self-willed. I had wonderful ideas for reform and the sisters seemed so obdurate and unwilling to contemplate change.' She smiled briefly at a memory. Blaise had once sent her a picture postcard of a flock of sheep, standing immovably in the middle of a moorland road, staring rather balefully towards the camera. On the back he'd written: 'Community life?' He'd understood her difficulties though he'd been sad that she hadn't persisted. 'It's not easy, you know, to surrender yourself wholeheartedly and generously. Whether the relationship is with God or with another person, there's a great deal of giving-up of self involved in it. I couldn't do it.'

'Not for anybody?'

Hester glanced at her, a sharp bright look: 'Are we playing "Truth"?' she asked lightly. 'You didn't warn me first, you know.'

Clio flushed. 'Sorry. It's just interesting to me, especially at the moment, when you talked about surrendering yourself.'

Hester's gaze softened. 'I might have managed it once. But in the end it wasn't required of me. Now let me ask you a question. If Peter were to leave the agency would you be content to continue to work there?'

Clio stared at her, the colour in her cheeks fading as she contemplated her answer. 'No,' she said slowly. 'I don't think so. I'd almost decided to leave when Peter arrived. I felt I'd done it all, if you know what I mean. I wanted something fresh. But then Peter needed help to settle in and it was exciting somehow, showing him the ropes, and then . . . well, so then I stayed,' she finished rather lamely.

'So if he were to go?'

'But why should he go? Or are you asking if I'd go with him?'

She looked confused, as if Hester were posing a difficult question – or even setting some kind of trap – and Hester shook her head.

'There's no hidden agenda here. I simply ask whether you stay for Peter or for the job itself, that's all.'

The telephone bell saved Clio from finding an answer and she jumped up quickly.

'Hello. Oh, hi. How are you? We're fine. Yes, honestly, she's doing really well. Hang on a minute. Hester's right here. It's Amy,' she said, and saw Hester's look of surprise as she took the phone to speak to Patricia's granddaughter.

Carrying her mug to the window, half listening to Hester, Clio stared out into the garden. Away from London, at a distance from her job and from Peter, she was beginning to see just how precarious their relationship was and she was dismayed. No longer mesmerized by the radar-like beam of his personality, she was able to question her feelings for him – or was she simply overreacting because she was hurt by his rather curt cancellation of the trip to Bridge House?

Sipping at her drink, listening to Hester's side of the conversation, Clio was unexpectedly subject to a violent stab of envy for Amy. This was foolish, she told herself. After all, she had no desire to be married to a naval officer, who spent a great deal of time at sea, or to be left at regular intervals with the care of three boisterous children.

Yet Clio knew very well that Amy wouldn't have changed a single thing in her life. She didn't even mind Alan's absences. She'd inherited the family trait of detachment and admitted to being grateful for some space to herself. Amy and Alan had a kind of knockabout, laidback attitude to themselves and their children, supported as they were by a sprawling network of relations.

Clio doubted that she would cope so well in Amy's position – and had said so.

'I'm just doing what I like best,' Amy had responded. 'I couldn't do what you do. Good grief! I wouldn't last five minutes. I know I don't have any brothers or sisters but our house was always full of children. I can't count my cousins, there's so many of them. I was brainwashed from an early age. Not like you, Clio. You're so clear-sighted and focused.'

It was true that her own experience had been very different. Hester's company and influence had given Clio, an only child of peripatetic parents, a sense of self-worth that derived from being independent. Hester had shown her god-daughter that self-esteem was grounded in confidence and encouraged Clio's capabilities in the hope that she would not have to depend on other people's approval to make her feel valuable.

So far Hester's influence had borne good fruit but now Clio wondered if she had become too dependent on Peter, despite the fact that she knew just how peripheral she was to his life. She remembered her disappointment when he'd misread her invitation to Bridge House – and the short, sharp words with which he'd cancelled the visit. Yet his letter had been so full of need and love. Clio was filled with confusion and longing: she must see him again before she could come to any sensible conclusions. She would text him to confirm that she was coming back and await his reaction.

Putting her mug down on the table, leaving Hester to her conversation with Amy, Clio went to find her mobile phone.

Later that evening, after supper, the telephone rang again. This time it was Jonah.

'Just to say thanks again,' he said, 'and wondering if Hester has a few days free any time this month. How are you? Shall I see you too if I come down?'

'I'm going back to London this weekend,' she told him brightly, hoping perversely that he would be disappointed.

'Great,' he said cheerfully. 'Then I'll take you up on that suggestion you made. Is Hester there or are you her social secretary at the moment?'

Clio laughed. 'I can hear it in your voice,' she told him. 'You're convinced that there's a story here, aren't you?'

'Something like that,' he admitted, 'but it's a bit more personal this time.'

'Hang on,' said Clio. 'I'll get Hes and check her diary.'

There was a brief consultation and then Hester took the telephone.

'Hello, Jonah. Have you spoken to Lucy?'

'I have. She says OK.'

'Are you both quite sure?'

'She was a bit shocked at first but she has agreed. I think it's time; she does too. I asked if she'd like to phone you but she says, "Not yet".'

'Very well. This weekend might be difficult. Perhaps the next one?'

'That would be terrific. I could come down on Friday and stay until Tuesday if that's not too long? The thing is, I'm not driving just at present. Will that make difficulties? I can get a taxi out to you, can't I?'

'I shall be able to pick you up from the station,' Hester said. 'I can drive quite well again now.'

'That would be very kind. I'll check train times and phone again. I can't tell you how much I'm looking forward to it.'

'So am I,' said Hester. 'Goodbye, Jonah.'

'What was that about driving?' asked Clio suspiciously.

'He isn't, at present.'

'Why not?'

'I didn't ask,' replied Hester serenely. 'It didn't seem relevant.'

Clio snorted. 'Drinking or speeding,' she pronounced. 'Will you be OK?'

'I doubt that I shall be in any danger with Jonah, especially when it comes to speeding or drinking. I'm sure I shall be quite safe.'

'You know what I mean,' said Clio crossly – and went to stack the dishwasher. She was surprised to find that she felt rather put out, as if she were being excluded from something rather special.

CHAPTER NINE

In the little cottage in Litten Terrace, Jerry was preparing to walk into the town to fetch the newspaper. This period of the morning was the best time of the day for him, when he might manage some gardening or letter-writing and, if he were lucky, enjoy a brief respite from pain and the self-defeating weariness that dogged him, sapping his courage. The familiar route to the newsagents – crossing the recreation ground, passing through the park that lay beneath the city walls – generally raised his spirits. This morning he hesitated, watching Lucy who was sitting at the table jotting down an address.

Ever since Jonah's telephone call she'd been slightly distracted and he feared that she might be concealing something. He struggled with a growing anxiety that she was beginning to feel the need to shield him. Jerry stiffened at the thought of it:

every instinct fought against such a humiliating prospect. He who had always been the strong one, the protector, was now in a position of weakness and he was finding the process of coming to terms with it very difficult.

He pulled on his jacket, picked up his stick with a hand that was beginning to claw because of the pain in its joints, watching her preoccupied face out of the corner of his eye.

'You've been a bit quiet since Jonah phoned, Luce,' he said at last. 'Are you sure he's OK?'

'He's fine.' She put down her pen, turning to him quickly, reassuringly. 'Honestly. It's just that whilst he was down on Exmoor with Lizzie Blake he came across someone I knew in the war. Hester Mallory. I stayed with her family after Mummy died and before I came here to live with Aunt Mary. I was just amazed at the coincidence and I can't quite get it out of my mind, that's all. And just then I was thinking about Aunt Mary.' This wasn't strictly true but she had no wish to tell him about Jonah's proposed visit to Bridge House – not yet. 'Do you remember when you first met her, Jerry?'

'Of course I do.' He put his keys in his pocket and came back into the room. 'She was very kind to me.'

'And to me. I don't know what would have

happened to me without Aunt Mary. You don't regret that we stayed with her? Lots of young men wouldn't have been able to cope with a crotchety, sick old woman in the first months of their marriage.'

'I think we all managed very well and, anyway, it would have been a pretty poor show to leave her alone after all those years she'd looked after you.'

Lucy smiled at him: Aunt Mary had approved of Jerry.

'He's tough,' she'd said. 'Don't underestimate him, Lucy, or mistake his kindness for weakness. He's a good man.'

'What are you smiling at?' Jerry asked.

'I was thinking about the Lambert Barnard paintings in the cathedral,' she said, lying to him for the second time. 'And the way we met.'

He laughed, forgetting his anxieties. 'Ah yes. Good old Barnard. All those Bishops of Chichester looking exactly alike.'

She got up suddenly and went to him, putting her arms around him and holding him tightly.

'I've had an idea,' she said, looking up at him. 'Why don't we go out this morning? In the car, I mean. We could go to Stansted House and give Tess a walk and then have coffee and one of those delicious caramel slices in the tearoom. Shall we?

You always say that all your beastly drugs and tablets ruin your breakfast coffee. It's such a lovely morning and this weather can't last much longer.'

She spoke so pleadingly that he was touched. It didn't always occur to him to acknowledge the ways in which this wretched disease had closed down on their lives. Most of the time he was too busy struggling with his physical deterioration, the after-effects of the drugs and the bouts of depression, which were so contrary to his natural disposition.

'Why not?' he said. 'I'll drive. I feel up to it this morning. We'll pick up a newspaper on the way.'

She didn't make a fuss or argue with him: asking him if he were sure it wouldn't tire him too much. She simply nodded, gave him a quick kiss and went away to call Tess in from the garden. Jerry took a deep breath, his spirits rising. All was well.

Sitting beside him as they drove out through Chichester, heading west, Lucy was still thinking about the Barnard paintings. She'd seized on them by chance, seeking to distract him from questions about Hester, and then found that the memory had been so fresh, so strong, that she'd been over-whelmed by her feelings. Suddenly it seemed to her that to spend the morning apart would be a terrible waste; that there might not be so many sunny mornings left to share. This was not a new idea. Ever since systemic lupus erythematosus and Hughes syndrome had been diagnosed, and they'd been made aware of the implications of the disease, they'd both bravely resolved to try to maintain a positive attitude.

This morning, looking at Jerry, she'd remembered the young, strong fellow she'd met in the cathedral quite by chance nearly forty years before. The memory, rather than saddening her, had filled her with an odd sense of revitalization: a strong feeling that nothing – not even this terrible disease – could destroy the true essence of those two people who had once gazed at the paintings together. As she looked sideways at him, at the tweed sleeve of his jacket, she recalled that this was the first thing she'd noticed about him: his tweed-covered arm holding the guidebook.

She sees him out of the corner of her eye, standing to one side and very slightly behind her. This morning she's come into the cathedral on a whim, seeking some kind of inner strength from that deep-down peacefulness that is the natural result of nine hundred years of prayer. It's not that caring for her frail aunt is particularly demanding, it's just that sometimes she feels very lonely in the little cottage in Litten Terrace and then she is over-whelmed by a need to be a part of the bustle and activity in the town. Once she's settled Aunt Mary with a book and a cup of coffee she has a little time to herself: to potter in the town, do some shopping and go to the library. Today she is drawn into the cathedral, wandering in the quiet aisles, pausing in the north transept to look at the sixteenth-century paintings of the Bishops of Chichester by Lambert Barnard. After a moment she becomes aware of someone nearby, holding a guidebook.

Glancing round she is struck by the expression on the young man's face. It is one of an almost comical dismay. He looks at her, ready to share his surprise.

'It's a bit odd, isn't it?' He's lowered his voice to a kind of respectful whisper. 'Have you noticed? All the faces are exactly the same!'

He nods towards the paintings, clearly baffled, and she can't help chuckling at his astonishment. He looks at her more closely, rather as if he has discovered something else of interest apart from the paintings.

'I'm new to all this,' he says, slightly on the defensive, brandishing his guidebook. 'I've just moved from Surrey. I work at the new college over in Westgate Fields, in the science department, and

118

I'm finding my way around before term starts officially. Gerald Faringdon.' He holds out his hand, as if to show that he isn't trying to pick her up but is anxious to put this meeting on to a respectable level at once, and she takes it, liking his open, good-humoured face and broad shoulders.

'I'm Lucy Scott,' she says. 'I live with my aunt over the other side in Litten Terrace. How do you like Chichester?'

She's glad now that she decided to change into her new apple-green linen shift dress and the pretty sling-back shoes before she came out, her long thick brown hair brushed so that the ends flick up à la Jackie Kennedy. She'd been rather pleased with the overall effect and now, looking at him a little shyly, it is clear to her that he appreciates it too.

They stroll away together, talking casually, neither of them quite knowing how to make the next move. As they come out into the bright sunshine they each covertly take stock of the other. She likes the look of his crinkly reddish fair hair and bright blue eyes. He has a reassuringly kind smile but he is stocky and well-built – and there is a natural confidence in his straightforward gaze and the set of his shoulders that appeals to her.

He glances down West Street, towards Market Cross, jingling the coins in his pocket.

'I was planning to have some coffee,' he says. 'Do you fancy a cup? I saw a rather jolly place on my way here. Just across the road down there. Very old, I gather. It's in my guidebook but I expect you could tell me all about it.'

So it is that they find themselves having coffee in the Dolphin and Anchor Hotel: the first of many meetings.

Now, she would have liked to touch his arm, cover his poor clawed hand on the wheel, but she restrained the impulse. Jerry had never been able to respond easily to impulsive, loving gestures; kind, yes, and always thoughtful for her security, he wasn't an emotional man. Affection, in his experience, was shown in deeds, not in flowery speeches and romantic gestures. Love was demonstrated by keeping the car properly serviced, bills being paid on time and sensible precautions taken for the future. In these ways he cared for her and protected her. There were moments of tenderness – generally after he'd had a pint or a gin and tonic when his self-control was relaxed a little – and he had an oddball sense of humour and a passion for modern jazz that had sustained a youthful liveliness. Lately, however, he'd begun to suspect unpremeditated acts of affection as manifestations of her pity and, as

120

a result of the terrible thrice-daily cocktail of medication, he could be irritable and moody.

She wanted to say to him: 'We haven't really changed, not deep down inside, have we? We still carry with us those two people, the Jerry and Lucy who stood together in front of Barnard's paintings,' but she knew that he would not be able to confirm her instinct that the true essence of the human spirit is unchanged by age or suffering. He might remember the occasion with affection but he would feel uncomfortable if she were to press the subject further.

Instead she sat back in her seat, thinking now about Jonah.

'It was so strange,' he'd said. 'First, you mentioning Hester's name, then finding that Piers has known the family for ever, and then this girl Clio telling me that she's her god-daughter. It was just so bizarre that I felt that it was meant, if you know what I mean?'

His voice had been almost pleading, willing her to understand and not be cross, but she'd been surprised by an oddly peaceful sense of inevitability.

'It's OK,' she'd said. 'Really it is. How is Hester?'

'She's great. Fantastic. But I had such a strange feeling while I was there, and she . . . told me things, Mum. About Grandfather being a friend of the family. She's said I can go and stay and I'd really like to do that, if you don't mind. She was very clear about that – you knowing about it and agreeing to it, I mean. Would you like to telephone her, you know, just to check things out?'

'No,' she'd answered quickly. 'No, not yet, but you go if you want to, Jonah. Honestly, I think you're right about it being meant, and if Hester really wants to talk . . .'

He'd been so relieved, so grateful, that she'd felt the usual guilt and fear twist her gut. She'd kept silent for so long, despite Jonah's longing to know about the past.

Well, it was out of her control now. Staring out at the passing countryside, Lucy wondered what Hester would tell him, what questions might arise from their meeting, and her gut flipped again at the prospect. Yet, beyond the guilt and fear, a calm certainty took possession of her: it was time.

CHAPTER TEN

The letter was lying beside Hester's place at the breakfast table. The sight of the spiky writing on the recycled envelope, along with its second-class stamp, caused her heart to beat with pleasurable anticipation but it wasn't until Clio had finished her toast and set off to see Lizzie at Michaelgarth that Hester opened her letter.

St Bede's Convent
All Souls' Day

Darling Hes,

I've been thinking about you particularly during these last few days and not only because we've been holding you closely in prayer since your operation. It's the time of year, isn't it, when we think of all those people we've loved but who 'now worship in a greater light and on a farther shore' and I've been remembering our family

123

especially. Little cameos from the past, recalling happy holidays at Bridge House, student days at Cambridge and more sombre thoughts about the boys, killed so early in the war, and then, later, dear old Edward and Michael. What a terrible time it was. And, before that, your parents, Hes: Aunt Emily and Uncle Nicholas.

Just lately I've been thinking a great deal about Uncle Nicholas and what a terrible blow it must have been to you especially, Hes, when he died. There are certain people – just one or two if we're lucky – that seem to be vouchsafed us on our journey: people who truly know us and not only love us but *enjoy* us, if you know what I mean. Your father felt like that about you, Hes. He understood you, and enjoyed your imperiousness and curiosity and passion for truth; and your oblique take on life which was immensely endearing and made you a difficult but fascinating child and, later, characterized your books about John Clare and Christopher Smart. I think it was clever of you to draw the parallels between the two, showing how their 'madness' was grounded in their passionate response to the physical world. How proud your father would have been, Hes, to read your work.

I can see why, when he died, you transferred

your love to Edward. He was so like him, wasn't he? Not only physically but he had that same intuitive understanding for looking beyond the surface of people and an appreciation for the finer points of character. I always felt that your mother's love was too concentrated on her sons (and I was included in that love, for which I thank God!) to appreciate her daughters properly – and that is why she gave up, poor soul, when the boys were killed and Edward taken prisoner.

It was a blessing, I suppose. Seeing Edward, best beloved of all her sons, so broken and destroyed when he finally came home, would have been terrible for her. I'm only just beginning truly to understand how appalling it must have been for you, Hes. Edward valued you in the same way that your father valued you and oh! how we need that real true kind of loving to grow up properly. Without that particular kind of valuing, which has nothing to do with spoiling and smothering the child with possessive affection, it is difficult to develop with confidence and self-esteem. Most of us have to do our best without it.

You are so much in my mind, Hes, you and all the others, and I'm so glad that you are recovering well – but how do you feel about the long journey up here for Christmas? It wouldn't be the same without you – and I know the sisters feel the same – but I'm rather worried about you driving so far, especially at that time of the year. Would it be wise this year to come by train? Is Clio still at Bridge House? How sweet of her to take her holiday time to be with you, although I expect that she's glad to have the opportunity to show her gratitude for all the things you've done for her. You valued Clio in the way that I wrote about just now and it shows in her. Give her my love.

On a different note, we have a new convent cat. He has appeared from nowhere and the sisters have taken him in joyfully, having been in mourning for weeks for dear old Mouser. On being applied to for a name – and having in my thoughts your book on Christopher Smart, which I was rereading – I said he should be called Jeoffrey. Remember Smart's lines 'on his cat Jeoffrey' from the *Jubilate Agno*?

For I will consider my Cat Jeoffrey
For he is the servant of the Living God duly
and daily serving him.

Anyway, I'm hoping that the name will inspire our newcomer and that he will remember that, according to Smart, 'the mouse is a creature of great personal valour'. I wish I could introduce Jeoffrey to St Francis.

Let me know how you are, Hes,

Love as always,

Blaise

Hester put the letter down, folding it automatically, smiling at Blaise's choice of name for the cat whilst, at the same time, rather shaken that the letter had been written on the day when Jonah had first arrived at Bridge House. She was moved by Blaise's references to her father's feelings for her, and to her work.

Thoughtfully she put the letter back into its envelope, thinking now about Christmas. Ever since Blaise had retired from his parish duties to take up the position of chaplain to the sisters at St Bede's she had driven up to Northumberland each year to spend Christmas at the convent. Usually she took the journey in stages, stopping off at Cambridge and Lincoln to see friends and colleagues. Just at present, however, the thought of the long drive north filled her with trepidation. Yet the prospect of Christmas alone, without seeing Blaise or the nuns of whom she had become so fond, was a bleak one.

St Francis leaped onto the table. He gazed hopefully at the butter dish, which Hester immediately picked up. She got to her feet and began to clear the table, ignoring his look of reproach.

'There is a new cat at the convent,' she told him. 'His name is Jeoffrey and we must hope that he is a more efficient rodent controller than you are, old friend. Or they might be saying, "Poor Jeoffrey! The rat has bit thy throat."' She smiled again as she remembered Blaise's words, already forming a reply in her head; framing phrases and sentences and quotations that would make him laugh. She shared with Blaise the passion for words that she'd once shared with Edward.

'I'm only just beginning truly to understand how appalling it must have been for you, Hes.' Was that what was puzzling her: that Blaise should be thinking so much about the past again and especially that particular period of time that she was beginning deliberately to call up so as to communicate it to Jonah?

Hester was surprised by the quick uprush of joy at the mere idea of seeing Jonah again, of talking to him and sharing with him. She saw suddenly that it was a great privilege to find someone to whom she might pass her history and the history of her family – someone who was passionately interested and deeply involved. The story must be accurate, the details clear and without confusion or muddle.

Distracted by this thought, Hester abruptly abandoned the clearing up and went to her study. There was work to be done before she was ready for Jonah.

Alert and hopeful, St Francis watched her well out of sight before he jumped up onto the draining-board and began to eat the butter.

CHAPTER ELEVEN

'Clio has returned to London,' Hester wrote to Blaise on Sunday evening.

Her departure was rather horrid; just like going back to school years ago. I can only imagine that it's because she's been here for four weeks and this has given her the opportunity to look clearly at her situation both at the agency and with Peter. If it hadn't been for Peter I think she would have made a change a year ago, but falling in love does rather cloud the judgement and, now she's had the chance to think about things, she gives the impression that she's rather fearful that she made a mistake in staying at the agency. That's what is horrid, Blaise, watching her going back to London and knowing that she's lost her confidence in what she's doing. Clio is usually very positive, as you know, so it shows when she's having a wobble. On the other hand, I should be deeply relieved to hear that this affair with Peter is over. Naturally I can't interfere but you know how unhappy I have been at the thought of Clio involved in a relationship that can have no future. Having had my own similar experience all those years ago I'm in no position to throw stones at Clio but I worry that there are so many people who could be hurt. Not least the children. Anyway, I really have hopes that she is seeing clearly now.

Your last letter was so very much in tune with what was happening here that I've been wondering how to reply to it. Michael's grandson has been here, Blaise. Clio met him – I won't bother you with how or where at the moment – and brought him to Bridge House at his own request. Something very odd happened. It was as if at some emotional level he tapped into his whole history, and he's coming again next week. He wants to know about those war years. His mother up until now has refused to talk about it – and who can blame her? – although he's seen old snapshots of us all. I remember sending photos to Michael during the war, so as to keep him in touch, and Jonah (that's his name) specially remembers one of Lucy with Jack and Robin.

He's clearly a very intuitive boy – well, he seems like a boy to me, probably thirty – and he had a very strange experience on his arrival here.

She paused, wondering how to explain Jonah's experience and her own reaction to it, and at that moment the telephone rang and Hester put down her pen and went to answer it.

It was odd, she reflected in the few seconds that this took, that though she used the computer for most of her correspondence she still wrote to Blaise by hand, with her fountain pen and sitting at the table in the breakfast-room. Before she could come to any conclusions about this, she'd picked up the receiver and said as she always did, 'Hester Mallory.'

'Hester.' The familiar voice was warm, flexible and very charming. 'How are you?'

'Robin.' She spoke his name on a little gasp of surprise. 'I can hardly believe this! I've just this minute written your name in my letter to Blaise. How extraordinary.'

There was a tiny pause before he said: 'Oh?' A chuckle. 'Nothing defamatory, I hope?'

'Of course not. I've been looking at some old photos of you and Jack. How are you, Robin?'

'I'm very fit. No problems there.'

Hester took the telephone to the table and sat down. The inflexion was slight but she knew Robin of old and she grew alert.

'So where *do* you have a problem?'

'Oh, Hes. I never could fool you, could I?'

His voice was rueful now, self-deprecating – almost the voice of the small boy caught taking more than his fair share of the sweet ration, spoiled by his mother and by Nanny. Their voices echoed in her head.

'Now, you mustn't be too cross with him, Hes. He's too young to understand. You're sorry, aren't you, Robbie? There, you see. Give Jack a hug and he shall have an extra sweetie next time.'

'Come to Nanny, there's a good child. He's a bit unsettled now that Lucy's arrived. It's only to be expected. It's not his fault.'

'I hope you wouldn't want to fool me, Robin,' she answered, putting the memory of the small, engaging boy out of her mind. 'So what is it?'

'Well, it's the usual thing but rather more serious. I owe a bit of money, Hes, and things are a trifle tricky.'

'My dear, I told you last time that I have no more money to lend you. I'm living on my pension now and it doesn't go far.'

She forbore to point out that he never repaid her

'loans' and tried to bear in mind that since his wife had died Robin had lost the one person who had been able to keep his impracticalities and extravagancies under control.

'I know that.' Her nephew's voice shifted key; became conspiratorial. 'It's a bit different this time and I don't want a loan. I've had a different idea. It's to do with the house. I need to sell my share and I have the feeling that Amy might be rather glad to sell hers. She could do with some extra cash just now with her rapidly growing family.'

Hester straightened in her chair, holding the telephone tightly, but she did not speak.

'I was wondering,' he went on rather tentatively, 'if you'd begun to think about selling up.'

'Sell Bridge House?'

'It makes good sense if you think about it.' He spoke rapidly, as if the idea were more palatable if the words were said quickly. 'It's a big place for you to keep going and, as you've said already, it must be a bit of a struggle on your pension, especially as you pay me and Amy rent.'

'I see you've thought it all out,' she said drily. 'You make it sound as if you'd be doing us all a favour.'

'Well, don't you think I might be?' He sounded

almost jaunty, jollying her along. 'I'm quite sure Amy could do with the money and wouldn't you find a little cottage or a bungalow in Dulverton much more convenient, especially now, after your operation? Surely you must have thought about moving, Hes? After all, at your age it's bound to happen sooner or later, isn't it?'

It was as if he'd slapped her: she felt old and shocked and humiliated.

'I know you've lived there since you retired, Hes,' his voice continued sweet and persuasive in her ear, 'but the bottom line is that it's a family asset: it belongs to the three of us. And it's not as if you'd be homeless.'

'That's a relief.' Her own voice was as sharp as a lemon. 'But how can you be so sure, after the proceeds have been split three ways, that there will be enough for my little bungalow. Or was it a cottage?'

He laughed, reassured by her astringency. 'Well, as to that, I asked a friend of mine who was down on holiday to have a quick glance at the place. Only from the road, of course, but he's a chartered surveyor and he had a look at the local agents and he said that we're sitting on a little goldmine down there by the river.'

Hester tried to control a sense of revulsion: she'd

135

been spied upon by some stranger assessing Bridge House, weighing it up, looking upon it as a commodity to assist Robin out of his gambling debts. Momentarily possessed by anger and fear she was unable to speak.

'But if you're really against selling up then why not think about a mortgage, Hester?' He was wheedling now, as though he guessed that he'd made her angry. 'Equity release is really worth looking into. The mortgage company would take it over and you wouldn't have to pay a thing. They give you the cash, the interest rolls up and they sell the house when you die. It means that Amy and I could have our share now and you could continue to live in the house.'

Suddenly she remembered Amy's unexpected phone call; her solicitous enquiry after Hester's health and her anxiety that the house and garden would be too big for Hester after her operation.

'Have you spoken to Amy?'

'Well, to be honest I have. She's quite keen, actually. Her oldest boy is off to school soon and it's going to be a real squeeze for them.'

'She's always said that she's looked upon Bridge House as a last resort: a kind of insurance policy against her old age. That's what Jack intended when he transferred his share to her. After all,

136

they're not badly off. You've always said the same, Robin.'

'I know I have. But let's face it, Hes. I'm not that far off old age and I'm in a real mess. It was OK for Jack; he was lucky. He never needed financial help, so he was able to pass on his share to Amy, but I never had his flair with investments. To tell you the truth I've overreached my luck this time and it will be seriously embarrassing if I can't raise the funds soon. I wouldn't ask it otherwise. You know how it is.'

'*Now, you mustn't be too cross with him, Hes. He's too young to understand. You're sorry, aren't you, Robbie? There, you see. Give Jack a hug and he shall have an extra sweetie next time.*'

'*Come to Nanny, there's a good child. He's a bit unsettled now that Lucy's arrived. It's only to be expected. It's not his fault.*'

'It doesn't sound as if I have too much choice if you're both decided.'

'Oh, don't take it like that, Hes.' He wanted her to be kind to him; forgiving his weaknesses and making it easy for him. 'We'd hate you to be upset. To be honest we both thought that this was the right time, after your operation. It must be a hell of a place to keep up, and Amy and I can't help much when it comes to running repairs.' A little hesitation

137

here. 'My chap said that the roof is looking pretty dodgy and I don't think any of us could afford a new roof at present.' Casually said, it had the air of a trump card though his voice invited complicity: an agreement that property was a financial nightmare.

'You've made your point, Robin. I'll have to think about it.'

'Of *course* you must.' He was generous in his relief. 'All I need to be able to say is that I own this asset, which will be turned into cash as soon as possible. Look, take your time and I'll phone again in a day or two. Think it through and don't forget the mortgage option if you're set on staying. Bless you, Hes.'

The line went dead.

Hester took a deep, deep breath. Presently she went back to her letter. Picking it up, she read it through; but somehow she hadn't the heart to finish it.

When the telephone rang again she hesitated for a moment before answering it. This time it was Clio to say that she was safely back in London.

'It seems odd after being away for so long.' Her voice was rather wistful. 'Are you OK?'

'Of course I am. Don't worry about me. I'm getting ready for Jonah.'

'There can't be much to do.' Clio sounded almost indignant. 'His bedroom's ready and the freezer's full.'

'Oh, yes, of course. I'm not talking about those kinds of things, Clio. You've been wonderfully practical and done all the hard work for me. This is to do with his history. I keep remembering odd things about the past and making notes. I know it's foolish to try to second-guess what he wants to know, but I need to be prepared. I'm trying to put it down on paper sensibly.'

Clio laughed, a genuinely amused sound. 'It sounds to me as if you're writing a script for him,' she said. 'Jonah's the last person you need to do that for, Hes: he writes his own scripts.'

Hester chuckled too. 'I know that but I can't help myself. I want to show him things too. To take him to all the places Michael knew when he was young. We used to have such fun. Of course, Lucy never went too far afield. It was much more difficult in wartime with the petrol rationing, but I'm so looking forward to showing it all to Jonah.'

'He'll love it. I know he will. Just don't overdo things.'

'I promise I won't. Good luck for tomorrow.'

A tiny pause, then: 'What do you mean?' Clio asked rather defensively.

'Well, just starting back to work after a long break. It can feel odd, that's all.'

'Oh, I see. Thanks. Well, I shall be thinking of you and Jonah. I'll phone at the weekend to see how it's going. Bye, Hes.'

Hester sat down again. Clio sounded like a child that has been excluded from a party but is trying to be brave about it, and Hester wondered how she would have reacted if she'd told her about Robin's plan for Bridge House. It had been impossible to mention the subject lightly – apart from the fact that she knew Clio would worry about it – but it also seemed just as difficult to write the words to Blaise.

'Robin's just telephoned with a not wholly unexpected suggestion . . .'

'Do you think it's time to sell Bridge House and look for something smaller . . . ?'

'I feel old and vulnerable, Blaise, and I need your help . . .'

None of these approaches was the right one and, in the end, Hester decided that it should be left until morning. There was unfinished business at Bridge House and nothing could be decided until after Jonah's visit. She went back to the study, losing herself in her work preparing for his arrival.

CHAPTER TWELVE

Afterwards, Jonah remembered his stay with Hester in a series of mental images that were composed of light and air and water – and always accompanied by the unforgettable sound of the river. Everywhere they went, driving in Hester's little car, there was the noise of water: rain clattering down in soaking torrents, the roar of fast-running rivers in broad, open pastureland and the gurgling of brooks in narrow, wooded valleys. He peered dizzily down into tree-clad, steep-sided combes to see, far below, small secret streams tumbling, white-tipped, over rocks, and watched swift-flowing water sweeping knee-deep across narrow stony fords. When the rain ceased, the louring cloud-banks fell apart to show amazing skyscapes: scraps of rainbow arching diaphanously between soft, moisture-laden woolpacks; inky-coloured rags scudding across patches of tender blue; and, here and there, golden vapour trails arrowing across the sky.

He stood on grassy cliffs whose precipitous sides plunged down into restless grey water, and looked across the Channel to where Wales huddled, half hidden in pearl-soft fleece. Then, homeward-bound along a quiet road, he saw a gush of white water issuing out of the very rocks, and crying, 'Stop!' he climbed out and stared up, head back, so as to see the source of the waterfall that plunged down the high bank. Just here, where the water spouted and tumbled, the black, ridged rock was worn smooth and shining while on either side clustered hart's tongue and pennywort and bright green ferns.

And each morning on waking and every night before he slept, the constant, surging voice of the river.

At Bridge House they spent most of their time together between the breakfast-room and the book-room. Jonah especially liked the book-room. It was cosy in the evening, with the fire lit and the curtains drawn, the photograph albums open on the small table and Hester gazing into the flames whilst she talked.

As he listened, cameos of the day's journey

seemed to mingle with her words and add colour to her stories. In his mind's eye, as Jonah watched scenes unfolding, characters developing, he was aware of tiny dramas weaving together, growing like a tapestry into a larger picture. Sometimes he wished he had a tape-recorder, despairing of ever remembering each detail she described so accurately, yet with another part of his mind he knew that, mysteriously, the story was being stitched by her precise words into the fabric of his memory: a tiny piece of history being passed from her to him.

Sometimes he would interrupt, asking for more personal information: 'But what did Nanny look like?' and, 'How did Patricia cope with her husband away fighting?' or, 'Yes, but what do you think Eleanor actually felt when she heard that Edward was posted missing, believed killed?' and so on. It dawned on him that, however accurate Hester might be, however truthful in her recounting, she was less sure when it came to people's emotions and reactions. He guessed that her detachment, which made her such a restful and fascinating companion, had given her a blind spot here.

Nevertheless, each time she described Edward and Michael, her animation contained all the passion and admiration she'd once felt for these

143

two young men and, as she told of amusing escapades and described their love of poetry and the English language, Jonah knew that a real sense of his grandfather was developing and he began to identify strongly with him. In Hester's stories of the past, the young Michael lived again: sensitive, driven by the creative impulse, fearful for his small child.

Jonah discovered too a great deal about Hester. Some things she disclosed quite unconsciously in her telling of the past; others he learned simply by living with her. He liked the way that she didn't fuss over him. Her whole concentration was focused on a need to convey to him certain things that were part of his heritage and she treated him exactly as if he were a very old and valued friend. Her mind – keen, tough, alert – distracted from her physical frailty and her ready humour kept any kind of self-pity at bay.

She talked to him of Michael's love of the poetry of John Clare and of the way he and Edward used the poet's words – 'haynish' for awkward, 'clumpsing' for numb with cold – and on one occasion she picked up a book and read to him. Her voice barely changed, continuing quick and light, so that for a second he didn't realize that she *was* reading:

'Just by the wooden brig a bird flew up,
Frit by the cowboy as he scrambled down
To reach the misty dewberry – let us stoop
And seek its nest – the brook we need not dread,
'Tis scarcely deep enough a bee to drown . . .

. . . Five eggs, pen-scribbled o'er with ink
    their shells . . .

. . . They are the yellowhammer's . . .

'Your grandfather loved the bird poems best,'
she told him – but she did not urge him to read
them for himself for that was not her way. He saw
that she made no effort to control any situation or
impose her own views; she simply related what she
knew and left him to make up his own mind. Nor
did she question him. She never asked him what
he was thinking about, though he often sat for
long periods, staring into the flames and building
scenes in his head. He couldn't help himself:
his imagination seized on anything that might
feed it and now it felt as if he had been waiting
for this ever since he'd seen the photograph,
all those years ago in the attic room, of his mother
with Jack and Robin in the garden at Bridge
House.

'Don't you think it's odd,' Jonah burst out
suddenly, 'that Mum never wants to talk about her

father? He sounds a really fascinating person, and you all seem to have had such fun together.'

'Ah, but you mustn't forget that by the time Lucy arrived here things were rather different. Her mother had been killed and Michael was very anxious about her.'

Hester fell silent and he glanced at her shrewdly. 'You haven't told me about that yet.'

'Not yet,' she agreed calmly. 'I thought that it was best to continue chronologically. I have the feeling that it's not only Michael's story that is interesting you.'

'You're quite right,' he said thoughtfully. 'He is a part of the whole. Obviously, to me, a very important part but I need to see the overall scene, including him, in context. I can imagine something bigger happening here.' He looked at her quickly. 'Please don't think that I'm not treating it seriously, though. I see it as a jigsaw puzzle that I'm piecing together but I can't visualize the whole picture yet by any means. For instance, that night I arrived. I saw that man run out. I *saw* him, Hester. I had the strongest sensation that this had happened before: a man running out into the wind and rain crying for help. It happened, didn't it?'

She nodded slowly. 'I'm not being deliberately reticent,' she said at last. 'It's a very important part

146

of the story, which is why I want you to feel familiar with the cast before I tell you about it. I hope that you will be able to see it whole so that you don't misjudge any of us.'

He smiled at her use of the word 'cast', but he said: 'That sounds a little ominous.'

'It wasn't meant to be.' She stood up and touched him lightly on the shoulder. 'I'm off to bed,' she said. 'Goodnight, Jonah.'

He watched her go, liking the way she never gave him instructions: 'Don't forget to make the fire safe' or 'put the cat out' or 'switch off the lights'.

St Francis padded in through the half-open door, jumped into Hester's vacated chair and turned round and round on the cushion before settling to sleep. Jonah watched him, thinking that the cat's air of benign detachment reminded him of Hester. He remembered her telling him how her mother had liked this room and he glanced about, trying to imagine how she'd sat here, by the fire, enduring the pain of losing two sons whilst knowing that a third, her favourite child, was a prisoner of war.

It was as if he was looking at her through the lens of his mind's eye, her shade called up by Hester's words, and briefly he was able to connect with her agony. Round her other figures moved and gesticulated; children cried and called to one another. With his eyes closed he could see and hear much more clearly and he settled back in his chair, feet stretched to the fire whilst he watched.

Slowly the story took shape visually: scene following upon scene, building to some shadowy climax that he could not yet see. If he were directing such a story he would want it to start before the war with the boys coming home from Cambridge to the family at Bridge House, their own small dramas being played out in this peaceful corner of Exmoor whilst, on the larger global stage, much darker and more violent actions were escalating towards the war in which they would all be entangled.

Between Hester's stories and his own imagination it seemed that he moved amongst them. Soon it was impossible to distinguish between the two worlds and presently he slept.

CHAPTER THIRTEEN

The next morning the wild showery weather had cleared away and the sun shone from a tranquil sky.

'We shall go to Dulverton,' Hester decided, carrying the breakfast things into the kitchen and opening the dishwasher. 'We'll have coffee in Woods or a glass of wine.'

Jonah followed her out, carrying their fruit juice glasses. He looked around the kitchen, knowing now that the breakfast-room was a fairly recent addition and that, during those earlier years, all the family's meals had been eaten in the room that was now Hester's study. She had described the original kitchen to him and he could imagine exactly how it had looked with the ancient solid-fuel range and the butler's sink and Nanny's pots of geraniums on the window-sill. Today there were still several pots of geraniums, sitting in a row on rather beautiful old hand-painted plates, and as he glanced at them something else caught his eye: a white plastic tub that had once contained ice cream. A label was stuck on its lid and he bent closer to read the printed words: 'DO NOT DISTURB. SOMEONE IS SLEEPING HERE.'

'Hey, Hes,' he said, startled. 'Who's sleeping in the ice-cream tub?'

She raised her eyebrows, as if puzzled at the question, and then her brow cleared. 'It's a butterfly pupa. Much safer there. Let me have those glasses.'

He laughed, experiencing a moment of brief uncomplicated happiness before a thought struck him.

'I realized last night that there's simply not going to be time for you to tell me everything, is there?' He passed her the glasses, his face downcast. 'I feel I've only just started and I have to go back tomorrow.'

Hester looked at him, surprised. 'But you'll come again, Jonah. Very soon, I hope. This is important, isn't it?'

'Yes, it is important. Not only for me personally, but because there's another side to it.' He hesitated whilst she watched him with her bright intelligent gaze. 'How would you feel if all this finished up as a play, perhaps for the television or maybe the theatre? Would you feel that it was being trivialized?'

'Trivialized? No, I don't think so. I've been aware that part of your mind is shaping it, if that's an accurate expression. I feel quite strongly that both Edward and Michael would have approved, provided you are truthful.'

'That's wonderful. Fantastic!' He was almost euphoric with relief. 'It's been so difficult to separate the two things and it's beginning to haunt me. Of *course* I'd want it to be truthful. Gosh, Hes! We've got a long way to go yet.'

'I realize that.' Her own enthusiasm shone in her eyes. 'But it can't be hurried. And the landscape in which the events happened is just as important as the story.'

'I'm sure you're right but I'm impatient to know what comes next.'

'I know you are. I only hope it won't turn out to be an anticlimax. It's a very familiar theme – just a love story that went rather tragically wrong.'

'It was Eleanor and Michael, wasn't it? Don't worry, I'm not trying to rush you with the story but I wonder if that's why Mum won't talk about it.'

Hester frowned. 'The odd thing is,' she said, 'that I can't really imagine that Lucy knew anything about it. She was only a child.'

'Oh, but children pick up so much, don't they? And adults often don't notice that they're around. Perhaps she saw something that upset her?'

'Perhaps. An embrace? An argument? It's possible. Will you tell her what you've discovered?'

'I'd like to, if that's OK with you?'

'Of course it is. I'd rather want you to, in fact. She might be able to provide some other side of the story for you now.'

'I'm hoping so.' He grinned at her with pure pleasure. 'This is so exciting, Hester, isn't it?'

'Yes, it is exciting,' she agreed. 'And necessary, I think.'

He liked Woods Bar, with its beamed partitions and terracotta-coloured walls. The bistro atmosphere was reinforced by the impressive array of bottles reflected in the long mirror behind the bar and a soundtrack of Mama Cass singing 'California Dreamin''. Two large young men, perched on the stools at the bar, were drinking beer whilst an elderly lady sat at a corner table sipping coffee and reading a newspaper. Although sunshine splashed on the white-washed walls of the house opposite, a fire burned in the stainless-steel beer cask that had been made into a stove and stood in the inglenook and, beyond the adze-cut wooden partitions, he could see a young couple enjoying an early lunch in the dining-room.

'It used to be a bakery,' Hester had told him. 'Delicious home-made cakes. I have to say the standard of the food is still just as good.'

She'd gone off to the library, leaving him to drink his mocha alone, and once again he was grateful for her ability to give him space to think his own thoughts and absorb the atmosphere of the life around him. In this need for solitude he and Hester were alike and he wondered if it was the reason she had remained alone. His own relationships had foundered on this stone: this requirement for space to allow for the creative life of his imagination.

Both of the girls with whom he'd shared his life so far had accused him of detachment: of not caring, not listening, not being able to put them before his work. To begin with, each relationship had followed the same pattern once the initial physical attraction had drawn them together: a declared fascination in the creative process, leading to encouragement and real belief that one day he'd write the 'big one', which slowly degenerated into impatience, accusations of neglect and declarations of feeling cut off.

'You're not listening to a word I'm saying. I know that glazed expression. You're "writing", aren't you, inside your head? I might as well be talking to myself.'

It was a perfectly reasonable accusation and he'd had no defence so, after a few stormy weeks of trying to change and failing, he'd be alone again. He was fascinated by women but realized that in his attempt to understand how they thought and felt he was actually doing himself no favours.

'And anyway,' one of his girlfriends had said acidly, 'you're not really interested in me, you just want to use me as copy for your next female character.'

There was a grain of truth in this – someone had once described this syndrome as the splinter of ice in the heart of the creative person – and he was unable to convince her otherwise, so it seemed better to let it go at that. He saw that women were very complicated people – unable to experience simple happiness without guilt or anxiety coming hard on its heels. In bed: 'Was it really good for you?' a contented cuddle, then: 'You don't think I'm too fat?' At the theatre: 'Isn't Richard Griffiths brilliant?' a sip of wine, then: 'Did I remember to take the chops out of the freezer?' And it seemed difficult for them to accept that men could be truly peaceful whilst simply staring at their shoes. 'What are you thinking about?' 'Nothing.' 'But what are you doing?' 'Staring at my shoes.' Those moments of joy that were uncomplicated or unaffected by the state of a relationship appeared to be unknown by women. Even in the aftermath of a row – amidst silent sulking and glares of recrimination – it was possible to be amused by something on the television or absorbed by a book, which caused further resentment; as if it should be unthinkable, even reprehensible, to experience any emotion that was not related directly to her.

Jonah finished his mocha and ordered a pint of beer: he'd decided that he simply wasn't good partnership material and that it was best to remain alone – until he'd met Clio. He'd been rather taken with Clio. He'd mentally tried out one or two opening remarks in the hope of finding out a bit more about her from Hester. It hadn't worked.

'Clio's an amazing girl, isn't she?' he'd ventured. 'I rather like her.'

'So do I,' she'd agreed amiably – and that had been that.

He chuckled as he took his pint back to his table. Hester was the perfect companion, no doubt about it. Pity she wasn't forty years younger. And here she was, standing before him.

'Oh, good, you've had your coffee. I shall have

a glass of wine and I recommend a Woodman's Lunch. My treat.'

He raised his glass to her. 'I think I am in love with you, Hester,' he said.

'Splendid,' she replied. 'Though there was no need for the declaration; I would have bought the lunch anyway. It's my turn, if you remember.'

CHAPTER FOURTEEN

When Clio telephoned, Jonah had gone back to London and Hester was alone again.

'So how did it go?' Clio asked – but she sounded remote, as if Jonah's visit had happened in another sphere of time to which she no longer was connected.

'Very well. We didn't speed and we didn't drink, at least not to excess, and it was a very productive meeting.'

There was a little silence, as if Clio were puzzling over the words, then she laughed. 'I'd forgotten for a moment,' she said. 'Sorry, Hes. I'm glad it went OK.'

'And you?' asked Hester lightly. 'The last time we spoke you said that it all felt rather odd after such a long break.'

'It did. Still does, actually.'

'Still?' Hester was surprised but she was reluctant

to press for information. 'I'd imagined you were back into your routine by now.'

'The point is . . .' Clio hesitated. 'Well, the thing is, Peter isn't in the office at the moment. His wife is ill and I've only seen him once or twice very briefly when I first got back, so the routine bit hasn't happened. Obviously there's a flap on but I feel rather disorientated, to tell you the truth.'

'But you enjoy a flap,' Hester pointed out. 'It's what you're best at.'

'I know it is, but this is different.'

'Is it different because Peter isn't there?'

'Something like that. Do you remember asking me whether I'd stay if Peter left the agency? Well, I'm beginning to think that the answer is no. And I'm not terribly certain that I want to stay even when he gets back.'

'Is this to do with your being away for so long?'

'In a way. I began to view things a bit differently when he didn't want to come down to Bridge House. It made me take a few steps back and I saw our relationship more clearly.' Clio hesitated and when she spoke again her voice was brittle. 'His wife's had an ectopic pregnancy. She's been very ill and naturally he's terribly worried about her.' A longer pause. 'Stupid of me to believe him when he said there wasn't anything like that between them any more, wasn't it?' she asked bitterly.

Hester reacted involuntarily: 'Not a bit stupid! We need to believe it. I am so sorry, Clio . . .'

'It was a shock. He's always seemed so detached, you see. Oh God, I feel such a fool and I feel angry too. I feel cross with myself for being taken in, and guilty. But that doesn't make me stop missing him. It's hell, Hes.'

'I know it is and it's no consolation to tell you that it will pass. Try to be glad you found out before you were any deeper in.'

'Well, it might sound rather selfish with his wife so ill but at least it's made me see that I've been living a totally ostrich-like existence. Let's face it, the relationship was never going anywhere, was it? I'm coming to the conclusion that I don't want this any more, Hes.'

'Will you look for another job?'

'That's the idea, except that I'm rather tired of being a PA. I'd like something different.'

'In what way different?'

'Oh, I don't know. I'm probably being irrational but I just feel rather stale. I see now that it wasn't my work that was giving me a buzz but having Peter around. I have to get over that. Anyway, Hes, I just wanted you to know. After all, you might have some kind of inspiration about what I should do next.'

'I'll give my mind to it. I imagine you want to stay in London?'

'I'm not even sure about that at the moment. I was going to ask you a favour, actually. If I decide to give in my notice at work and at my house, would it be possible to stay with you for a bit if I needed to? Just until I sort myself out? I've got savings, of course, but I just thought – a kind of sabbatical?'

'Is it wise to give up your little house? You are so fond of it and it's not easy to find accommodation in London, is it?'

'The point is, Hes, the house is so tied up with the whole Peter thing. I moved in just after I met him, if you remember. I needed to have a place on my own, so that he could come and go, and now I just don't see myself separating him from it. I know that sounds muddled but I'm sure you know what I mean. I feel that for the last year I've been obsessed and I want some space to step right out of it and get a clear vision of what I want to do and where I want to be. I've got a few friends I could go to but they wouldn't be capable of giving me that kind of space. It's not only physical space but the other kind too. They fuss and advise, and if I'm sharing their homes I'd feel a kind of obligation to

160

listen to them. It would be such a comfort if I could think I could come to you for a very short time.'

'Of course you can come, Clio, and I promise not to fuss or advise. You can stay for as long as you need; that is, as long as I'm still here. I wasn't going to worry you with this just at the moment but Robin wants his share of the house in cash and I have to decide whether I want to buy something smaller or take the equity release route.'

'*What*? Are you kidding?'

'Sadly, no. And Amy is of the same mind so I don't have too much choice.'

'I can't believe that Robin and Amy would turn you out.'

'That's rather melodramatic. I hoped it wouldn't arise, of course, and that the house would remain a kind of insurance for them for a while yet. Knowing Robin's tendencies there was always the chance that it would happen sooner rather than later, and they both have a perfect right to ask for their share, but I don't quite know what to do, which route to take. He rightly pointed out that since my operation I might feel happier in a smaller place. I admit that I feel rather more vulnerable but not quite enough to move into a sunset home.'

'Surely he didn't suggest that?'

'Not quite but nearly. Anyway, like you I am

thinking about my future. However, you are more than welcome here, Clio. I don't imagine I shall be flung out into the snow quite yet. However, please, don't do anything in a rush. Give yourself time, talk to your friends and don't be pressurized by your emotions, especially negative emotions. If you decide to leave London it should be because you feel you are going towards something better, not because you are trying to leave Peter or the agency behind.'

'I realize that. Thanks, Hes.'

And to be fair, *she wrote later to Blaise*, I don't really feel anxious about Clio taking a sabbatical. To be honest I am just so deeply relieved that she's free of her obsession with Peter at last that I can't worry too much about her having a short holiday. Poor Clio! How painful these things are. But she's not at all the sort of person to become idle or unmotivated and she's worked very hard ever since she left university. Do you agree with me?

Regarding the other problem, I should be glad to know your thoughts. Bridge House is a big place to keep in good repair and with Amy and Robin out of the financial equation it might rapidly deteriorate. If it is to be passed over to the mortgage company when I die you might well say, 'Does it matter if it does?' I simply cannot decide. Meanwhile, I have arranged to have it valued, and Amy and I have agreed to sign some kind of document so that Robin can then raise a loan against his share of the property. I hope this is the right thing to do. He sounds rather desperate and I don't want Bridge House sold in a tremendous hurry simply so that he can meet his debts. Apparently his bank is happy with that arrangement.

As for Jonah's visit – I enjoyed it very much, Blaise. He is so like Michael, and not just physically, that it made it easier to recapture the past. Do you ever wonder what happened to Eleanor after she followed Michael to London? After he was killed we had that brief message saying that she was going to the States, if you remember, but I wonder how she survived. Lucy, apparently, remained with that aunt of Michael's who lived in Chichester and she has continued to live in her house. I am slightly puzzled by her refusal to talk to Jonah about her childhood. It was a terrible thing to lose both her parents in such a violent way but it seems odd that she has tried to wipe us all from her memory. She was so fond of us all. I'm now beginning to wonder what might have happened with Eleanor and Michael in London in those few months before he was killed and whether Lucy was affected in some way. At least she has given her permission for me to talk to Jonah: a big step on her part. Jonah thinks that she's facing some sort of crossroads in her life since his father has become ill and is trying to come to terms with various aspects of her own character. Jonah senses that she is fearful of the future and is attempting to cast off this fear. He is clearly deeply attached to her – to them both.

Jonah wants to take our story and make a play of it. Naturally he would change names, places, etc. Can you see any harm in it? After all, it wasn't a particularly unusual little drama, was it? War touches us all, whether we are away fighting or at home: lives are battered or destroyed, and loves and loyalties are put to the test. Anyway, he will be coming back again as soon as he can. He script-edits for one of the television soaps and has two or three weeks' work ahead but I am looking forward to seeing him again and also, I will admit, to the prospect of having Clio back. I miss her. When we are old the presence of youth has an invigorating effect: their confidence and fun and vitality rub off on us a little and bring warmth. As I've had young students about me for most of my life, I've been used to the privilege of connecting with their minds and enthusiasms.

I'm sure that something will come along for Clio and I am so thankful that her liaison with Peter is over. Pray for us all, Blaise, with all these changes happening in our lives.

How is Jeoffrey? Is he like his namesake, '. . . a mixture of gravity and waggery. For he knows that God is his Saviour'?

Give the sisters my love. An idea! If Clio is here at Christmas she might well offer to drive me up to Hexham. She's going out to Greece to see her parents for the New Year but I'm sure she'll agree providing you can manage both of us in your little flat. What fun it would be. Let me know. I simply cannot get Lucy out of my mind. What will Jonah tell her of his visit, I wonder. Will she be able to accept it?

St Francis sends his felicitations to Jeoffrey.

And mine of course to you,

Hester

165

CHAPTER FIFTEEN

In Litten Terrace, Jonah and Lucy were sitting at the table: Jonah at one end with Lucy at right angles to him, facing out into the garden. Jerry was having his afternoon's rest in bed and Lucy had waited until now to talk to Jonah about his visit to Bridge House. So it had often been, Jonah reflected; this kind of mutual recognition between them that certain subjects were best avoided until they were alone together. His father had never been able to enter easily into the world of the imagination that Jonah had inhabited from a small boy upwards. His mother, however, had always related to his creative needs, taking him seriously, encouraging him, whilst managing to prevent his father from feeling excluded.

'So you liked Hester,' she was saying. 'She was kind to you.'

Jonah watched her. There was a guarded quality

about her, though she clearly wanted to know what had happened.

'She was brilliant,' he answered warmly. 'She showed me a photograph of you and her together, like those ones you've got in the attic.'

He'd decided to be perfectly open with her, hiding nothing and hoping that this would allow her to speak freely. Lucy nodded but made no response, merely sipping her tea thoughtfully, so he elaborated a little more.

'She was obviously terribly fond of you and of Michael.' Since he'd been with Hester it seemed more natural to call him Michael: this man he'd never met and of whom he knew so little. 'She told me how he used to stay with them when he was at Cambridge with Edward. Do you remember Edward?'

She set her mug down, biting her lips, and he was aware of a brief reaction of fear.

'Yes,' she said after a moment. 'Yes, I remember Edward but not terribly well. After all, Jonah, I was very young, only four when Edward came back.'

Her voice held a note of pleading – as if she were asking him not to press her too far – yet, at the same time, he could see that she wanted to talk. It was she who had introduced the subject, after all. The creative force within him was always ready to sacrifice finer feelings if there were a story that needed to be told but he had no wish to hurt her.

'It's very young, isn't it?' he agreed reflectively. 'I can't remember much about my life when I was that age. Before starting school, just a bit, and one or two people. It's impressions that you remember, though, isn't it? The feel of things; atmosphere. Memories of people are much more to do with the reactions they engendered – fear or joy, for instance – rather than what they looked like.'

'That's right,' she agreed eagerly. 'When I first saw Hester I knew that she was what I called a "safe" person, so was Patricia, but Edward was frightening. I realized, ages afterwards, that he'd come back very damaged from the prisoner-of-war camp but at the time . . .' She shook her head, her eyes wide with memories. 'His fits of temper were frightening and his behaviour was extremely odd, although he rarely took any notice of me. But there was a kind of turbulence around him: an uncertainty of what he might do or say. I was afraid of Edward. And of Eleanor.'

She fell silent and Jonah waited. He didn't want to disturb the flow of these revelations although he was anxious to hear the story from her perspective.

'Eleanor,' she went on slowly, 'was rather like an animal who works from instinct and has no thought for any kind of human morality. I can see that now. She was in love with your grandfather and she wanted him. It didn't matter about Edward or me or anyone.'

This time the silence was rather longer.

'But you were happy there to begin with?' Jonah asked gently. 'At Bridge House with Hester and Nanny and the boys?'

Lucy smiled. 'Nanny.' She repeated the name affectionately, as if she'd forgotten her until this moment. 'Nanny was very sensible. She treated me as if I were a perfectly ordinary little girl who'd had a bit of a misfortune but wouldn't be allowed to milk it. She pointed out that the boys' father was at sea and that they worried all the time that he might be killed and, since we were all in the same boat, we must simply get on with it. She was very good for me. Normality is so important for children. Patricia spoiled me terribly, she had such a soft heart, but Nanny kept me straight. Nanny and Jack. Jack was my friend. I had nightmares, you know. They put me in a little room next to the boys and Jack used to come in if I cried out.' She smiled again, rather sadly. 'I was such a nervous child by then. I was afraid that Daddy would be taken away too, you see. I can remember that I was afraid of the dark and of the old people behind the curtain.'

'What old people?' In his surprise he interrupted her and she looked at him, her eyes clouded now with anxiety.

'I'd forgotten so much,' she said rather desperately. 'And now it's beginning to come back to me. Just lately I can't seem to prevent it but I still can't decide if it's right to disinter the past or just a form of self-indulgence.'

'I have this feeling that you think it might be right,' he said carefully. 'That for some reason the time has come to face what happened back then.'

'It's to do with your father,' she said at last. 'I feel frightened when I think of the responsibilities I'm having to shoulder. I'm not talking about silly things like paying the bills and remembering the MOT, but being strong and tough enough to keep him going through his pain and despair. I panic easily, especially at three in the morning when I can't sleep, and I'm beginning to feel that need to understand myself better so as to be able to cope with whatever is ahead. It would be easy to say, "This is me. Don't expect too much," but Jerry needs a great deal of support and I *want* to give it to him. All these dreadful drugs are making it impossible for him simply to grit his teeth and bear it bravely. There's the terrible depression, for one thing, which is so unlike him. You can see his fear,

170

Jonah – you've remarked on it yourself. I don't want to worry you or to be a burden – you do what you can for us – but I need to find some extra strength from somewhere and I have this feeling that if I could control my own fear then I could help Jerry more. Fear is such a stupid, disabling emotion but it comes before you can prepare for it and then you feel guilty for being unable to conquer it. For a little while now I've been thinking that if I can't change myself then I might not be able to help Jerry when things get really bad. I want to know why I am instinctively afraid of certain things and I began to wonder if it's to do with what happened when I was a child. Then you phoned and said you were going down to Exmoor and it seemed as if I were being shown that I was right to be thinking about the past after all the years of denying it. Even so, it's not easy to change: perhaps it's not possible.'

Jonah was silent. He was beginning to be anxious that he was opening Pandora's box and he might not know how to handle the results. He had an unshakeable belief, however, that communication must be a good thing. Lucy was already beginning to face up to things she'd kept hidden. At least he could assist her to confront them. Not for her, though, Hester's methodical, scholarly way of approach: she needed to be drawn gently along the path of remembering, exploring byways on the journey.

'Tell me about the old people behind the curtain,' he suggested at last. 'Were these people in your imagination?'

To his relief, she laughed. 'It was the shoes, you see. There was an alcove in the corner of the room with a hanging rail and a curtain pulled across to hide the clothes. Some shoes stood below it so that it looked as if a row of people were hiding behind the curtain. I knew there was nobody there, of course, but when it grew dark I imagined them standing there, listening. I was afraid that if I made a noise they'd come out.'

'Did you tell the boys? Jack and Robin, wasn't it?'

'That's right. They were sweet to me when I first arrived, on their best behaviour because they knew about Mummy being killed. Hester was there . . .' She put her elbows on the table, cradling her mug, looking back almost eagerly into the past, and suddenly Jonah was able to relax. All was well here, and, as she talked, describing odd related incidents and sensations, he could weave Hester's version of the story with her own as he listened.

CHAPTER SIXTEEN

'You'll be quite safe here,' Daddy tells Lucy
when they arrive at Bridge House on that sunny
September day in 1944 – and the first person she
sees is Hester. Hester does not immediately rush to
take her in her arms, as Patricia does later on. No,
Hester looks at her steadily and then goes down on
one knee to be at Lucy's own level. She says, 'Hello,
Lucy,' and stretches out her hand to touch Rabbit's
grey ear, smiling at Lucy, so that Lucy suddenly lets
go of Daddy's hand and holds out Rabbit to Hester,
knowing that what her father says is true and that
she feels safe.

Hester takes Rabbit and strokes his soft, plush
ear and says, 'Do you know the Little Grey Rabbit
books?' which surprises Lucy out of her shyness and
fear. She loves Grey Rabbit and Squirrel and Hare,
all living together in their little house.

'Jack and Robin love Little Grey Rabbit too,'

Hester tells her. 'They'll show you their books if you ask them. Oh, and here they are.'

And two little boys come into the room looking rather shy and awkward. Lucy is beginning to get used to the fact that grown-up people behave differently to her since Mummy died in the bombing. They speak with hushed voices and say, 'Poor little mite,' and their children are told to be kind to her. She hates it: it makes her feel singled out and even more frightened. So when Nanny comes in and says matter-of-factly, 'Oh, you've arrived, have you? That's good. We're just going to have tea but Jack and Robbie can show you your room first,' she feels a huge sense of relief: no hushed voice or long face – just good down-to-earth normality.

'You're in the room next to us,' the bigger boy says, clattering up the stairs in front of her. 'It's very small but I like it the best because it's right at the end of the house. I'm lending you my teddy just for tonight to make you feel at home but Robbie wouldn't let you have his. I tried to make him but he cried and Nanny said it was because he's young yet.'

Along a corridor, past their bedroom – 'We're in here but you can look later' – and then she is here in what is to be her own little room with its narrow bed and small painted chest. A teddy sits on the quilt and Jack bounces on the bed, seizing the teddy and rolling over with him.

She watches him cautiously whilst Robin stares at her, thumb in mouth, and she feels a sudden, terrible longing for her mother. The room is cold and bare, and nothing like her own bedroom at home in London; even the loan of Jack's teddy doesn't help to make it seem less strange. Before she can cry, or run back down the stairs to find her father, Nanny arrives carrying Lucy's little case.

'Now then,' she says briskly. 'Who will help me unpack?' and very quickly, helped by both boys, Lucy's own things are put about the little room. The pretty frame, with a photograph of Mummy and Daddy in it, is stood upon the chest along with Lucy's brush and some little china animals. Her nightgown is laid on the bed, her few books put on the shelf and her clothes in the drawers of the chest.

'Well done,' says Nanny. 'All ship-shape. Now we shall have some tea. Shall Rabbit sit with Teddy on your bed, Lucy?' But Lucy shakes her head, staring up at Nanny pleadingly with Rabbit clutched to her chest. 'No? Very well, he can come down to tea today.'

Immediately Jack seizes the teddy bear. 'Teddy wants some tea,' he shouts. 'He wants to have tea with Rabbit.' And he races ahead with Teddy, down the stairs, whilst the others follow more slowly. As they pass the boys' room, Robin unplugs his thumb and announces that his teddy would like some tea too, and Nanny says, 'Very well, just this once, to welcome Lucy.' She smiles at Lucy as she says it, and quite suddenly Lucy feels that it might be possible to be happy here after all, even after Daddy has gone back to London.

'Can we show Daddy my room?' she asks – and Nanny says, 'Yes, of course,' but by the time they get back downstairs there is another person with her father – not Hester but a dark woman who is tall, as tall as Daddy, and who smiles widely with a bright red mouth. Her eyes dart quickly at Lucy and then back again to Daddy. She looks greedy, Lucy thinks, rather like a witch who might gobble her father up. She pats Lucy on the head, as if she is a dog, and dismisses her.

'That's Aunt Eleanor,' says Jack, dancing Teddy upon the dining-room table, pretending that he is drinking Robin's milk. 'She lives with us now that Uncle Edward is away.'

And, just for a moment, Lucy feels frightened again: she does not like Eleanor. When Patricia arrives, however, carrying a plate of bread and butter, Lucy knows that she has found another safe person. Patricia puts the plate down quickly and hurries round the table to give Lucy a hug. For one terrible moment Lucy fears that Patricia might say something about Mummy but she doesn't, though Lucy can see that there are tears in her eyes. Instinctively, her own eyes begin to fill but Nanny is at hand, pouring Lucy's milk into a mug with rabbits on it whilst Jack is shouting to his mother to look at Rabbit and the teddies having tea together, and the moment passes.

The other grown-ups come into the dining-room but even though her father smiles at Lucy and waggles his fingers at her she can see that he is much more aware of Eleanor, who hovers close beside him. Watching him over the rim of her mug, Lucy feels that he is in some strange way afraid of Eleanor, yet how can he be? He's a soldier: brave and strong and fearless. Some instinct forces her to distract him – to demand his attention – and she joins with Jack in a noisy game with the toys whilst Robin laughs and laughs until he chokes and Nanny has to speak severely to them.

Jack spills his milk over Robin's teddy and, whilst Robin screams and everyone is mopping up and talking at once, Daddy comes over to Lucy to crouch beside her chair and asks if all is well.

She nods. 'Will you come and see my bedroom?'

she asks. 'Jack says it's the best one.' She puts her arms round his neck possessively, as if in some way she is protecting him – or herself – from Eleanor's dark stare, and he strokes her long thick brown hair and holds her tightly.

'You'll be safe here,' he mutters fiercely, almost as if he is begging her to agree and not to make a fuss. 'And I shall come to see you often. You'll be happier here than with Aunt Mary, won't you?'

And Lucy nods vehemently. It is much better here, with Jack and Hester and Nanny, than with Aunt Mary, who is very old and who lives in a house where things called V-2s are falling and there are so many things she, Lucy, is not allowed to touch. Yet she knows that soon her father must go away and a now-familiar terror seizes her: suppose a bomb kills him too? Her arms tighten about his neck but before she can begin to cry, Nanny is saying that they may all get down and go into the garden where there is a surprise for Lucy.

With the tears drying on her cheeks she scrambles down and they all go out together into the garden. With the river flowing by and the expanse of green grass it is almost as if she is back in the park in London but her attention is riveted by the sight of a little red and cream pram standing all by itself on the lawn. It is not new but it has been repainted and polished. Inside, tucked up tidily under a miniature blanket, is a rag doll.

Lucy stares at it, silent with delight, transfixed by the attention to detail. It is exactly like a real pram. Jack is already showing how the hood is raised and kept in place, and how the brake works, and Robin has brought Rabbit with him and now tucks him in beside the dolly. Her father gives Lucy a tiny push. 'Go and try it,' he says, smiling, and she lets go of his hand and runs across the grass.

'Nanny says that we may take it for a walk along the river path if you want to,' Jack says. He watches her eagerly, delighted with her pleasure. 'It used to be Mummy's when she was little but it's yours now for keeps. Shall we put the teddies in too? They can go for a walk as well.'

And when her father comes to kiss her she hardly notices because she is so busy taking off the fitted cover so as to put the teddies in at the foot of the pram; and finally the children with Hester and Nanny set off along the path between the trees, headed by Jack on his tricycle.

By the time they arrive back at the house her father is gone.

CHAPTER SEVENTEEN

Once Jonah had returned to London, Lucy found that she was thinking more and more about the past and her own reaction to it. Apart from talking to him at length about her arrival at Bridge House there had been no other opportunity to describe those later events, the memory of which still filled her with an instinctive horror. It seemed odd to her that Hester could talk calmly about that period of time without thinking of its culmination: the fight in the drawing-room, Edward knocked backwards into the river and her father fleeing with her back to London.

She was certain that Hester had not yet told Jonah the full story and she was interested now to find out exactly how much Hester would tell and how she would explain Edward's death to Jonah. Of course, she didn't know that there had been a witness that terrible evening but, even so, Hester was clearly more than ready to talk about the past. This was so extraordinary that, if those blows and cries had not been etched so clearly on her own memory, Lucy wondered if she might now begin to believe that the whole thing had been the figment of one of her nightmares. Yet she knew it wasn't: the scene was too real, following too close on the breaking of the Midsummer Cushion to be a dream.

'Ask Hester about the Midsummer Cushion,' she'd said to Jonah, spurred by an inexplicable desire to test the veracity of Hester's account of the past. How foolish that the mere speaking of it aloud should have the power to make her heart knock in her side.

He'd looked puzzled. 'The Midsummer Cushion? What's that?'

'Ask Hester. See if she remembers it.'

She saw that she'd aroused his curiosity but that he was deliberately controlling his eagerness to know more. He'd let her set the pace and was determined not to press her. Lucy was grateful. After a lifetime of denial it was very difficult simply to talk about it all as if it were an amusing little episode to be told across the dinner-table. She could see that Jonah was fascinated by Hester's accounts of his grandfather and that already he identified and sympathized with the man whom he instinctively called 'Michael'.

At what point, Lucy wondered, would she be obliged to say: 'Yes, but he killed his oldest friend, you see. He'd been having an affair with Eleanor and when Edward found them together there was a fight and Daddy killed him. And then ran away'?

Lucy folded her arms tightly across her breast and rocked herself in an attempt to contain the pain of the memory. The pain was still fresh, driving up from its hiding place, piercing her heart as she tried to make sense of it. Nothing more terrible for a child, she reminded herself, than to see a beloved parent fearful and ashamed. In some strange way her father's fear and shame had seemed more terrible than watching him knock Edward backwards into the river. How wild the river had been that night: the waters raging and uncontrollable, mirroring the violence of the scene inside the house.

It was because the river's voice had been so noisy, so clamouring, that she'd been unable to sleep and so had crept out onto the landing and seen the light on in Hester's room and the door open. Hoping that Hester was there she'd gone in, ready to plead for a story or a drink, but the room was empty and she'd been drawn as usual to the Midsummer Cushion.

What terrible luck, Lucy thought now, that it should be on that particular evening that she should scramble up to look at it more closely, reaching on tiptoe to trace the bright flowers beneath the cold glass so that the stool wobbled unsteadily and she'd instinctively clutched at the tapestry. If it had not crashed to the floor, smashing the glass, the dried flowers withering instantly to dust, would events have been any different? Certainly she would not have gone downstairs looking for Hester and, hesitating in the hall, heard the voice coming from the drawing-room.

Even now she could remember the quality of urgency in the whisper: the desperation. She'd gone quietly in, pausing in the doorway. The chiaroscuro of light and shadow between the lamp and the firelight made it difficult to see where the two people sat close together in the semi-darkness. The voice had ceased now and there was silence. Another voice spoke, harder but just as urgent.

'It's because of Lucy, isn't it? If it weren't for her we could get away. You're a fool, Michael. Something terrible is going to happen and it will be because of Lucy.'

She'd slipped quickly behind the sofa, heart

hammering, and then everything had happened at once. Hester had come swiftly in from the hall, switching on the light and then exclaiming as if shocked at the sight of the two figures embracing on the sofa. At the same time the French doors leading from the terrace had been wrenched open and Edward stood confronting them. Peeping from her hiding place she'd seen that his dark, mad eyes were fixed upon Eleanor and her father, who'd risen from the sofa.

He'd shouted words unintelligible to her, seizing Eleanor by the shoulder so that her father grabbed at him in an attempt to restrain him whilst Hester tried to intervene. Then suddenly the two men were struggling together, grunting and panting like animals and stumbling against the furniture. Eleanor had begun to scream and Lucy had hidden her face in terror.

Even now she could recall the suffocating fear and the trembling of her limbs.

'Are you OK, Luce?' Jerry had come in and was watching her curiously. 'Have you got a pain, clutching yourself like that?'

'No, oh, no. I'm fine.' Quickly she got up and went to him, putting her arms about him. 'Just a silly moment. You know how it is.'

He held her tightly, imagining that she'd been

worrying about him and their future, and as he comforted her she despaired that she would ever be able to change. Her decision to confront the past had been in the hope that she would become the stronger partner. Instead it was Jerry who, unknowingly, was giving her the courage to face it.

Looking up at him she was struck by his expression: it was clear that he was glad to be comforting her. Her need was enabling him to show his own strength – frail sometimes though it might be – and it was necessary to his pride for this still to be required of him. She saw that the change for which she hoped in her own character need not be at the expense of Jerry's mental toughness and natural protectiveness; nor must she be so ready to believe that her weaknesses had become a burden to him.

Briefly she wondered if she might share her secret with him, talk to him about the past and the effect it still had on her – but instinctively she shied away from it. Jerry had never been a natural confidant, personal revelations embarrassed him, and she simply couldn't face a verbal pat on the head – 'I'm sure it wouldn't have been that bad, Luce. Perhaps you're imagining it' – as a response to something that was so crucially wrapped about her deepest sense of self.

He was already turning away lest the embrace

should lengthen into mawkishness, talking about it being time for a cup of tea and bending to stroke Tess who'd been slumbering in her basket by the fire. Lucy accepted that the moment was over and went to make the tea.

Jonah, unable to contain his curiosity, telephoned Hester from the train to London.

'I've been talking to Mum,' he said, keeping his voice low, shoulder hunched to his travelling companions. 'She told me all about her arrival at Bridge House. It was great. I mean, she seemed very ready to talk about it. There wasn't time for much but she asked me to ask you about the Midsummer Cushion. Does that mean anything to you?'

'*The Midsummer Cushion* was the title given by John Clare to a body of work which he collected together for a fourth volume of poetry. A friend persuaded him to change it to the more conventional title of *The Rural Muse*.' Hester sounded puzzled. 'I can't imagine that Lucy would have known about that. Certainly not when she was with us.'

'It seemed important to her.' Jonah was urgent in his disappointment. 'Maybe there's another connection.'

186

At this point he lost his signal and, unwilling to entertain his fellow travellers with any more of his conversation, he switched his phone off and gave himself up to contemplation.

Later, waiting for his train to the north, he switched his mobile on again and saw that there was a message on his answerphone. Hester's voice was very clear.

'So stupid of me, Jonah. Lucy must have been talking about the tapestry we had once. It was a very beautiful thing, embroidered wild flowers, with a particular reference to John Clare that I'll tell you about at another time. The point is that the string wore very thin and frayed through and I discovered the tapestry in pieces on my bedroom floor. It was very precious to the family – a kind of heirloom – and we as children, and then Patricia's boys, were always threatened with dire results if any of us should touch it so I imagine that's what Lucy can remember. I recall that she loved it and I used to pick her up so that she could have a close look at it. How fascinating! I'm looking forward to your next visit so that we can talk it over properly.'

The message finished as abruptly as it had begun. Hester wasn't the kind of person to send affectionate greetings or indulge in drawn-out goodbyes, and Jonah was left feeling distinctly dissatisfied. On an impulse he phoned Clio, only to be told that there was no-one to take his call. Frustrated, he boarded the train and settled down to the long journey north.

CHAPTER EIGHTEEN

Hester wakened suddenly from a vivid dream. In the dream she'd been standing in the doorway of the drawing-room, just where she'd stood sixty years before. It looked exactly the same: mysterious shadowy corners, golden pools of lamplight spilling across polished wood, bright reflections in the mirror above the fireplace where blue and orange tongues of flame licked hungrily at the wood in the grate. A newspaper, casually flung down, was sliding from the chintz-covered cushions of the long sofa under the window, where damson-coloured damask curtains had been pulled against the wild night, and it was there, from just behind the sofa, that something pale but bright flickered suddenly out into the firelight – and just as suddenly disappeared.

In her dream she'd switched on the light just as the French doors burst open and Jonah appeared, calling out, soaked to the skin – and she'd wakened, heart thumping and with that familiar sense that something was not quite right. St Francis was curled in a large warm ball at the back of her knees and Hester continued to lie on her side for a moment, trying to control the feelings of distress that the dream had invoked.

She raised her head to peer at the little illumined face of her clock – half-past three – and groaned inwardly. Such a terrible time to be awake: a time of fear and terror and despair. Insidious images, general and particular, haunted the mind: of the lonely vulnerability of old age, of the anguish in the world, of a dear old friend who'd suffered a stroke and whose witty, clever mind was now imprisoned, still agonizingly alive and aware, in the weighty cage of her immobile body. All these horrors could be offered up in prayer, held in a silent intercession of sharing, and Hester knew that this could bring its own kind of peace. Tonight, however, her vivid dream pressed upon her consciousness: that scene in the drawing-room, the unexpected flash of colour and Jonah bursting in crying out something about the Midsummer Cushion being broken.

Hester climbed out of bed and reached for her shawl. She remembered how she'd woken recently, on the night of the storm, with this same sense of panic: the wind knocking the photograph to the floor and smashing the glass to pieces, just as the Midsummer Cushion had been smashed all those years ago. There was no storm tonight. The moon sailed cold and free above the black silhouette of the trees, and mist lay along the river so dense it looked like drifts of snow. Thick-sown stars glittered, sharp as tiny jewels, dazzling with an icy brilliance above the silent, frosty fields, and even the river's voice was hushed, muted by its fleecy coverlet.

Huddling in the woollen warmth of the shawl, Hester leaned out of the window: how cold it was. The ruts and puddles were freezing over – 'crizzling', John Clare would have called it – and the garage's frosted thatch glimmered whitely in the moonlight. Hester drew her head back inside and closed the window. The sight of the thatched roof reminded her of Robin and her decision, yet to be made, as to whether she should stay at Bridge House. Shivering, she pushed her feet into moccasins and went downstairs to make a hot drink.

Resenting the icy blast of air, missing her warmth, St Francis insinuated his bulk beneath the quilt and resumed his slumber.

*   *   *

The day finally dawned chill and bleak. The mist rolled silently along the valley, drifting up to obscure the pale December sun and hanging faint and ghostly in the bare black branches of the tallest trees. Later in the morning, a very welcome distraction arrived in the form of a letter from Blaise.

St Bede's Convent

Darling Hes,

Thank you for your letter. You are constantly in my mind at present. So much seems to be happening around you: Jonah, Clio, Robin all needing help, and you in the middle of them all wondering what you should do and where you should go. I'm glad that you've arranged the means for Robin to pay his debts without having to make a speedy decision about moving. You need time to think about such an important change and I have a strong feeling that this should be a period of consideration rather than action. After all, it *is* Advent: a time of waiting.

I've just taken a few moments to reread your letter. First, Clio. I think you are quite right to say that Clio won't waste any time feeling sorry for herself and I am sure that it will be an excellent thing for her to have a brief respite with you – a time of waiting for her too – before she decides what to do next. This is an important step for her, now that she is – we hope – emotionally freed from a relationship that had no future, and you'll enjoy having her with you. Your idea about asking her to drive you here for Christmas is inspired. If you think she could face Christmas in a convent we should all be very happy to see her, if you don't mind sharing the spare bedroom with her. Since you know the accommodation I have here I can only assume that you've already thought of that.

You know, Hes, when I began to read what you'd written about Jonah I couldn't help but visualize Michael as I knew him all those years ago: that sensitivity to atmosphere that you described – how interesting that he should have 'seen' his grandfather on the bridge – and his strong creative impulse that makes him want to take this piece of history and reshape it into a play. It all sounds very like the Michael I knew and I'm not in the least surprised that Jonah's a scriptwriter and a playwright. How very suitable for Michael's grandson. I'm glad that Lucy has broken her silence on the subject. As far as I remember, I never knew her, shut away as I was in Bletchley Park for the duration, but it does seem odd that she has been so reluctant to discuss his grandparents with Jonah, or for that matter her time with you all at Bridge House unless, in some odd childish way, she felt that you – the family – were in some way responsible for Michael's death. Apart from a natural resentment of her father's affection for another woman, especially so soon after the death of her mother, it's possible that she imagined that his relationship with Eleanor affected his ability to do his work safely – perhaps they continued their affair more openly in London – and all of you have remained tied up with Lucy's unhappy memory of Eleanor. It's rather an unlikely suggestion but the only one I can come up with at the moment. We often attribute far too much importance to small events, or misunderstand things we see and hear, when we are children. Now, at least, you might be able to discover what has been weighing so heavily on her. It is interesting too that Jonah thinks she is trying to cast off her fear so as to face the future more ably. It struck a particular note, as it happens. I have been rereading *The Impact of God*: St John of the Cross tells us that we can step free from the things that cripple us – fear, hatred, lust, selfishness, guilt – if we allow God the initiative to set us free by his grace. He goes on to say how very difficult this can seem, that it can take a lifetime to open ourselves up, emptying ourselves so that God can enter, but to remember, at the darkest moments when nothing really seems to be working, that we *want* to be free of whatever it is that is holding us back from peace or joy. I find that it works: just remembering my desire to be free pulls me off the demoralizing suction pad of a bad memory, hopelessness, or fear of some future event and enables me to lift my desire for freedom up towards God again.

I'm not absolutely sure, Hes, why I'm writing all this to you – apart from the fact that I've always written out my thoughts to you – but I feel I have been especially led to do so today.

I've thought a great deal about Jonah's idea of making a play of this small part of your history and after much reflection I can see no real reason why some kind of story shouldn't be created about it, as long as Jonah has all the facts accurately and – very important – assuming that Lucy has no objection. After all, apart from you and Lucy, nobody is left who can be directly affected. As you rightly say, tragic though it was, it mirrors hundreds of small dramas that were happening everywhere at that time. I write all this, however, having no true knowledge of Jonah's character or being able to judge how he will react once he knows the whole story. We – you and I – look back at that time with the compassion and wisdom that hindsight bestows: the pain has been dulled by forgetfulness and overlaid by the business of living.

I paused for a little while there, Hes. I suppose that niggling away at the back of my mind is the wish to know the real reason for Lucy's self-imposed silence. I still feel that there is something to do with Eleanor here that we might not know about. The question is: can Jonah handle the truth about his grandfather? Has he identified with Michael very closely and sympathetically – you say he is very like him physically and clearly there are similarities of character – and might he therefore find it difficult to accept Michael's behaviour at the end? It sounds as if his grandfather – because of the mystery surrounding him and his tragic death – has been built up in his mind to some rather heroic figure. The young can be so puritanical, can't they? That's all I want to say and, remember, I'm writing as usual from a position of ignorance. I'm sure you wouldn't have taken part in all this if you hadn't been sure it was right.

After all, there has already been so much filmed and written about the war that if Jonah feels there is something new to say then it's up to him to say it: that's his decision. I can well imagine both Edward and Michael spurring him on!

As for Jeoffrey! He is much loved. As Christopher Smart puts it: 'For there is nothing sweeter than his peace when at rest. For there is nothing brisker than his life when in motion.' Poor Christopher, thrown into the mad-house for his compulsive praying in the street! Speaking of which, of course I shall hold you in my prayers – when do I not? – although not in public!

My love, dear Hes,
Blaise

As the day passed, Hester reread the letter several times with a growing sense of unease. She'd taken seriously Blaise's phrase 'as long as Jonah has the facts very accurately' and was trying to remember everything she'd already told him and deciding how very carefully she would have to explain Edward's mental and physical condition when he'd returned to them from the prisoner-of-war camp: those tiny, terrible details of the way he stole and hid food and his incandescent rages if anyone touched his belongings.

Remembering these things sent Hester at once to the study to record her thoughts and to note down the final sequence of events that led to the fight and Michael's return with Lucy to London. Confident that she'd assisted Jonah to build up a true impression of the characters of all the people involved, combined with his natural feel for that brief, relevant period of the war that she'd described to him, she could only hope that he'd view the rest of the story with understanding and compassion.

When she next saw him, however, she was filled with doubt. Jonah was as eager as ever; his longing to know the whole of the story was undiminished. If anything, Lucy's disclosures had simply added fuel to the flames of his curiosity and Hester saw that nothing would satisfy him now but to know everything. The first thing that he asked about, however, was the Midsummer Cushion. Hester was relieved to be able to tell him how John Clare had described a very old custom among the villagers, which was to stick wild field flowers into a slice of turf and place it as an ornament in their cottages. These were the 'Midsummer Cushions' and the custom had so delighted one of Hester's ancestors that she had translated it into a tapestry.

'It was very beautiful,' Hester said, 'and I can well imagine that Lucy would remember it. For some reason it utterly enchanted her and she would ask to be lifted up so as to see it properly.' She hesitated. 'Did you feel that she was quite happy to be talking about all this at last, Jonah?'

'I felt so. It hasn't been a complete *volte face*, don't think that – she's approaching it very cautiously – but when I talked about Nanny and the boys she told me all about her arrival here, as far as she could remember it, and it seemed to be a very happy experience. Of course, you'd described it too, so I was able to see it as a whole picture. I have to say that having two sides of the same story is fascinating.'

Yet Hester still hesitated to plunge in as she'd done so readily on his previous visit: the warning in Blaise's letter continued to haunt her. The stark fact was that Jonah's grandfather had conducted an affair with his best friend's wife for a year before Edward's return and it had been the sight of them together that had driven the already unstable Edward to violence. How to explain the loneliness of the years between Edward's capture early in 1942 until his unexpected return late in 1945 so that Jonah should not judge Eleanor – or Michael – too harshly? After all, she'd long given up hope that her husband was still alive and it was easy to understand how both Michael – still grieving for Susan – and the lonely Eleanor might be drawn to each other for comfort.

At this point Hester pulled herself up sharply. These were not the 'accurate facts' of which Blaise had written. To describe the events so might be more palatable for Jonah but it in no way gave any truthful picture either of Eleanor's predatory determination to possess Michael or of the gradual weakening of Michael's will. He hadn't loved Eleanor but he could not, in the end, resist her. Hester saw, with a kind of horror, how very easy it would be to distort the facts. She began to fear her ability to achieve telling the whole story honestly without leaving Jonah with a rather unsavoury portrait of his grandfather.

As they sat beside the fire in the book-room, with St Francis draped lovingly across Jonah's chest, Hester started to describe the uncertainty of those years after Edward's capture, and the anxiety and fear that had haunted them all – especially Eleanor. Her physical passion for Edward had been very real and she'd missed him terribly so that Michael's arrival with Lucy had found her in a lonely and very needy state.

As Hester negotiated these dangerous waters she soon realized that Jonah was not at all predisposed to judge his grandfather: he was ready to accept that Michael and Eleanor had both been vulnerable and therefore open to temptation. Hester could truthfully show that it was Eleanor who'd made the running, even if she were aware of Jonah's growing recognition that Michael must have allowed himself to be manipulated – up to a point.

The sticking point, beyond which he would not budge, Hester told Jonah, was Lucy's safety and happiness. It was at Bridge House, with Hester and Nanny and the boys, and Patricia, that Lucy had found some kind of normal life again and Michael refused to move her away though it was clearly impossible to have an affair before the gaze of such a large family. Any leave he had was spent at Bridge House, which though it had its advantages for Eleanor, was also deeply frustrating.

'I'm sure that Lucy was happy with us,' Hester said, though now sounding rather doubtful. 'And though it could be said that Michael and Eleanor behaved badly, it's necessary to remember that for three years Eleanor – all of us – half believed that her husband was dead. The danger really began when poor Edward came back and neither Michael nor Eleanor would make a clean break one way or the other. To be fair, Edward frightened all of us and I wouldn't have blamed Eleanor if she and Michael had decided to cut their losses and had simply gone away together. Afterwards, I wished they had.'

'Afterwards?'

'He came on them unexpectedly one evening.' Hester decided that she could tell him this much. 'They were together in the drawing-room. I think Eleanor was pleading with Michael to go away with her. She was holding on to him and he had his arms round her. Perhaps, in his dark, confused mind, Edward already suspected something between them. Anyway, he lost control and attacked Michael. They fought, it was very violent and horrid, and afterwards there was no question but that Michael should take Lucy at once and go back to London. Eleanor decided to go with them.'

Jonah was looking rather shocked. 'Mum didn't say anything about this.'

'Lucy wouldn't have known. She was in bed, asleep. Eleanor had to wake her up so as to dress her and hurry her away. It must have been very frightening for her and I don't know what Michael and Eleanor told her. Perhaps there was something they said which accounts for her long silence. Shortly afterwards Michael was killed. The whole period was terribly traumatic for her. I feel now that we let her down. I said that she was happy here and I'm sure she was, at least until Nanny and the boys left when Patricia's husband came back after the war. After that she must have been lonely, poor little soul, though she had become used to us by then, and Michael was reluctant to move her to his old aunt in Sussex. When Edward came back, and we saw that he was unstable and deeply disturbed mentally, we should have acted. I see that now, in retrospect, but life is never quite so clear when one is living it, is it? We all dithered, getting through each day, trying to come to terms with this new development. We didn't have counselling in those days. We just got on with it as best we could. Most of the time Edward was very quiet but odd things would upset him and one could never be sure what they might be: certain noises or even colour combinations distressed him. Nowadays he'd have been locked up, of course, or on very powerful medication.' A pause. 'Did Lucy talk about Edward?'

'Only in passing. She said that he frightened her but took very little notice of her. She said . . .' Jonah frowned, remembering, 'she said that there was an aura of turbulence around him and that he had violent fits of temper but she said that Eleanor also frightened her. She said that you and Patricia were "safe" people.'

Hester smiled gratefully. 'I'm so glad that she felt that and that she remembered Nanny and the boys with affection. Tell me what she said about the Midsummer Cushion. It clearly had an effect on her.'

'Actually, she didn't talk about it as such. She mentioned it right at the end, when I was leaving. "Ask Hester about the Midsummer Cushion," she said.'

'I've been thinking about it,' Hester said, 'and I remember that it broke very soon after Michael and Lucy left us. I found it in pieces on my bedroom floor. The string was worn very thin and had broken. Probably some vibration finished it off. I'm glad she didn't know about that. She loved it so much.' She hesitated, watching him, trying to gauge his reactions. 'Do you think that she might come here, Jonah? Now that you've broken the ice? I would so like to see her again.'

He smiled at her. 'I'd like to think she would,' he said warmly. 'I'm sure it would do her so much good now that she's begun to open up. I'll certainly mention it when the moment seems right.'

'Good.' Hester stood up. 'I thought we'd have a drive tomorrow. The forecast is promising and I think you need to keep the landscape in your mind, as well as the emotions. There will be plenty of time before you catch your train.'

'That'll be great. My turn for lunch, though.'

'Splendid. We'll go to the Royal Oak at Winsford. Your grandfather enjoyed a pint there. Goodnight, Jonah.'

She went away and he sat on for a moment, piecing the story together, seeing visions in the flames. There was a great deal to think about and, though he was conscious of some missing element in Hester's recital, he was too tired and comfortable to worry about it.

CHAPTER NINETEEN

She knocked on his door next morning, opened it a little way and spoke through the gap. 'The boiler has indigestion. Best put on an extra jersey. Dave can't come until tomorrow.'

His curiosity was sufficiently roused for him to ask sleepily: 'Who's Dave?'

'Dave is the boiler's personal physician. He does clever things to its little insides and then it feels much better. Meanwhile it's rather cold.'

It was whilst they were drinking a third cup of coffee each, and the usual early morning silence was being gradually broken, that Hester told Jonah that she might be leaving Bridge House. During breakfast he'd been brooding on all the things she'd told him, especially the details of Edward's mental condition, and weaving them all into a comprehensive whole that he could see developing quite clearly and satisfactorily in his mind's eye.

This news, however, shocked him so much that his thought process was completely broken.

'Leave?' he repeated. 'But why? I mean, sorry, it's none of my business. It's just that . . .'

'Just what?'

'Well, I feel I've just found you after all these years. Not just you, of course, but all of them: Michael, Edward, my mother even. It sounds weird but I do feel that I'm learning at last about my own family. And Bridge House too. It's all been a part of it for so long, you see. "Lucy with Jack and Robbie in the garden at Bridge House." It became a part of the whole mystery of it. And now, just when I've found you all, you say you're going. How can you do this to me, Hester?'

She smiled. 'It's not quite that straightforward. I don't have any particular desire to go but the fact is that I'm not the sole owner of Bridge House. My mother left it equally to Patricia, Edward, and me. Edward left his share to me and when Patricia died she left her share divided between Jack and Robin. We've all used it as a family home for holidays and emergencies until I retired and since then I've lived here most of the time although the family still come for holidays. Now, my nephew Robin is rather in need of ready cash so it looks as if the time has come to sell up.'

'But that's rather tough on you, isn't it? After all, it's your home. Where would you go?'

'That's a very good question,' Hester answered lightly. 'I only wish I had an answer to it. I think that Robbie thinks it would be more sensible for me to be in a smaller place, less to look after and so on, especially now that I've had a hip replacement. To be honest, I feel better than I have for years but that's not the point. The upkeep would be beyond me without the others to share some of the costs. I'm sure you've seen the state of the roof. A new thatch would cost a great deal of money.'

'You couldn't afford to buy them out?'

She laughed. 'On my savings and pension? No, my dear Jonah, I couldn't. I was an academic, not a footballer. Do you know anything about equity release?'

He frowned. 'Not much. Is that where the mortgage company gives you part of the value of the house in return for the property when you die?'

'Something like that. You continue to live in the house using the money they've given you. In this case, a third of the money would go to Robin and Amy.'

'Who's Amy?'

Hester explained the intricacies of the family

tree whilst Jonah watched her with an expression of mingled dismay and indignation that amused her.

'It's quite fair, really, you know. They are entitled to their inheritance. It's my own fault for not looking too far ahead. I lived in university accommodation, you see, and when I retired it seemed a natural move to come to Bridge House. Everyone was happy about it and I pay Robin and Amy a proportional rent. It was good to have the old place used full time, and any of the family could come here when they felt like it so I grew complacent. My difficulty about staying here is the prospect of keeping up with the costs. I'm not certain that my share from equity release will support Bridge House and me for the rest of my life.'

'So if you don't take that route where might you go?'

Hester shook her head. 'I really can't decide. Bridge House seemed to be a natural centre when I retired, it was home, but now I feel rather rootless. I have old friends in Lincoln and in Cambridge but I don't particularly feel drawn to moving back to either place. I could buy a smaller place in Dulverton.' She sighed. 'I'd decided to put it on hold until Clio comes back. She's so clear-headed that I hope she might help to see it all more positively. Sometimes we need someone who isn't so involved to show us a path out of our muddles. Don't look so upset, Jonah.'

'I am upset,' he declared. 'Especially if you don't want to go. There must be other ways out of this.'

'I'm glad you arrived when you did,' she told him. 'Let's just be grateful for that. And if you can persuade Lucy to come for a short visit I should be very happy.'

'I shall certainly try. When you say Clio is coming back do you mean for the weekend?'

'No,' she answered. 'That's another story.'

This opened a new direction of discussion that lasted them through the drive to the Royal Oak at Winsford where Hester introduced Jonah to Graeme, who pulled him a pint of Butcombe. At the bar, several locals were discussing a shoot and, having made a fuss of two black Labradors, who waited patiently with noses on paws, Jonah and Hester took the menu and their drinks to the table in the bay window. After they'd eaten they sat long over their coffee, enjoying the warmth of the fire, and presently went out into the winter afternoon. Already the sun was low but the sky was still clear and the air had a frosty chill to it.

Jonah settled himself happily in his seat, preparing himself to be receptive to the glory of the

210

scenes that Hester would show him. She drove slowly, stopping at certain points, occasionally telling him a little story that involved Michael and Edward or some other member of the family and, just as before, he was aware of the impact of light and air and water.

The quality of the light, particularly, was extraordinary: the winter sun, shining obliquely across hill and water, touched the countryside with vivid, rosy radiance. Even the dying bracken and dry brittle cages of heather took on a new and glowing life. Puddles lay like bloodstains beside the road and the bright bare twigs of the graceful, ghostly silver birch burned crimson.

On a steep hillside sheep stood toe-to-toe with their slab-sided shadows, grazing peacefully whilst a flock of starlings swirled over the field and settled in a chattering crowd on a wind-twisted thorn. In the west a low bank of cloud lay massed across the land behind which the sun was slowly sinking, its power gradually evaporating as if it were being extinguished by the watery vapour. Across the Channel tiny lights began to prick into the growing twilight: an insubstantial, flickering necklace strung out along the coast.

Jonah, utterly absorbed by the mysterious beauty, was surprised when Hester began to turn the car.

'If we're quick,' she said, 'we'll see the rest of it up on Dunkery. It should be pretty impressive.'

The road, descending from the hills, passed between beech hedges and dry-stone walls, plunging downwards into the little town of Porlock where friendly lamps twinkled and shopkeepers were bustling out to bring in their wares from the pavements. The unusually truncated church tower showed black against the brilliant sky and Jonah twisted in his seat to stare back at it as the town was left behind and they raced on through deep lanes and between woodland that crowded thick on every side. So dark was it in these combes that when the car burst out again upon the high moorland road Jonah gasped in surprise. Up here the light was still radiant and the rocky cairn on Dunkery Beacon showed starkly outlined against a duck-egg-green sky that was streaked with cloudy banners of flame and scarlet and gold.

Hester parked the car and they both climbed out. Jonah stared at the spectacle in silence. Each moment the sunset colours changed and glowed with a greater intensity and, as he watched, a grey plume of thunderous cloud funnelled up and drifted like smoke across the blazing sky. The brilliance began to fade; already in the north the mist lay soft and white, though hard-edged, with an indigo scrawl on the horizon where the land rose as if out of a distant milky sea.

He glanced at Hester who smiled at him, tipping her head as if to draw his attention to some new wonder, and he turned quickly. In the east the moon was rising, all shredded about with wisps of cloud, luminous and magical above the darkening land. Jonah found that he was swallowing hard, moved beyond anything he had ever known, and then Hester was beside him, touching him lightly on the shoulder.

'Come,' she said gently. 'We have a train to catch.'

CHAPTER TWENTY

It was as the train was approaching Reading that he received a message from Lucy: Jerry was in hospital following a severe cold that had set off a flare-up of symptoms including fever, shortness of breath and a rash. He'd been admitted for blood tests, she told him. If all went well he might be home in ten days. She sounded distressed and very tired, and Jonah said that he would come straight to Chichester, getting down as soon as he could. His train was on time, he told her, and, with luck, he should be able to catch the nine-seventeen from Victoria.

He arrived at Litten Terrace just before eleven o'clock. Lucy was waiting for him. He gave her a hug and she held on to him tightly for a moment whilst Tess struggled out of sleep and left her basket to come wagging to greet him.

'Bless you for coming,' Lucy said. 'It's been a rather terrible day but he's fairly comfortable now.

On top of everything else, he's had the most excruciating joint and muscle pains and no appetite at all. They've had to put him on a three-day course of intravenous steroid and even after that the daily oral dose of prednisolone will be raised for a while. Then there will be the withdrawal symptoms as he struggles to decrease it to a safer long-term level. God, I hate this vile disease.'

She made him some supper and they sat together at the table whilst he ate it.

'So how was Hester?' she asked suddenly, rousing herself from her unhappy thoughts and looking for a diversion. 'Did you ask her about the Midsummer Cushion?'

'Yes, I did.' He was glad to be able to distract her. 'She described it to me and said how much you'd loved it.'

'Yes, I did. It was very beautiful.' She paused. 'So did she say anything else about it?'

'Well, yes. I wondered whether to tell you, actually. It's rather sad. The string holding it up frayed through and it fell off the wall and smashed. She said she was glad that you didn't know about it.'

She was staring at him. 'Didn't know about it?'

'It happened after you'd gone, she said. After you and Michael went back to London.'

'Is that what she told you?'

215

Jonah looked puzzled. 'Isn't it true?'

'No.' Lucy was too tired to prevaricate: too tired and too angry. Seeing Jerry in such terrible pain, combined with her fear for him and of their future, had all fused with her own exhaustion and, with an almost luxurious violence, freed her from the restraint and silence that the past had imposed upon her. 'No, it isn't true. *I* broke the Midsummer Cushion. I climbed up on the little stool and touched it and it fell down. Of course it might be true that the string was frayed and I simply hastened the process. My God, how ironical!' She struck her fist lightly on the table. 'All these years I've felt as if I committed a terrible crime and that what followed was a punishment and, after all, Hester calmly says that she thought that the string had frayed.'

'What d'you mean, "What followed"?'

'The fight. Did Hester tell you about the fight?'

'Yes, she did. She explained about Michael and Eleanor, and how Edward found them together and they fought. That was why it was decided that Michael should take you away. Of course, she knows that you never knew why you had to leave so suddenly. You had to be woken up and taken away. It must have been very frightening.'

Lucy laughed – an unexpectedly explosive sound

that contained no mirth. Jonah stretched out a hand to her and held her wrist.

'What's wrong, Mum? Should we be talking about this now, what with Dad and everything . . . ?'

'Yes,' she said angrily. 'Yes, we should. You've always wanted to know the truth and now I want to tell it. We didn't leave Bridge House because there was a fight. Oh, there *was* a fight. Hester's telling the truth about that. Daddy and Eleanor were together in the drawing-room and Edward came in off the terrace and found them. He was quite distraught. He ran at Daddy and grappled him.' She broke off to stare at Jonah with a kind of horror. 'There's something so terrible about men fighting,' she said. 'All that intense struggling and their expressions of hatred.'

She fell silent, remembering; too distressed to proceed.

'But how did you know about it?' Jonah asked at last. 'Hester said you were in bed asleep.'

Lucy folded her arms on the table and breathed deeply, composing herself.

'She would have assumed that. The truth is that I couldn't sleep that night; the wind and the river were making so much noise. So I got up hoping I might persuade Hester to read me a story. Her bedroom light was on but the room was empty and

217

I went in to look at the Midsummer Cushion. I climbed on a stool and overbalanced and that's when I broke it. It made such a mess and so I went downstairs wondering if I should tell Hester or whether I could clear it up. Something like that, anyway. I was very frightened because I believed I'd done something very bad. I heard voices in the drawing-room and I went in. That's when it all happened. I hid behind the sofa and saw it all. They struggled and Eleanor rushed at Edward and he let go of Daddy and took her by the throat. By this time they were near the French doors and my father pulled Eleanor away and punched Edward in the face. He reeled backwards across the terrace and fell over the low wall into the river.' She glanced at Jonah. 'Hester didn't tell you that?'

He shook his head silently.

'Hester rushed out and leaned out over the river,' she continued, 'but Eleanor seized her and held her by the shoulders. Daddy stood quite still, as if dazed, and then he raced out along the terrace and over the bridge. He was shouting for help. Hester went after him. She was calling, "Michael, wait. There's no point." No point, you see,' repeated Lucy rather desperately, 'in trying to save Edward because he was already dead. And she and Daddy came back together, and Eleanor brought him into

218

the house. That's when I ran upstairs and got into bed. I was afraid that they would see me and that it was all my fault because of the Midsummer Cushion.'

Jonah remained silent. He was remembering now the detail missing in Hester's recounting of the fight. She hadn't spoken about Michael running out of the house and over the bridge.

'So then Eleanor appeared by my bed,' Lucy went on. 'She shook me but I was curled up tight in a ball, pretending to be asleep, and she had to shake me quite hard. "We've got to go to London," she said. "Get up, Lucy. Be quick." And I said, "I'm not going," and her face grew quite angry and she said, "Oh yes, you are." But I fought her and began to cry, and suddenly she took me by the shoulders and began to speak very quietly and venomously and I was hypnotized by her and by the pain of her fingers digging into my shoulders. "We're going to London," she whispered, "because your Daddy has killed Edward. Now do you understand? If he stays here he'll be caught and taken to prison. Now get up and get dressed quickly and never say a word of this to anyone. Not anyone, not even your father. Do you understand?" And I was so frightened that I did as she told me and we went downstairs and as soon as I saw Daddy's face I knew it was true. He looked as if someone had broken him. All the way to London I was waiting for a policeman to catch us up. And Daddy took me to Aunt Mary in Chichester and a few months later he was killed exploding a bomb. I was almost glad. It took some of the strain away, you see. At least he wouldn't be caught and put in prison. I was almost *glad* . . . Oh my God! Can you imagine how horrible that was? To feel like that about someone I loved so much?' She stared at him. 'So Hester didn't tell you that bit?'

'No. Hester didn't put it quite like that.'

'I'm sure she didn't,' said Lucy bitterly. 'They wanted to hush it all up. I suppose, after all this time, Hester simply looks back on it as a kind of tragic aftermath to war, which is why she is prepared to tell you about it. At least, the edited version. That was the other thing that was so terrible to me: that Hester was prepared to go along with it. To collude with it.'

'But it's impossible,' he burst out – yet he suddenly remembered Hester's words: '*I want you to feel familiar with the cast . . . so that you don't misjudge any of us*' – and he fell silent.

She watched him. 'I still can't decide, you see,' she said at last, 'which is the worst: to know that my father – who was my idol – was an adulterer or a murderer or a coward. I could forgive him for

220

wanting Eleanor and, to be strictly truthful, it was manslaughter not murder. But when I remember his face that night, with its expression of self-disgust and humiliation, then I believe that running away was the worst act of them all. Eleanor and Hester between them turned him into a coward and he allowed them to do it.'

They sat in silence together.

Presently Lucy stirred. 'I'm going to bed,' she said. She glanced at Jonah and was struck by his bleak expression. 'Oh, darling, I'm so sorry. You see now why I kept silent about it all.'

'It's not your fault,' he said. 'It's just a shock, that's all. I've felt so close to him; to Michael, I mean. From the minute I arrived at Bridge House it was as if he reached out to me and, from then on, Hester made it all come alive for me.'

She watched him compassionately. 'I encouraged you,' she said. 'Oh, yes, I did. I remember when you phoned and said you were going down to Exmoor. I should have kept my silence then. I had a feeling that the time had come to face it all but I see now that I was wrong. Perhaps, after all, it isn't wise to attempt to confront the past. I'm just so sorry that you've got involved. Do you have to contact Hester again?'

'I don't quite know. I suppose I shall have to tell

her that I know the truth but that there's no question of . . . going on with it.' He saw her look of puzzlement. 'I'd wondered if I could make a play out of it, you see. Different names and places, of course, but she'd agreed to help me.'

'Make a *play* of it?'

She looked so shocked that he felt the need to defend himself. 'I had no idea about Edward. I suppose I was concentrating mostly on Michael. And you when you were little. Hester was trying to build up the characters of you all because I wanted to know how the relationships had begun, that kind of thing. We'd hardly talked about the ending. It was my idea that I might make something out of it but maybe she thought that it was a kind of exorcism: a way of putting the past to rest.'

'It is quite unbelievable.' Lucy shook her head blankly. 'That Hester could agree to it, I mean. Of course, she's an academic, isn't she? She writes about dead people and the past and, I suppose, in the end she views everything with that same kind of detachment, even her brother's murder. OK – ' she saw his instinctive reaction – 'his manslaughter, if you prefer it. Even so, I notice that she still wasn't prepared to talk openly about it. She left that to me. Perhaps she imagines that fictionalizing it makes it more palatable.'

'I don't know what to say. Or do. I shall have to think about it. I'm really sorry, Mum.'

'So am I.' Lucy stood up, kissed him and moved to the door. 'Try to sleep. I'll see you in the morning. And thanks for coming down, Jonah.'

Jonah continued to sit at the table. Eyes closed, he tried to remember everything that Hester had told him. He was surprised at how miserable it made him feel to believe that she had lied to him – or, at least, withheld the whole truth. He could understand now why Lucy had been so devastated and why she'd kept it secret. Even after such a short acquaintance with Hester and with only an embryonic identification with his grandfather, Jonah nevertheless felt a keen sense of loss and an odd sense of betrayal. He wondered how Hester would react when he told her that at last he knew the facts, though he shrank from the prospect. Her words repeated themselves in his head.

'*It's a very familiar theme – just a love story that went tragically wrong.*'

'*I want you to feel familiar with the cast . . . so that you don't misjudge any of us.*'

'*Edward frightened all of us and I wouldn't have blamed Eleanor if she and Michael had . . . simply gone away together. Afterwards, I wished they had.*'

At what point, Jonah asked himself, would Hester

223

have finally disclosed the truth? He found that he was thinking about Michael: the young man whom Hester had described with such affection and who had gone running out into the wild, streaming night to fetch help for his one-time closest friend. And Hester calling after him, 'Michael, wait. There's no point.' She'd seen Edward's lifeless body in the water, no doubt, and her one thought was to get Michael and Lucy away. Jonah wondered what Hester had done afterwards. How had Edward's death been glossed over and explained? An accident, perhaps? After all, it wouldn't be all that surprising if Edward should fall into the river, given his mental state. She might even have allowed it to be known that he'd committed suicide.

'When Edward came back, and we saw that he was unstable and deeply disturbed mentally, we should have acted . . . Nowadays, he'd have been locked up.'

He tried to imagine exactly what had happened after the others had fled away. Perhaps Hester might tell him if he ever had the courage to confront her. At least there was no question of Lucy going to see her now. Jonah frowned, trying to work out what benefit Hester could have imagined accruing from such a visit.

'The whole period was terribly traumatic for her,' Hester had said. 'I feel now that we let her down.'

Jonah felt guilty of that too. By pursuing the past he'd forced his mother into a very vulnerable position, and at a difficult time when his father was so ill. A period of respite was needed – for all three of them. Yet he knew, lodged deep inside him, there was a driving, seeking element that wouldn't let him rest: an absolute requirement to discover the whole truth.

PART TWO

BRIDGE HOUSE: SEPTEMBER 1944–
SPRING 1946

When Eleanor first sees Michael in the drawing-room at Bridge House she knows at once that he is going to be terribly important to her. Her friends might laugh at her passions but they have no idea of how deeply she experiences this love that overwhelms her. Oh, she admits that there have been rather a large number of men with whom she's fallen so passionately in love – but that doesn't mean that her feelings aren't genuine and painful. She loved Edward once – how long ago it seems – but how can love survive war, separation and, now, the conviction that he is dead? Love requires two people, she insists; it can't survive without nourishment.

In the two years since Edward was posted 'missing: presumed dead' – during visits to London to see her friends – there have been one or two small romances, nothing too serious, but when she sees Michael she knows that this time it is different.

'Well, isn't anyone going to introduce us?' she asks – and is instantly aware of Hester's antagonism. Well, she is used to that. From the beginning she's felt Hester's cool gaze upon her and it keeps her on her mettle: nothing is so critical or puritanical as the judgement of a young girl. Usually Eleanor is able to break down any resistance to her charm – she much prefers to be loved than disliked – but with Hester all the usual tactics fail. She is a success with Patricia and the boys, even Nanny succumbs, but Hester remains aloof, almost as if she fears that she, Eleanor, is a threat to Edward.

Of course, Eleanor reminds herself, Hester has no idea what it is like to have had a physical relationship with a man and then be denied it: she cannot begin to understand the neediness and the longing. She is Edward's sister, not his wife or lover, and so her anxiety for him is quite different from Eleanor's own feelings. Despite this antagonism she prefers to make her base at Bridge House. If she goes home to her parents they badger her to be useful, they expect her to be stoic and dutiful, and she finds it difficult to settle back into the role of a child, having been a wife. At Bridge House she is treated with respect, she is Edward's wife: nobody questions her occasional visits to London and nothing is required of her – apart from her ration book – when she is with them. Patricia is full of compassion and sympathy for Eleanor's plight, Nanny spoils her, and the little boys are rather sweet though sometimes she could scream with the boredom of it all.

So, 'Isn't anyone going to introduce us?' she asks when she sees Michael in the drawing-room – and, quite suddenly, she intuits that her life is about to change.

Of course, she knows very well who Michael is. Good grief! There's been enough discussion about him and little Lucy and the tragedy of his wife's death during the last few weeks, though Eleanor has kept rather quiet on the subject as to whether or not Lucy should come to Bridge House. She feels that it would be tactless to suggest that two children are more than enough to have about the place and, anyway, she quickly sees that her opinion is not going to be sought – but she watches and listens with interest.

'Of *course* Lucy must come,' cries Patricia, eyes brimming. 'Poor child, poor little girl. How terrible for her to lose her mother.'

She clasps little Robin tightly and he gazes up

at her anxiously, eyes wide, whilst Nanny clucks disapprovingly lest he should be distressed at the sight of his mother in tears.

'We don't want to upset the little mite,' she says firmly, removing Robin from Patricia's embrace. 'Let's try to remain calm, dear. Of course Lucy must come if there's nowhere else for her to go. You'll like that, won't you, Robin? Having a little girl to stay with us?'

'Of course he will,' says Patricia quickly, affectionately. 'He's such a loving little boy, aren't you, Robbie? You'll be very kind to Lucy, won't you?'

Robin looks from one to the other and even Eleanor can see that he is already calculating how this new situation might be used to his advantage. She prefers Jack, who is more direct and much more generous, but to be honest she is not really interested in either of the boys though she knows it is in her interest to make a pretence of affection. What surprises her is how readily Patricia, and even Nanny, are taken in by this. They are so besotted with the children that she can only imagine that they expect everyone else to feel the same way.

'And poor Michael,' says Patricia, trying to prevent more tears welling up, though Nanny has now taken Robin to find Jack so that he won't be further distressed by his mother's emotion. 'How is he going to manage? He must be so cut up about it. Poor Susan. She was so young and they were so happy. Do you remember that sweet letter she wrote to Mother after their wedding, Hester? And then again when Lucy was born? I know we never met her but I felt that she was part of the family too. I'm so glad Michael feels he can turn to us. He won't feel quite so desperate.'

At least he knows she's dead, thinks Eleanor impatiently, bored now by all the histrionics. He can get on with his life. Not like me . . .

She lights a cigarette, slightly ashamed of her reaction but still irritated. Oh, she knows he is Edward's oldest friend, and much loved by everyone, but frankly she is getting rather tired of the plans and arrangements and the excitement that Patricia and Hester – especially Hester – feel at the prospect of seeing Michael again after all these years.

Yet, as soon as she sets eyes on him, she is struck by something beyond his good looks: there is a vital quality, a nervous energy that reminds her of Edward and makes him very attractive.

'This is Michael,' says Hester almost reluctantly, but Eleanor cares nothing for Hester's watchfulness, though she doesn't like it when Hester adds rather too pointedly, 'And this is Edward's wife, Eleanor.'

Hester refuses to accept that Edward has perished – and so, clearly, does Michael.

'Edward's my oldest friend,' he says warmly, taking Eleanor's hand. 'It's wonderful to meet you at last.'

His look is sympathetic but she doesn't want his sympathy – or, at least, only in so far as it engages his interest and makes a natural stepping-off place to what must follow. Nevertheless, she is intelligent enough to see at once that there can be no short cuts here: Michael is a sensitive man. It is clear that his grief for Susan and her anxieties for Edward must be given their due respect. She makes some suitable greeting, her look conveys understanding – 'We two are in the same boat,' it tells him – and then Patricia is breaking in with some remark about the good old days and Eleanor waits for her next chance to make her claim upon him.

When Lucy appears on the scene Eleanor is taken aback. The child has an intelligent and penetrating look – rather like a childish version of Hester's – and she sees that no easy conquest is to be hers. It is as if the child immediately grasps the situation and already sees her, Eleanor, as an enemy. Michael is sweet with her, Eleanor is touched by his care for his child, and it is obvious that Lucy adores him: tact and patience will be required.

When the children rush out into the garden after tea to show Lucy her surprise, Eleanor hangs back a little, smiling at Michael in a way that underlines the fellow-feeling that she hopes she has already awakened in him. He smiles back at her almost ruefully.

'It's such a relief to know that she'll be here,' he says, 'but I shall miss her terribly. I think it's the right thing to do.'

For a moment she is taken aback: her own feelings for him are already so heightened that she has assumed that he will seize an opportunity to make some kind of remark that relates to the similarities of their situation: something of a personal nature. She recovers swiftly – so swiftly that he notices nothing – and tells him that they will all be making sure that Lucy is kept happy. She manages to imply that because of her own loneliness it will be her special care to watch over the child and he looks at her gratefully. Yet, even in that look, she sees awareness of her beauty and a response to her situation.

'I am so sorry,' he begins to say, 'about Edward. It must be . . .' He hesitates for a suitable phrase and she cuts in very quickly.

'I've grown hardened to it. It's been two years now and I know I shall never see him again.'

Somehow he has taken hold of her hand, protesting that she mustn't give up hope, but she resists his attempts to change her mind by simply shaking her head and indicating that she'd rather not discuss it. Hester suddenly appears, Michael drops Eleanor's hand abruptly, and they all go out into the garden together.

If Eleanor hopes to further her plans by cultivating Lucy's affection she is doomed to disappointment, for the little girl resolutely keeps her at a distance. It is Hester whom Lucy loves most: Hester and Jack. Robin is gentler but Jack is straightforward and open, and Lucy feels safe with him. It is to Jack, finally, that she confides her fear of the old people behind the curtain. To begin with she keeps her terror to herself. She doesn't know any of the family well enough to feel that she can explain properly. She suspects that any grown-up will simply throw back the curtain and show her that there is nobody there – she can do that for herself when the sun shines brightly in through the window – but when it gets dark, what she knows no longer counts. The night-time brings with it a different world where shadows emerge, creeping and changing shape, and there are muffled sounds and urgent rustlings in the silence.

Lying in bed, the blackout down, hardly daring to breathe, she seems to hear the old people in the alcove somehow becoming visible, *growing* into the shoes, which shuffle about and creak as if the old people are standing on tiptoe, getting ready to advance into the room. It is Jack who finds her one night, weeping with fright, huddled under the blankets. Even then, she doesn't tell him and he simply thinks that she is crying for her mother. That's when he shows her the Midsummer Cushion, so as to comfort her.

'Come on,' he whispers. 'Everyone's having dinner and Nanny's listening to the wireless. It's *ITMA*, her favourite. Come on.'

She follows him out on to the landing, breathless with excitement and fear, and waits with him as he hesitates outside Hester's bedroom, head on one side, listening.

'It's all right,' he says, and they go in together.

The blackout is not drawn down and the room is filled with late summer evening light, quite bright enough to see the frame hanging on the wall.

'But it's not a cushion at all,' she begins, surprised and disappointed, but then Jack draws her closer to it and Lucy catches her breath with delight. The flowers are perfect: each tiny petal is lovingly delineated in coloured silks so that they look fresher, more alive, than the faded, pressed blooms that lie amongst them. Cornflower blue, poppy scarlet, buttercup gold, grass green – Lucy is captivated and Jack shows her how to stand on the little stool so as to see it better.

'But you must never, never touch it,' he warns her. 'It's very old and precious, and Nanny says if we touch it something really bad will happen.'

Jack watches her almost proprietorially, enjoying her pleasure, proud to be the one bestowing the honour upon her whilst at the same time frightening her by the prospect of retribution, just as he and Robin have been warned in the past.

'What sort of thing?' she asks fearfully, still staring up at the tapestry. Instinctively she thinks of her mother and her little rituals to ward off evil.

Jack shrugs – no particular punishment has been described – but he doesn't want to lose his power over her.

'It's an heirloom,' he says importantly. 'So if it broke it would be very bad luck for someone in the family.'

'An air loom.' Lucy puzzles over the words. She associates them immediately with air raid and remembers that this is how her mother died: in an air raid. An air loom sounds a dangerous thing, yet she is not frightened away from the Midsummer Cushion, rather it draws her back again and again to gaze upon the bright, delicate scene.

In gratitude to Jack she makes him a present of her fear, entrusting it to him though she knows he might use it against her to tease her or tell the grown-ups that she's a scaredy cat; an expression with which he often stigmatizes Robin. He doesn't, though. He takes it very seriously and offers to come in one night and wait with her in the dark.

'If they come out,' he tells her, 'I shall run them through with my sword.'

Lucy looks at his silver-painted cardboard sword with respect. The hilt is set about with pieces of coloured glass and the scabbard is carved. She knows that she will feel braver with Jack beside her. So it is that one night they sit together, huddled under Lucy's eiderdown, the faint, flickering beam of Jack's electric torch aimed upon the alcove curtain. As the plumbing gurgles menacingly behind the walls, and mice scamper through the dark, secret pathways of their territory beneath the floorboards, the children wait. The weak pencil of light roves to and fro, up and down, and it seems that the curtain *does* move, that it bellies a little and ripples, as if the old people are taking shape behind it. Lucy's terror communicates itself to Jack so that a sudden noise – no more than a mouse skittering behind the skirting-board – precipitates them into action. Jack leaps from the bed, glad to expend his fear in physical violence, and assaults the curtain with stabs of his sword and cries of, 'Avaunt thee!'

The door is flung open, the light switched on, and Patricia stands there, eyes wide with apprehension, staring in amazement at the scene. Jack is tangled up with the curtain and the shoes, hot and overexcited, and Lucy clutches the eiderdown tightly in fear of the impending row. Patricia, however, seems to understand that there is something more than simple high spirits here and she hurries to help Jack out of the tangle in the alcove.

'What is it?' she asks. 'Whatever are you doing, darling?' and she smiles reassuringly at Lucy, who feels weak with relief. Jack is explaining that they thought they heard something behind the curtain and manages to bring the shoes into the story so that, still rather puzzled, Patricia picks up a pair of brogues. Somehow, Jack has managed to convey some measure of their childish horror to her and, though she doesn't quite understand, she piles the shoes into a small suitcase and closes the lid.

'These belonged to Grandpapa and Granny,' she

tells Jack. 'I can't imagine why they are still here. I'll get rid of them. It was quite right of you to look after Lucy, darling.' She pulls the curtain right back. 'There's nothing there now, Lucy. See? Only your nice party frock and your winter coat hanging on the rail. Shall I leave it open for tonight?'

Lucy nods wordlessly and Patricia hurries to her and gives her a hug. 'Poor darling. Nightmares are so horrid, aren't they? Now, what about some milk to help you off to sleep again? I'll bring some up and we'll have a little picnic here in Lucy's room, just the three of us.'

She goes out, taking the case with the shoes in it, and Lucy and Jack stare at one another, silent with relief. Once again, Lucy feels that she owes Jack something; this time for freeing her from her nightly terror.

'You were brave,' she tells him admiringly, still huddling beneath the eiderdown and trembling a little from the excitement.

Jack sheaths his sword carelessly but he looks gratified. 'Lucky it wasn't Nanny,' he says mischievously – and, at the mere thought of Nanny bursting in upon the scene, they both begin to giggle. Relief spurts out of them in muffled squeals of laughter – though neither of them knows quite what it is that is so funny – and when Patricia comes back with mugs of milk she finds them fully recovered from whatever it was that had frightened them so badly.

To begin with, Eleanor's reaction to Michael goes unnoticed in the general excitement of having him with them again. The whole family are delighted to see him on those rare forty-eight-hour passes, which give him just enough time to hurry down to Bridge House to spend the best part of two precious days with his daughter. Leaving the train at Brushford Station, he walks the few miles to Dulverton and then takes the road beside the river that leads to Eye Marsh.

All through that autumn, whenever he walks to Bridge House with his eyes upon the gleaming water and his ears tuned to the birdsong echoing high up in the woods, he tries to control his feelings for Eleanor. His stomach churns with excited anticipation yet he is shocked that he can feel like this so soon after Susan's death; though it is not love, he tells himself quickly, nothing like love. Yet the fact that he has fallen prey to this consuming sexual infatuation is almost more terrible to him than if he'd fallen in love. It is shaming that though he knows that Eleanor is shallow and grasping and self-centred, he nevertheless remains in thrall to her physical attractions. He wonders if this is how Edward felt about her – she is so clearly *not* Edward's ideal mate – and whether the scales fell from his eyes during the short period of time they had together.

Michael strides on, reciting John Clare's poetry in an attempt to distract himself, yet the excitement persists like some overwhelming addiction and he curses himself for disloyalty to both Susan and Edward. At least, he comforts himself, he has had enough control to conceal his feelings from Lucy and Hester and the rest of the family. At the thought of how good they have been to him his heart expands with love for them: it is unthinkable that he should betray them. He can never forget how warmly their mother welcomed him, Edward's friend, and how she encouraged him in his studies. His unclaimed love had been instantly given to them all: to the serious yet loving mother and to the gentle, maternal Patricia, as well as to the two noisy, younger boys and small Hester with her tough mind and uncompromising look.

As for Edward . . . Michael sighs with regret at the loss of his old friend. He realizes that he is coming to accept that Edward is dead but whether that is because he genuinely believes this to be the case, or

243

whether it is because it soothes his conscience, he does not wish to know. He thinks instead about his gratitude to the Mallorys for welcoming Lucy so wholeheartedly. Lucy: at the thought of her his heart lurches with anxious love. It is inconceivable that she should be harmed and he knows that, whatever his feelings for Eleanor, Lucy shall never be sacrificed for them. She is safe here, with the family at Bridge House. When he crosses the little bridge that spans the Barle they will be waiting for him.

Although they all accept that it is Lucy he comes to see, nevertheless each one of them is overjoyed to have Michael home. Patricia and Nanny like to fuss over him, to make special meals for him; it feels more natural to have a man about the place. He plays cricket with the boys and rags with them on the lawn – though Robin cries if it gets too rough – and Patricia and Nanny tell each other that it is good for the boys to have a male influence. They ask him his opinion on the latest war news and when he thinks it will be over, although they are just as reliably informed by the newspaper reports or wireless bulletins, and he reassures them and raises their spirits. He is the nearest to being the head of the house that they have and some instinctive need within them responds to his presence with relief.

For Hester it is a more simple, if poignant, joy. Michael reminds her of happier times. They talk about Edward and her mother, retell little anecdotes and laugh over old jokes. She longs for him to be the Wilfred Owen of this war, and encourages him to write, but Michael seems reluctant. His always dilatory muse has deserted him, and she doesn't press him too far. Just to have him here is enough.

Lucy is in seventh heaven: it is *her* daddy who is the cause of so much excitement and affection, *her* father who is so handsome and popular. She is so proud and happy she can barely contain her emotions. Though she feels possessive about him and clings to him like a limpet, she tries to be unselfish where the boys are concerned – but she is not prepared to share him with Eleanor. It doesn't take Lucy long to understand that, frightening though the old people behind the curtain were, Eleanor is a much more dangerous threat to her happiness. Instinctively Lucy realizes that, unlike the other women in the household, Eleanor puts herself first. Her care is not for the children, or even for the small community as a whole, it is for Eleanor. She pursues her desires with an almost childish clear-sighted single-mindedness that Lucy recognizes – and fears. Eleanor is prepared to grab what she wants no matter what it costs; and what she wants is Michael.

Abnormally alert to her father's reactions, Lucy senses that Eleanor unsettles him. He is not so natural with her as he is with the other women, and in her anxiety Lucy tries to force some kind of scene that will show Eleanor that she, Lucy, is his favourite. If Eleanor manages to engage him in private conversation Lucy climbs on to his lap, she wraps her legs about his waist and her arms around his neck; she kisses him lavishly and holds his hand possessively – and all with one eye on Eleanor. Her father reacts with generous love, believing that his daughter is missing her mother and is naturally making the most of every moment that he and she can spend together.

Lucy's watchful brown eye detects that this irritates Eleanor but that she cannot let Michael know that it irritates – that would be to show herself unsympathetic, unwomanly. Instead she smiles with a saccharine, understanding expression that deceives Michael but not his daughter, who is aware that he is in some way grateful for the protection she affords. She doesn't understand that her father is not ready for the advances Eleanor is making, that he is bewildered – almost shocked – by this direct approach. She only knows that he welcomes her shows of affection and makes no attempt to shoo her away.

Lucy has no idea of the strength and danger of the undercurrents. She is working purely on instinct, responding as a small animal that is threatened might, but she knows that Hester is on her side and this knowledge increases Lucy's love for her.

Hester watches with disbelief as the affair begins. In her innocence she has believed that neither Eleanor nor Michael will betray Edward, even though it is clear that Eleanor is not above flirting with Michael, yet soon it becomes evident that the situation is moving out of control. During the winter and into spring Michael manages only a few visits to Bridge House but when the war ends everything changes. When Patricia's husband returns home, and she and Nanny and the boys go back to their home near Plymouth, Hester and Lucy are left alone with Eleanor.

Travel becomes a little easier, Michael gets his car back on the road, and Eleanor makes one or two trips to London. Hester imagines that she is seeing her parents and old friends but, when Michael makes his next visit to see them, Hester sees a change in him. In his presence, Eleanor has a triumphant air – she is glossy with satisfaction – and the way she looks at him is unmistakable. Hester is quick to guess what has happened on one of those visits to London but she is unwilling to believe it. That is, she can quite believe such behaviour of Eleanor but not of Michael.

In the possession of Eleanor's body Michael has sacrificed some element of self-worth: he is no longer free. His eyes follow Eleanor almost furtively, even his voice sounds weighted with shame. Now, when Hester talks about Edward – which she does with almost indignant insistence – he can hardly bear to answer her. It seems that they have both denied his existence and she burns with anger and resentment on his behalf – and on Lucy's.

For now, Michael's unwilling passion for Eleanor colours his feelings for his child. He is no longer natural and happy with her. Though he still accepts her hugs and kisses it is clear that she has become a problem to him and his love for her is stained by Eleanor's presence.

Hester wishes that Eleanor would go away – for what can keep her at Bridge House now? Why should she make her home with the family of the husband she has betrayed? Yet she cannot bring herself to confront Eleanor even though, woman-like, she blames her for Michael's fall from grace. She can hardly bear to look at him, so embarrassing is his lack of pride as he watches Eleanor like an anxious puppy waiting on its master's command. And, anyway, there is Lucy to consider.

Michael holds her as a shield, a defence against Eleanor's rapacity, and Hester guesses that although Eleanor's physical attractions are more than he can resist he is not prepared to commit himself utterly to her. Meanwhile, Hester works hard to make sure that Lucy is happy. She knows how much the child is missing the boys, especially Jack, and she tries to keep her occupied. Michael makes no attempt to take Lucy back to his aunt in Chichester, though it is quite safe there now, nor does he have any plans for making a new life for her. Soon, Hester decides, soon she must make a move, ask him what he plans to do, but she postpones the moment of truth. All through that summer she feels that she is waiting: Eleanor and Michael may have given up on Edward but Hester hasn't.

When they hear that he is coming home Eleanor is silent with disbelief and horror. She has convinced herself that Edward is dead and simply cannot accept that he is returning to ruin everything that she has worked for with Michael. In contrast, Hester feels weightless with joy and relief; Edward is alive and his homecoming will put everything to rights. He will be back where he belongs. It is only after the first rapturous sensations of happiness that she begins to wonder how, exactly, problems will be resolved.

It is Michael who persuades Hester to allow him to meet Edward from the troopship at Southampton and drive him down to Bridge House.

'Just in case,' he says. 'Please, Hes. There are some very disturbed men coming back from the Far East at the moment. Good God, think about what they've been through! Well, you can't, of course. We're only just beginning to know the truth of it. He's been a prisoner in appalling conditions for three years and the adjustment might be much more difficult than you can imagine. I know I'm not in your good books at the moment but please let me do this. I've got some extended leave due and I'd like to spend it with Lucy anyway.'

So it is Michael who meets Edward from the troopship at Southampton, who makes a hasty telephone call to tell Hester to make up the beds in Edward's room that Jack and Robin have been sharing.

'He's a bit disorientated,' he says. 'To be honest, he looks terrible, Hes. I've had a chat with the MO and he's given me some stuff for Edward to take. He had a few bad moments on the ship but he's OK if he's kept calm. For God's sake warn Eleanor. Don't expect too much.'

His appearance shocks all of them. His dark hair is liberally streaked with white, he is bone-thin and malnourished, and his grey-tinged skin – the result of beriberi – is scored with deep furrows. He is not yet thirty and he looks sixty. Even more worrying than this is his behaviour. He is clearly bewildered, withdrawn, and he looks at them warily as he comes in with Michael. Despite the shock, Hester hugs him warmly though he barely responds. It is as if he has forgotten how to behave normally and Hester feels chilled. This gaunt, frightened man is not the brother she remembers and she is glad now that, against her better judgement, she agreed that Michael should be here for the homecoming.

Now Edward's sunken eyes shift uneasily, flicking away from direct contact, although he stares fixedly at Eleanor for a few seconds who cannot help but shrink against Hester as if for protection. He has made no attempt to greet his wife – nor she him – and it seems that now their opportunity for some kind of natural reunion has passed.

'Come on.' Michael puts his hand on his shoulder and Edward reacts suddenly, shaking him off violently and then seizing his arm so aggressively that Michael winces; but he carries on calmly enough. 'We've got your old room all ready and I'm sharing with you again,' he tells Edward. 'I've been looking at your books. Remember how we used to read to each other in the old days? We'd take bets who'd drop off to sleep first.'

Still talking, he leads Edward very slowly towards the door as if he guesses that any sharp movement will unsettle him. Hester hesitates, then steps forward and kisses him lightly on the cheek.

'Goodnight, Edward,' she says. 'Sleep well.'

The gesture seems to calm him and he smiles; barely more than a little flicker of the muscles around his mouth. His eyes slide round again to study Eleanor as if wondering who she is. She holds her breath, trying to outface him calmly, terrified that he might confront her, but his eyes slide away again and she gasps silently with relief.

He shuffles out with Michael, whose voice can be heard as he guides him upstairs, and the two women stare at each other in shocked anguish.

'Oh, the poor darling,' whispers Eleanor. 'Oh God, Hes. That was terrible.'

'He'll need time,' Hester says quickly, defensively. 'Time to adjust,' but she is frightened.

'Thank God Michael's here.' Even at a moment like this, Eleanor cannot quite hide her feelings. 'He was wonderful with him, wasn't he?'

And Hester cannot deny it: she too is grateful for Michael's presence.

Eleanor thrusts her arm within Hester's as if requiring physical support. Hester can feel that she is trembling, and when she looks at Eleanor she sees that her eyes are dark with distress and fear. In that moment, Hester connects. Though she has no experience she can imagine how frightening it might be to meet again the man with whom you have had no contact for three years. A man, moreover, who not only has the right to expect affection and great intimacy but also looks as old as your grandfather and is clearly unstable.

They stare at each other and quite suddenly Eleanor's grip tightens and unexpectedly she smiles. It is a smile of great sweetness.

'Oh, darling,' she says ruefully, 'I'm not being very brave.'

'I can sympathize with that,' says Hester feelingly. 'He's not himself. Don't worry. Thank God we've got Michael.'

Eleanor regards her with a pleased surprise at

such a ready capitulation. 'Can you see how it is at last, darling? Can you understand? Oh, I know it's been hard for you to forgive Michael and me. You've been shut up here ever since you left school, first with your mother and then with the family. You've never been in love. I know all that. Just don't be too hard on us, that's all. Remember that Edward and I were married for only seven months, Hes. Seven months! And he's been away for over three years. I thought he'd been killed, I really did. Can you understand?'

This plea for clemency rather undermines Hester's new-found ability to connect; she is not ready for girlish confidences or intimacy, nor does she think that it's the time for them. The puritanism of youth, not yet softened by experience, reasserts itself at the sight of this over-emotional display. Nevertheless there has been a shift in their relationship: a shift towards friendship and a greater tolerance.

Eleanor reaches for her bag and lights a cigarette. She turns her head, blowing the smoke sideways, cupping her right elbow in her left hand.

'I'm frightened,' she says simply.

Hester sighs. She sees that Eleanor's feelings as Edward's wife must take precedence over her own as his sister. She experiences a sharp jab of resentment. She has lost a great deal in the last five years – her two younger brothers, her mother – and now Edward seems to be the last straw that might break her courage. Yet that brief moment of connection has had its effect. She knows that if they are to survive this calamity she must relinquish the dislike she's indulged for so long; that she must allow Eleanor to be fearful without judging her. As she struggles to reconnect, it surprises her to realize just how much her dislike of this woman has upheld her and how much more difficult it will be to love rather than to hate.

'It's bound to take time to adjust,' she says – but she speaks with no confidence, and Eleanor looks at her with brooding sincerity.

'But you must see that it will never work now with Edward and me,' she says. 'You can see that, can't you, Hester?'

And in this new awareness, this new maturity, Hester *can* see that it could never work again; that their brief, ill-matched relationship could never be resurrected.

'Perhaps not,' she says, 'but you can't just walk out on him. Not just yet.'

Eleanor watches her, still puffing at her cigarette, her eyes narrowed against the smoke.

'Are you sure that it wouldn't be wiser?' she asks quietly. 'Just to disappear quietly before he remembers anything properly?'

'Not if it means you'd take Michael,' answers Hester almost angrily. 'How can I manage alone? Just think, Eleanor. When Edward went away he had a whole family. And you. Now there's just Patricia and me. She can't come back to look after him. That leaves me.'

'Sorry, sweetie.' Eleanor pitches the butt of her cigarette into the fire. 'I'm trying not to be selfish but don't you see that it might just be me who will unsettle him most? He couldn't quite place me, could he? You, yes. You're still little Hes, you haven't changed that much, and Michael, the old school chum. That's OK. But where do I come in? Supposing he remembers and wants to . . . well, be husbandly.' She shudders deeply and with no affectation whatsoever. 'I couldn't do it, Hes. It's not just because of Michael. Not even just because Edward looks like an old man. There's something else, isn't there? When he took hold of Michael's arm he looked mad. Did you see how Mike winced? And his eyes, Hes . . .'

'I know.' Hester gets up and goes to her as she paces before the fire. 'Look, it's only the first day. Let's not be melodramatic.'

256

They turn, startled, as Michael comes into the room.

'The MO gave me something to help him sleep.' He looks bleak and very tired. 'He's out cold but I'm going back in case he disturbs and doesn't remember where he is.' He glances at Eleanor and looks away again. 'I shall lock our door,' he says. 'Just in case. I don't want him wandering about in the night and frightening Lucy.'

Eleanor stretches a hand gratefully towards him, as if she is acknowledging the real reason for his wariness, and Hester feels a stirring of the old irritation. Even at a moment like this, Eleanor must take centre stage; *her* feelings must be paramount.

'That's a good idea,' she says unemotionally, before Eleanor can speak. 'Thanks, Michael.'

'Goodnight then.' He goes out, his face grim, and the two women are left together.

In the days that follow, there are many occasions when Hester is grateful that Michael is on leave. Edward's lucid, calm periods become longer, he seems less confused, but Hester begins to suspect that he is suffering more than they have guessed. She comes upon him one morning, standing just inside the bedroom that once belonged to their mother and which Eleanor now uses.

Eleanor has gone shopping in Dulverton, Michael and Lucy are collecting wood along the river path, and the house is quiet. Only the river can be heard, turbulent after a night of heavy rain, tumbling and rumbustious as it streams towards its union with the River Exe further down the valley. Edward's head is bent, as if listening, and Hester wonders if the river's relentless sound is distressing – she remembers how her mother found it so when she was ill – and she lays a hand very lightly on his arm whilst speaking his name. They are all learning that it is dangerous to take Edward by surprise, to startle him.

He looks at her and his glance is clear and sane.

'I can't believe it sometimes, Hes. That Mother and the boys are dead. I didn't know about Mother and I kept forgetting about James and Henry. All those years when I was thinking of them as if they were alive and that one day we'd all be together again. Poor Hes. However did you manage?'

She bites her lip, carefully contemplating a reply that will not send him toppling over into the abyss where madness lurks.

'I had Patricia,' she says cheerfully. 'And the boys and Nanny. Nanny managed for me. You know Nanny!'

He smiles, as she means him to, and for a moment the empty eyes light with a happy memory, and his lips curve appreciatively.

'I'm glad you had Nanny and Pat,' he says.

'So am I,' she says, heartfelt, 'and they're all looking forward to seeing you when you're stronger.'

His smile this time is a bitter one. 'Don't you mean less mad?' he asks. His stare challenges her to answer truthfully and Hester is truly afraid.

'Probably,' she says bravely. 'You do have very odd moments, Edward. They'll pass, of course.'

'Will they?' His intensity is painful. 'Do you actually know that, Hes?'

He has seized her hand and his grip is painful but she doesn't show that it hurts.

'Yes,' she lies, staring him in the eye. 'The MO told us that it takes time and patience but that it passes. The really important thing is that you mustn't get excited about things, Ned. It sets you back.'

The little childish name seems to reassure him and he relaxes his grip. He turns and regards himself in the looking-glass that stands on the dressing-table.

'Look.' He's still holding her hand and now he pulls her round beside him. 'Look at me, Hes. I look older than our father did when he died.' They stand side by side, staring at their reflections. 'What must Eleanor think each time she looks at me?' He feels the involuntary tightening of her hand and laughs softly. 'Did you really believe I'd forgotten her? Did you, Hes? Don't you think I saw her expression when I turned up with Michael? What did you all expect me to do? Take her in my arms and demand my conjugal rights?' He drops her hand abruptly and turns away from the old man in the looking-glass. 'She's so beautiful, isn't she? I dreamed about her during all those years away from her – when I wasn't thinking about food, that is. You get obsessed with food when you're being starved, you know. You'd steal and cheat and lie for it. It's all that matters in the end: the desire for survival. And that means food, not sex. None of us cared about that. We used to plan menus, our perfect meal, that kind of thing. Eleanor represented beauty and cleanliness and sanity. She was the symbol of peace and all the small, homely, decent things. Coming back to her was the one thing that kept me going. Rather ironic when you think about it. Now we pretend that I haven't quite remembered that she's my wife. You see, there are chunks of time I can't account for and I'm afraid of what I've done. I got a bit violent once or twice on the boat coming home and I had to be restrained. I can't risk that with Eleanor.'

Close to tears, Hester remains silent. Her experience has not equipped her for this. Suddenly, rising up to the open window, echoes the rhythmical sound made by the noise of an axe on wood. Each time the blade makes contact it rings with an almost metallic blow and, with each strike, Hester notices that Edward winces, his face creasing into an anguished frown. Slowly he begins to shake his head, chopping at the air with his hands as if warding off blows and he makes tiny whimpering sounds, though his mouth is tightly closed. Still shaking his head, his arms now held up protectively before his face, he staggers across to the bed and kneels on it. He bends forward so that his forehead touches his knees, his arms folded over his head as if to close out the sound, and the dry sobs continue spasmodically.

Hester runs to the window and leans out.

'Michael,' she shouts urgently. 'Michael, stop!'

He appears below the window, staring up at her, and she shakes her head urgently, mouthing at him that Edward is ill. To her relief, Michael guesses at once and she hears him speaking to Lucy before he comes upstairs two steps at a time. He goes at once to the recumbent form, kneeling beside the bed, talking calmly to Edward though not touching him, and gradually the sobbing ceases and Edward collapses onto his side, his eyes tightly closed.

Hester goes out, closing the door behind her, and hurries downstairs to Lucy.

Studying Edward as she does, Lucy begins to see that there are two people struggling inside his head. It is rather as if he is playing a game, sometimes pretending to be someone else, as she and Jack did: Robin Hood and Maid Marian or Peter Pan and Wendy. In private they played out their parts with great conviction but in front of the grown-ups they had to be Lucy and Jack again. It seems that Edward can't always change over properly. Most of the time he is the Edward who talks quietly to Daddy and to Hester, though he seems to avoid Eleanor rather as if he is shy of her, and then, sometimes quite suddenly, the other Edward appears.

He doesn't seem to mind that the others are there, which makes her think that he is rather brave. She and Jack hated to be caught out by the grown-ups. 'And who are you today?' they'd ask, and it would spoil the whole game. If you had to explain who you were and what you were doing then you stopped feeling that it was real and you simply felt silly instead. Edward doesn't mind feeling silly, though all the grown-ups hate it. She's noticed that odd things bring out the other Edward. It might be a sudden noise or even a pattern. Eleanor has a frock with stripes in black and grey and white that seem to shimmer as she moves about. Only yesterday, when she was laying the table for lunch, swishing to and fro between the sideboard and the table, Edward kept staring and staring at the dress and his eyes slowly opened very wide so that he looked really frightening. Then he put out a hand very fast, just like a snake darting out its head, and caught a fold of the skirt, twisting it and twisting it and pulling Eleanor closer and closer, so that she screamed and Hester ran in and took hold of his hands and made him let go.

Lucy couldn't help wondering what game it was that he was playing and who he was pretending to be. She wishes Jack were still here so that she wouldn't feel quite so lonely – or so scared. With Jack around she wouldn't feel scared; it would just be another game. She's been told that Edward isn't very well and must be treated gently. She's not to shout or creep up on him and shout 'Boo!' like they used to with Nanny or Patricia.

'You know how it is with a car,' Daddy tells her. 'It has brakes to stop it if you are going too fast or someone walks out in front of it. People have brakes too. They stop us getting too angry so that we don't lose our tempers and hurt other people. They stop us telling lies and cheating and giving in to weaknesses. But sometimes the brakes don't work very well if people are ill or overtired. That's what's wrong with Edward. He's been kept prisoner and treated very badly and that's why his brakes aren't working properly. We have to get him better and mend them. Do you see, Lucy?'

And she did see: it was perfectly clear to her. She remembers how they used to rag with Daddy on the lawn; Jack and Robin would scream with laughter and get very red in the face as they rolled round and round, and then Nanny would say, 'That's quite enough now. You're going too far and someone will get hurt.'

Everyone's brakes always worked perfectly well, though sometimes Jack would protest, and nobody ever got hurt. She thinks about Edward's brakes and hopes they will be working soon so that nobody gets hurt now. Sometimes she thinks she would like to go away but then she knows she would hate to leave Hester and Bridge House, for where could they go but to Aunt Mary and the little house in Chichester where not very long ago the V-2s were killing people and it was very dangerous. But if she stays at Bridge House with Hester, then she knows she will see Jack and Nanny again. They have promised to come as soon as Edward is better.

She knows that Eleanor wants to go away, though. She hears her saying so to Daddy. They whisper together as she, Lucy, hides behind the door, holding her breath.

'I'm afraid, Mike,' Eleanor says. 'How much longer can we go on like this? You're going to have to make a decision soon, you know. Your leave won't last for ever. It's because of Lucy, isn't it? I can't see why we simply can't go to London . . .'

She doesn't hear any more because they go out through the French doors onto the terrace, but she feels frightened. Lucy believes that Eleanor's brakes aren't too good: not as reliable as Nanny's or Hester's or Patricia's. She has an image of Eleanor driving a car and putting her foot down hard on the accelerator pedal, going faster and faster so that people and cyclists fly out of her way or are caught under the wheels; but still Eleanor drives on and on with her hair blowing in the wind and a secret smile on her bright red lips. Edward and Eleanor are both dangerous because their brakes don't work properly.

*   *   *

Each of them is scared. Eleanor takes Michael's arm as they pass out into the garden and he glances round involuntarily, freeing himself quickly in case Edward is watching. Just lately, he has begun to fear that Edward has guessed the truth.

'It's not just because of Lucy,' he says, 'though I don't quite know what I'd do with her in London. It's Hester too. She's not able to look after Edward on her own just yet. Poor old Edward . . .'

His face crumples a little with compassion and Eleanor watches him thoughtfully, weighing his concern for them against his love for her.

'But you do love me, Mike?'

'For God's sake!' He's as jumpy as a new lamb, glancing up at the windows of the house, peering along the terrace. 'It's just not that simple . . .'

'I think it's fairly simple,' she says coolly. 'Lucy can stay with your Aunt Mary and you and I can get a little flat in London. You can see Lucy at weekends.'

He is secretly shocked by her ruthlessness. 'And what about Hes and Edward?'

'They must learn to manage. After all, you can't stay here for ever, can you?'

'And what about you? You are his wife, after all.'

'That didn't seem to bother us a few weeks ago in

266

London, did it? We can't let it get in the way now, why should we? The fact is that I hardly knew Edward when we married. It was all so quick and mad, a typical war-time romance that would have died a natural death at any other time. There's nothing to bind us now. No long years of marriage, no true deep love, no children. It might sound brutal but the truth can be brutal. It'll never work between me and Edward again. We must face up to the truth, Mike.'

She makes it sound so reasonable – and he knows that he is wriggling like a worm on a hook and despises himself for it – but he is unable to take the decision to abandon Edward and Hester. Yet Eleanor is right: something must happen soon. Edward is recovering his strength, he neither sleeps so late nor goes to bed early, and his presence amongst them is causing tension. He is beginning to be unable to hide his feelings for Eleanor, the sight of her exacerbates his madness, and Michael fears some kind of confrontation.

'I suppose you wouldn't consider going away for a week or two, to your chums in London or to your parents? Just to give Edward time to re-cover?'

She shakes her head, smiling at him as if she knows what he's thinking.

'You don't get rid of me that easily, darling. I'm staying with you. When I go I'm taking you with me.'

And Michael's heart sinks: he knows that he is caught in a trap – a trap of his own making but, nevertheless, a trap.

It is not just selfishness on her part, Eleanor tells herself, it is simply that she is trying to protect them all. The truth is that Michael can't stay at Bridge House indefinitely as some kind of sickbed attendant, and sooner or later Hester must decide what exactly is going to happen to Edward. If it were left to Eleanor herself she would simply put him in hospital – or the madhouse – because, let's be honest, the poor old boy is as mad as a hatter. Madder, because he's dangerous too. And surely they can see that it's asking for trouble to have him around with Lucy. Anything might happen. Oh, it's all very well for Hes and Mike to say that he takes no notice of the child and that she is actually very good with him but they must be able to grasp that he's about as volatile as a keg of gunpowder in a match factory. Much better to get Lucy away with Aunt Mary, even if she's as old as God and hasn't been anywhere since the war started. At least the kid will be safe with her and Mike can get down to

Chichester quite easily from London. After all, what else is he going to do with her? She's four years old and it won't be long before she should go to school, and he can't expect poor Hester to take her on. Certainly not now she's got Edward to worry about. No, the right thing is for the two of them to go to London, Lucy to Aunt Mary, and then Hes will realize that she simply can't manage and she'll be sensible and let Edward go into some kind of mental hospital. Then they can all get on with their lives again. And of *course* it's tragic about poor old Edward, of *course* it is, but that's the way war works. Some people die and other lives are ruined. It's ghastly, but it doesn't mean that everyone has to suffer because they feel guilty that they've survived. That's simply stupid. It's criminal, in fact, to throw away lives unnecessarily. An utterly pointless sacrifice.

And if Hester and Michael really think that they can sacrifice her along with themselves then they'll have to think again. In fact, rather than behaving in this hole-and-corner way, thinks Eleanor, perhaps the time is coming to force the pace: to push Edward nearer to the edge; oh, not too far, the poor sweetie, but just far enough to make certain that the decision is taken and they can all get on with their lives.

Edward and Hester sit together beside the fire. A volume of John Clare's poetry is open on Edward's knee from which he reads aloud. He stops at regular intervals so as to continue a conversation they are having about the past, interrupting the reading each time a new memory occurs to him. Outside, the rising wind soughs through the trees and whips the river into a foaming brown tide, which races beneath the old bridge and slaps against the stone piers as it passes.

Hidden behind the long sofa, Lucy plays with her doll and Rabbit: they are having a tea-party. She has saved a chocolate biscuit – a very great treat – and has broken it into small pieces. The teapot is full of milk, which she pours very carefully into the tiny plastic cups. She has begged the milk from Hester and, as she shares out the biscuit, she wonders if Edward steals food because it is part of the game he plays. She's seen him slip a bread roll from his plate into his pocket when he thinks nobody is looking and take another one to eat there and then, or it might be an apple and, once, an egg from the bowl on the dresser in the kitchen. She's watched him in Hester's kitchen garden – which they still refer to as the meadow because that's what it was before the war – kneeling beside the rows of vegetables and uprooting a carrot or a parsnip. He brushes the earth from it and puts it inside his jacket, glancing quickly over his shoulder to see if anyone is watching.

He is reading again now and Lucy sits quite still to listen because she loves Edward's voice and the words fascinate her. This is someone talking quietly to a friend as they walk along together, just as she and Jack used to, and she holds her breath as she waits to hear what they might discover.

'Up this green woodland-ride let's softly rove
And list the nightingale – she dwells just here.
Hush! let the wood-gate softly clap for fear
The noise might drive her from her home
   of love,
For here I've heard her many a merry year –
At morn, at eve, nay, all the livelong day,
As though she lived on song . . .

'Do you remember, Hes, when Mother read Hendy's report about nightingales over Bossington way and we went out one evening to hear them?' His voice is pitched very low and Lucy has to strain to hear him.

Hester chuckles. 'I was allowed to go as a treat, though Nanny said I was too young to be up late.

271

Mother insisted. "She might never hear one again," she said.'

'We all went in the end, except Nanny. Father piled us all into the car and we took Thermos flasks and rugs. I remember that it was jolly cold. It must have been the Easter holidays.'

'I don't think I minded too much about the nightingale. I just loved the idea of an expedition over the moor instead of going to bed.'

'We heard them in the end, in an orchard near Bossington. Magical.

'And where those crimping fern-leaves ramp
    among
The hazel's under-boughs, I've nestled down
And watched her while she sung, and her renown
Hath made me marvel that so famed a bird
Should have no better dress than russet
    brown . . .'

Lucy listens with delight. The phrases conjure up images of the wood in the summer; the path winding beside the murmuring river and the trees ringing with the sound of birdsong. Perhaps Edward has a secret house in the woods and an imaginary friend with whom he shares the roll and the egg. She and Jack have played games like that, taking food wrapped in a cotton handkerchief to eat later in the hollow of a big tree all hidden by its low, sweeping branches.

'The mind plays tricks,' Edward is saying. 'Poor old John Clare went mad, didn't he? Didn't know who he was in the end, poor devil. Do you remember that Gerard Manley Hopkins poem, "O the mind, mind has mountains; cliffs of fall"? I know what he means now. That's the frightening part about it all. You never know when you might suddenly be standing on the edge of one of those cliffs. Yet I can remember the nightingales.'

'Well, that's the important thing, isn't it? You have to hold on to that and wait for the other thing to pass.'

'And Eleanor? Is she prepared to wait too while we all play the pretending game?'

Behind the sofa Lucy is riveted with surprise: so the grown-ups know that Edward is playing games. They know how he steals food and about the other Edward that he plays at being and they don't really mind. In fact they are playing the game with him.

'It's just that the doctor fears that any emotional confrontation might be damaging,' Hester is saying gently. 'Do you remember what he said?'

'Oh, I remember. But, my God, Hes, can you imagine what a tremendous release it would be to make love to my wife. Can you possibly imagine the relief it would be just to do it? Oh, don't worry. I'm not likely to, not the way she looks at me. The sight of me disgusts her and I don't blame her . . . She and Michael seem to be very close.'

'We're all very close. The war has seen to that, and having Lucy with us has made Michael more like a brother than a friend. Go on with the poem, Edward.'

There is a little silence but when he begins to read his voice is calm again and Lucy relaxes. For one moment, when he talked about Eleanor, she'd feared that the other Edward might emerge.

'How curious is the nest: no other bird
Uses such loose materials or weaves
Its dwelling in such spots – dead oaken leaves
Are placed without and velvet moss within
And little scraps of grass and, scant and spare,
What scarcely seem materials, down and hair . . .'

Lucy can picture the nest. She and Jack found one once, so tiny it was, so beautifully made, and Jack climbed a tree and put the nest carefully in a fork in one of the branches but low down so they could see it from the ground. They waited and waited but no bird ever came to lay its eggs in it.

'What sillies you are,' Nanny said later, when she heard about the nest. 'The babies are all grown up now and flown away, that's why the nest was on the ground. It's not needed any more.'

'Deep adown
The nest is made, a hermit's mossy cell.
Snug lie her curious eggs in number five
Of deadened green or rather olive-brown,
And the old prickly thorn-bush guards them well.
So here we'll leave them, still unknown to wrong,
As the old woodland's legacy of song.'

The chocolate biscuit and the milk are all finished up but Lucy continues to sit, cross-legged, waiting. Some instinct warns her that it would be unwise to show herself. Luckily, Hester is stirring, talking about preparing dinner, and presently she gets up and goes out, leaving the door open. Carefully and very slowly, Lucy edges her way out from behind the sofa, leaving the tea-set but carrying her dolly and Rabbit.

A tiny sound alerts Edward to her presence and he looks round quickly. Lucy stands stiffly, clasping the doll and the rabbit to her chest, waiting for some kind of angry reaction from him. He stares at her and, to her surprise, she sees that his eyes are full of tears. They make his eyes shine in the firelight and one rolls down his sunken cheek. Lucy swallows, controlling her desire to run. The tears make her think of Jack, of Robin, of the frustrations and misunderstandings of the children's world and, instead, she holds out the doll to him.

Edward leans forward to take it and his face is gentle again. He sits the doll on the cushion beside him, smoothing her skirts and settling her carefully, and then stretches a hand to Lucy. She goes to him, scrambling up beside him, and they sit close together, sharing a wordless kind of loving.

What shall we do? Hester asks herself. Oh, what shall we do?

As she heats up the vegetable soup she wonders how long they can go from day to day simply postponing the moment of decision. Do they really believe that one morning Edward will wake, revitalized, normal, as he was four years before, and that, by some miracle, Eleanor will fall in love with him all over again?

The point is, thinks Hester, that I have to believe it – for what else is there to do? A tiny part of her mind tells her that Michael should take Eleanor and Lucy and go back to London; that Edward would soon come to terms with Eleanor's defection and that he would be more stable once Eleanor was out of the way. This might be so but has she, Hester, the courage to manage Edward, to have sole care of him? Nanny has offered to come back if she can be of any assistance – and that might be an option. Nevertheless, there are times when Michael's strength has been necessary to subdue Edward and Hester's heart quakes at the prospect of being alone with him, even with Nanny to assist.

Opening the oven door to check the rabbit stew, she thinks of the frightening episode that happened on the first day that Edward insisted on getting up in time for breakfast downstairs.

'I think he's beginning to get restless at being treated as an invalid,' Michael had said. 'It's best to let him, Hes.'

When he'd arrived in the dining-room he'd been carrying an old coffee tin. The lettering had been completely rubbed away and it was dented and shiny with constant handling. Edward placed it beside his plate and, sitting down, carefully repositioned his knife and fork, putting them together beside the tin. They have grown used to this behaviour. Each lunchtime – the only meal Edward has so far shared with them all – he tends to collect his cutlery together and becomes distressed if any of it is removed during lunch.

They've discovered that it's best to leave everything he uses at his place and then it is cleared only after he has left the room.

On this occasion, Hester had simply picked up the tin so that she could put his coffee cup beside his plate but his reaction had been instantaneous. He'd leaped up with a scream of rage, his chair flung backwards, and he'd seized Hester's wrist in one hand and wrenched the coffee tin from her with the other whilst desperate words bubbled unintelligibly from his lips. It was Michael who had come to her rescue, forcibly unlocking Edward's fingers, wrestling him away and back into his chair where he'd held him down whilst Edward wept uncontrollably and clutched his tin. Eleanor had simply fled the room whilst Lucy had disappeared under the table, waiting for the storm to pass.

Now, as Hester puts out some apples into a bowl, she wonders what other unconsidered action might bring down Edward's wrath upon her. How would she manage without Michael? She suspects that she simply doesn't have the will or the energy to make a decision; they will go on, from day to day, hoping for a miracle.

As it happens, the decision is taken out of her hands. Because it is not her nature to be either devious or self-seeking it does not occur to Hester that Eleanor has decided to pre-empt the situation. Their relationship is better than it has ever been but Eleanor does not confide her idea to Hester. She is careful to put her new plan into action only when Hester is nowhere to be seen and, if possible, when Michael hasn't seen Edward nearby or doesn't know he's within earshot. She begins so cautiously, so cleverly, that even Michael doesn't realize that she is deliberately inflaming Edward into some kind of response.

In his hypersensitive condition tiny things alert him only too readily: Eleanor's hand lingering overlong on Michael's shoulder when she leans across him to place something on the table; a quick reach up on tiptoe to whisper something private in his ear; a reluctance to leave a stolen embrace. Her quick ears and sharpened awareness seem to judge exactly when Edward will appear so that he sees just enough to arouse his emotions. After three weeks of anxious care, Michael's antennae are blunted and he is beginning to flag in his watchfulness. He cannot understand why Edward is less open with him; he seems silent and surly and Michael is at a loss as to what to do. Because they have all witnessed Edward's sudden, uncontrollable rages Michael never guesses for a moment that Eleanor might be actually hoping to precipitate Edward into an action that will force a decision.

As for himself, Michael is slowly coming to understand that there can be no future for him with Eleanor. To his shame and confusion he sees that he has added what he knew and loved of Susan to what he feels physically for Eleanor and in these few weeks constantly in her company he sees that he has been a fool. Eleanor is no Susan and he realizes now that they have little in common. She is not particularly interested in Lucy, except as a means to his own heart, and he is filled with a kind of paralysing horror at the thought of spending the rest of his life with her. He is also terrified at the prospect of telling her this – and, anyway, how is he simply to take Lucy and go back to London, leaving Hester with Edward? He knows now that there is no question of Eleanor remaining with her husband.

Although he is not aware of it, Eleanor picks up all the signs of his growing dilatoriness and is even more determined to make a push for her own future.

Events come to a head one stormy evening as she sits with Michael in the drawing-room. All day the rain has fallen in drenching sheets of water, teeming down the windows, streaming from the moors and fields into the rapidly rising river. Now, shortly before dinner, the downpour has ceased although the wind is rising. It rattles at the windows and echoes in the chimneys.

Eleanor has seen Edward go out onto the terrace a few moments before Michael comes in: the French doors are closed but the curtains are pulled back. Now, so concentrated is she on the darkness beyond the firelight that she doesn't notice Lucy slip into the room whilst she is pleading with Michael, persuading him to make the break. They sit close together, their knees touching and she takes his cold, unwilling hands in her own.

'I can't just walk out on Hester,' Michael is saying, in a low, desperate whisper. 'You must see that. And, anyway . . .'

His voice dies away but Eleanor is alarmed at the 'And, anyway', all her senses are alerted and she is determined not to allow any kind of doubt in his love for her to be voiced. She speaks urgently, her voice hard.

'It's because of Lucy, isn't it? If it weren't for her we could get away. You're a fool, Michael. Something terrible is going to happen and it will be because of Lucy.'

At this moment Eleanor sees what she has been waiting for: a flicker of white in the darkness on the terrace. Edward has returned and is outside the window, peering into the room. She puts her hands on Michael's shoulders and kisses him passionately on the mouth and, in the same second, Hester comes in and switches on the light just as Edward bursts through the French doors pursued by the clamouring noise of water.

Even in the face of his fury, Eleanor clings for as long as she can to Michael; she has staked everything on this throw and she is going to make the most of it. Edward seizes her by the shoulder, his fingers cruel and hard, and she cries out with the pain of it, and then Michael is grappling with him, dragging him away, aided by Hester, who is crying out, 'Oh, don't, Edward, please don't,' and hanging on to his jacket. Eleanor begins to scream, though she finds the violence of the scene faintly exciting, and the two men struggle together, crashing into the furniture and grunting with exertion.

They are near to the open French doors when Edward flings Michael off and turns again on Eleanor. This time she is truly frightened and, when he takes her by the throat, she realizes just what a risk she has taken. Edward might look feeble and old but there is the strength of the madman in his fingers. Michael rushes him, catching him off balance and punches him violently in the face. The blow completely unbalances Edward, who staggers back at a run, releasing Eleanor and stumbling on to the terrace. He falls, collapsing half over the low wall and then disappears into the swollen, tumbling water below.

Hester is there, almost as he falls, though Eleanor seizes her by the shoulders as if to restrain her physically from following him into the water. Below them Edward is struggling, trying to cling to the overhanging branches of a hazel tree, before being swept away by the current.

It is Michael, dazed, blood oozing from his mouth, who cries out in despair. He yells as if for help and goes racing along the terrace and out on to the bridge still calling just as the rain begins to fall again in torrents.

'Michael, wait,' shouts Hester. 'Wait. There's no point . . .' She goes after him, knowing he can't hear her above the river and the wind, and seizes him by the arm. 'Michael, wait. There's no point going along the road. Nobody will come that way at this time of night. And Edward will be carried downstream. Come and help me look for him.'

He suffers himself to be led back and Eleanor hurries to him, putting an arm about his shoulders and taking him inside, but now it is Hester who takes control.

'Go and wake Lucy,' she says almost angrily to

Eleanor. 'Pack her things and Michael's. You must go now, all of you. Whatever happens you must get away. We can't risk another confrontation. Come with me, Michael.'

They go together out through the house, running along the lawn to the end of the garden where the bank gives shallowly into the river and here they find Edward, lying halfway up the bank, soaked and exhausted. Even so, he rouses himself at the sight of Michael, shouting feebly and fighting his attempts to haul him out. Once they have dragged him across the grass and it is clear that he can stand, Hester gestures at Michael to let go of him.

'Go now,' she shouts at him, her words flung away by the wind, hardly audible above the river's tremendous voice. 'For God's sake. Just go now as quick as you can,' and he hesitates only for a second before hurrying into the house.

When Lucy hears Eleanor running up the stairs she clenches herself even tighter into a ball beneath the blankets. She is trembling with shock: first the breaking of the Midsummer Cushion, the dried flowers crumbling to dust, the glass splintering on the floorboards; then the fight between her father and Edward. Their hands, clutching and gripping, seemed swollen with violence and the final blow seemed all of a piece with the savage wildness of the

284

howling wind and the thunderous, surging water. She seems to hear voices in her head: first Jack's saying, 'If we touch it something really bad will happen,' and then Eleanor's saying, 'Something terrible will happen and it will be because of Lucy.' She *has* touched the Midsummer Cushion, she has broken it, and something very bad indeed has happened. Yet, even now, she can't quite take it all in. The events of the evening have been so appalling that she wonders if she has been having a nightmare: perhaps she will wake to find that it is one of her bad dreams.

Eleanor is real enough, though. She bends over the bed, speaking her name urgently, but Lucy squeezes her eyes closed and holds herself rigid.

'Wake up, Lucy!' Eleanor says in a kind of furious whisper. 'We've got to go to London. Get up. Be quick.'

Lucy unrolls herself, still clutching the blanket up to her chin, and stares up at her.

'I'm not going,' she says tremulously.

'Oh yes, you are,' says Eleanor, tugging the blanket away, and when Lucy struggles and begins to cry she takes her by the shoulders and her fingers dig in so painfully that Lucy stops crying and stares at her in amazement.

'We're going to London,' whispers Eleanor, her

face close to Lucy's, 'because your daddy has killed Edward. They had a fight and he's killed him. Now do you understand? If he stays here he'll be caught and taken to prison. Now get up and get dressed quickly and never say a word about this to anyone. Not anyone, especially not your father. Do you understand? Now where are your clothes? Put on plenty of warm things. Is this your case? Be quick.'

Too frightened to utter a word, Lucy begins to dress, pulling on her knickers and liberty bodice and her jersey while Eleanor opens the little painted chest and folds Lucy's clothes with quick movements. Lucy hurries to take her Little Grey Rabbit books from the shelf lest they should be forgotten and picks up Rabbit and her dolly, hugging them to her chest, and all the time she is shaking with fear. The terrible thing has happened and it is all her fault.

'Wait there,' Eleanor says, again in that fierce whisper and, shutting Lucy's door behind her, she goes away across the landing whilst Lucy, sitting obediently on the bed, still shivering with terror, can hear her opening drawers and closing cupboards.

When she's packed as much as she can for herself and Michael, Eleanor hears him coming up the stairs. She hurries to meet him, putting her finger to her lips and gesturing towards Lucy's door.

'He's OK,' he mutters. 'He and Hes are in the kitchen getting him dried off. He's pretty bashed about but he's OK, thank God. Hester needs some dry clothes for him.'

'Hester's quite right. We must get away,' Eleanor says urgently. 'If he sees either of us again he might go right over the top. Surely you can see that? Get those clothes off; you're soaked. I've laid some things on your bed. Go *on*, Mike. For God's sake, *hurry*.'

She goes with him, offering him a towel after he's dragged off his shirt and then watching in silence while he pulls on warm, dry clothes. All his movements are invested with a violent haste and his face is white with shock.

'You realize, don't you, that you must never breathe a word of this to Lucy?' she asks grimly, as if implying that it is Michael who is to blame but that she is prepared to forgive him as long as he does as he is told. 'Not a word. We must get her away before something worse happens. She's all ready.'

'What did you tell her?' he asks anxiously.

'Oh, just that you have to get back to London urgently and that you want her with you from

287

now on. She understands that so don't confuse her.'

He shakes his head obediently – the last thing he wants to do is upset Lucy – and they go out together. He hurries downstairs with the suitcases and some clothes and medication for Edward, whilst Eleanor goes to fetch Lucy.

'Come on,' she says. 'Daddy's waiting for us.'

Lucy follows her out on to the landing and down the stairs, shivering and frightened, though she is still hoping that Eleanor is wrong and that her father will come and tell her that this has all been some kind of nightmare. The moment she sees his strained, tense face, however, and his crushed almost subservient attitude, her heart beats fast with a different kind of fear. Her adored father looks beaten and frightened, and now she believes everything that Eleanor has said. She allows herself to be rushed out into the dark, wild night and packed into the car with the luggage. They drive out over the little bridge, and away towards London, and it is much later that she remembers that Hester has not come to say goodbye to her.

It is much later that Hester remembers that she has not said goodbye to Lucy. Her overwhelming instinct has been to get Eleanor and Michael away before any more damage is done and, though it will be a shock to Lucy, at least she will be out of harm's way. Hester cannot think beyond this yet. She has given Edward the sedative that Michael has passed in through the half-open door, along with some dry clothes, and he is now asleep where she first put him, in the chair beside the kitchen range. She sits at the kitchen table watching him. The river has washed away all the blood from his nose, though his face and arms are badly scratched, and he looks white and exhausted. No doubt the bruising will show up later. At least nothing is broken. He was too weak to fight Michael, as they half carried and half dragged him across the lawn to the house, but he screamed violent imprecations and struggled all the way.

As soon as the sedative began to take effect, Hester was able to get him into his dry clothes, and now he sleeps heavily whilst she watches him anxiously. Fear and horror keep her upright at the table, her hands in a continual wringing motion, whilst her brain begins to circle in one desperate groove of thought: what shall I do, oh, what shall I do? How will he be when he wakes?

When she knows that he is deeply asleep, she stands up and pushes the kettle onto the range. She has already made them some tea, though Edward resisted it to begin with, and now she goes through the familiar, comforting routine again. When she sits down she begins to think about her family, how it has been depleted in such a short time – even Michael is lost to her now – and she feels as if she has been utterly abandoned. She remembers those happy holidays when her mother and father were still alive, and the boys playing their silly practical jokes, and her heart aches with loneliness.

Help me! she cries to them silently. Help me! and tears rise in her eyes and run down the back of her throat. She drinks her tea, swallowing it down with her tears, and presently, overcome with fatigue, she puts her head down on her folded arms and sleeps. It might be a minute later, or an hour, when she hears the telephone ringing. Glancing anxiously at Edward she sees that the bell does not disturb his drug-induced sleep and she slips out into the hall, keeping her voice low as she speaks into the receiver.

'Is that you, Hester? It's Blaise. How are you? You sound very faint.'

'Blaise.' She can barely speak his name, so relieved is she to hear him. 'Blaise, where are you?'

'I'm in London. Did you get my letter? I was sent out to Germany from Bletchley Park and then on to America but it's over at last. I'm a free man, Hester.

I didn't pick up your last letter until I got back here yesterday. What's been happening down there? How's Edward?'

Quite suddenly she begins to cry, gripping the receiver, trying to explain whilst gulping down the tears, and Blaise is asking questions, his voice very different now, sharp and quick.

'I'll come down,' he says at last. 'Don't worry, Hes. I know someone who'll lend me a car. This is an emergency. I'll be with you as soon as I can.'

She goes back to the kitchen, her legs shaking, and sits down again. Edward is mumbling and stirring in his sleep but she no longer feels fearful: Blaise is coming.

When she first sees him she feels a sense of shock. He seems smaller than the tall young man she remembers: the older cousin, the one who kept the boys in order and had long discussions with her father. Yet his presence is much more commanding and, quite suddenly, she feels weak with reaction. She puts her arms round Blaise, burying her face in his Aran jersey, which smells of cigarettes and coffee, and she inhales luxuriously because this reminds her of her father.

Blaise holds her tightly murmuring, 'Poor little Hes. Poor darling,' and gives her plenty of time to

291

recover herself. She smiles up at him and suddenly realizes that it is not he who has shrunk but she who has grown. Just for a moment she is struck by the sharp planes of his cheekbones, the dark slate-grey colour of his eyes, and her heart gives an odd lurch.

'How is he?' Blaise is asking. 'I couldn't quite grasp what you were saying. Did Michael and Edward really fight? It seems so unlikely.'

He follows her into the kitchen where Edward sleeps, still asking questions, but when he sets eyes upon the recumbent figure his expression changes into a kind of compassionate horror.

'Poor old boy,' he says at last. 'Poor old Edward. Just for a moment I thought it was your father lying there, Hes. Though he never was so thin.'

He crouches beside the chair and takes the limp hand in his but Edward barely stirs and presently Blaise stands up again and looks at Hester. Now he studies her properly, smiling.

'You've grown up,' he says, as if making a discovery. 'How odd for us to be meeting again like this after all this time. I'm so sorry that you've had such a terrible war.'

'Everyone has,' she says, taking refuge from her confused emotions by beginning to make more tea.

'Oh, I've done well enough,' he answers lightly,

'hidden away in my cell at Bletchley Park. I haven't had a bad war.'

She glances at him quickly, detecting an almost bitter tone in his voice, but he smiles again: a smile of sheer affection and pleasure.

'I can't tell you how good it is to be here again, Hes, even in these circumstances. It's like a home-coming.'

They sit down at the table, the pot of tea between them, and Hester wonders how to explain exactly what has happened and where she should start. Blaise senses her difficulty and begins to ask questions that gradually lead her from the point when her mother died to the fight between Michael and Edward. Slowly, filling in the details as she goes, Hester tells him the whole story.

And when Edward wakes and sees Blaise sitting at the table he is at first puzzled and then delighted. He struggles to his feet, casting off his blanket, and the two men embrace each other whilst Hester looks on in relief and delight. After a while Edward frowns, clearly beginning to remember the events of the previous evening, and she waits, holding her breath. When he asks where Michael is, it is Blaise who answers him.

'He's gone, old chap,' he tells him calmly but very firmly. 'They've all gone. It's just you and me and Hester now. I've decided to take a very long sabbatical while I decide what I'm going to do now the war is over and Hester has agreed to let me stay. We're going to get you fit and well again.'

Blaise stands above him, smiling down at him, and it is as if he is imposing some sort of discipline on Edward whilst offering him a challenge: this is a new life, he seems to be saying, take it or leave it. And suddenly Edward nods his head, as if he is accepting the new order and is prepared to make the best of it.

So it is that Hester does not discover the Midsummer Cushion until the morning, when she goes upstairs to wash and put on clean clothes. She crosses the floor, murmuring, 'Oh, no. Oh no,' as if some new terrible calamity has taken place, and carefully picks the tapestry out of the wreckage of smashed glass to see if it is much damaged. The frame is broken, the wood splintered and, turning it, she notices that the frayed string has worn right through and snapped in two. She can see that the tapestry has not always been kept behind glass and away from sunlight, and that it is worn in places and rather faded. She shakes the canvas loose, folds it very gently in a scarf and puts it away in a drawer.

She stares at the splintered glass and quite

suddenly sits down on the edge of her bed and bursts into tears. It is as if the Midsummer Cushion is a symbol of everything she has known and loved: her happy family life is smashed to pieces, broken and spoiled. The bright future she once envisaged amongst her own people is destroyed. As she weeps she thinks suddenly of Lucy and wonders how she will cope with the new rupture in her small life; and she is glad that Lucy has not witnessed the breaking of the Midsummer Cushion. She loved it so much it would have upset her terribly.

Presently the storm of weeping passes and she feels indescribably tired but calm. She tells herself that this reaction is simply shock and her heavy heart lifts at the thought of Blaise, sitting downstairs with Edward. Quickly she strips off her damp, muddy clothes, pours water from the big flowered ewer into its matching bowl and sluices it over her face. As soon as they've had some breakfast she will bring up the dustpan and sweep up the glass – and one day, she promises herself, she will reframe the Midsummer Cushion. Meanwhile she is not alone. Blaise has come home.

The next few months are the happiest of Hester's life. With Blaise, Edward is rarely wild or uncontrolled, and slowly she learns to relax. Edward grows a little stronger and on fine winter days they are able to take short walks on the hills and by the river. The fight and his struggle in the water has had its effect on his weakened frame, though: Edward suffers from an increased short-ness of breath and a nagging little cough. Without the irritant of Eleanor's presence he becomes calmer; the need to be watchful and alert is no longer necessary.

He finds that he can tell Blaise a little about the camp but he knows that Blaise will never be able to understand the truth of it. Only those who have suffered the isolation of being utterly abandoned, locked in a bitter minute-to-minute struggle for basic survival, humiliated and degraded at every opportunity, could ever really understand. Even Blaise, who has a great capacity for entering into someone else's suffering, can only partly connect here.

'When the Americans rescued us,' Edward says, 'they were so appalled by what they found that they wanted to wreak terrible retribution. They couldn't understand that, after three years of being subjected to the most brutal violence and callous, inhuman indifference, we were far beyond the ordinary, honest, straightforward hatred that can find relief in simple revenge. Our hatred was woven into the very stuff of ourselves; it was pure, and theirs seemed childish by comparison.'

Blaise listens, and sometimes Edward finds relief in talking, but generally he is content in letting the past be. He cannot forget, never that, but he can concentrate on other things. It is the same with Eleanor's defection: he is coming to terms with it in his own way. He and Blaise have talked about Michael, Blaise carefully explaining Michael's particular loss and loneliness without condoning his behaviour, and Edward is slowly attempting to exonerate his old friend. He cannot blot him out of his memory, Michael is too bound up in his whole past and in his happiest memories, so Edward must somehow learn to contain him without descending into madness at the thought of that final betrayal.

He can accept that Eleanor would have been the moving spirit in the affair – he remembers her ways of old – and he knows that their marriage would never have worked; yet this knowledge brings a different kind of despair. It seems odd, now, that she'd remained such a powerful force through those endless years in prison; something for which to survive. He'd lived for her – and when he'd got home he'd seen at once that she no longer wanted him; that he horrified and disgusted her.

Now he has nothing, he sometimes tells himself

drearily. As soon as he thinks this, however, he reminds himself that it isn't true. He has Hester and Blaise, and the three of them are creating a small, safe world at Bridge House whilst the winter slowly passes.

Just before Christmas, Patricia and Nanny and the boys come for the day bringing presents. Patricia is shocked by Edward's appearance; so shocked that Hester realizes how hardened she has become to it. Patricia can barely keep the tears from brimming over each time she looks at her brother; Nanny is seized with rage at the treatment he has suffered and both of them are furious with Eleanor and Michael. Hester finds it difficult to deal with their reactions. She has managed to set aside these tragedies, to accept them as far as she is able, and she fears that their distress will simply upset Edward.

Blaise shields Edward from their shock and pity, joking with Nanny, sympathizing with Patricia in private, and playing with the boys. Watching him, Hester knows that she is in love with him and a tiny part of her is glad now that she was able to connect with Eleanor, however briefly or inadequately. She has begun to feel the terrible pangs of love: 'More like fangs,' she tells herself rather painfully, trying to laugh, wondering if there is any chance that he might feel the same way about her. Proximity has brought them close but he still behaves like the older cousin, or a very close, beloved friend, and there is nothing romantic in his approach to her.

'Thank God you've got Blaise,' Patricia says to her as they prepare the lunch together. 'But how will you manage when he's gone? Rob says that you must both come to us. It would be a squeeze but we'd cope somehow. We could sell this house and buy a bigger one. Oh, Hester, the poor darling. Isn't it terrible?' and she begins to weep again whilst Hester pats her on the back and mutters helplessly.

'Where did Lucy go?' Jack asks Hester when they are alone. He has been told that he mustn't mention her or Michael or Eleanor in front of Edward, and that she won't be coming back.

'She's with her father,' Hester tells him, 'in London,' and then wonders if this is true.

'I've got a Christmas card for her,' says Jack. 'Only Mummy doesn't know where to send it. Will you send it for me?'

'I'll try,' promises Hester. 'I don't quite know where they are living just at the moment but I'll find out if I can. Do you want to leave it with me?'

'As long as you send it,' says Jack belligerently.

He misses Lucy and is genuinely upset that he doesn't know where she is. 'I promised I'd come back to see her, you see. I *promised*. Her doll's pram is still in the shed.'

'Oh, darling, I know it is. It wouldn't go in the car, you see. I promise I'll find out where she is,' Hester tells him, giving him a hug. She puts the card on the dresser and the next day she puts it into a larger envelope, along with her own cards and a letter to Lucy and another to Michael, which ends 'Please let me know how you all are', and posts it to Michael's London address having printed 'PLEASE FORWARD' on the envelope.

A few days after the visit she receives a brief note from Eleanor; it has no address.

Dear Hes,

I have some bad news. Mike was killed last week, blown up by one of those bloody UXBs. I can hardly take it in and I feel in some way we've been punished for what we did to Edward. Anyway, I thought you ought to know. Lucy has been with Mike's old aunt down in Chichester ever since we left you and as far as I know she's fine. Mike's CO went down to see them, which was very decent of him. I didn't think they'd appreciate a visit from me!!!

My news is that I'm off to America with a girl I was at school with. Her father is an American, mother English, and she's decided to go home for a while. I'm going with her as a kind of paid companion, anything to get away from this dreary country. My parents have rather written me off, they can't really cope with me at all, but you could reach me through them if you need to. I hope Edward has recovered and I'm sorry, Hes, I really am. I don't suppose you'll want to hear from me again so I suppose I ought to tell you that I tell everyone that I'm a war widow. I move in different circles since Edward and I were together so it answers all the problems. Leila and her brother are being very kind and I'm looking forward to a new life 'Stateside'.

Good luck, Hes,
Eleanor

Hester's first thought is for Lucy: now she has lost everything. She wonders what she can do – if anything – and decides that it might unsettle Lucy if she should write to her. Perhaps she is trying to forget the unhappy memories that can only be revived if she, Hester, should get in touch again. Perhaps she should wait and see if Lucy responds in some way to the letter and the Christmas cards; no doubt her Aunt Mary will help her to decide what she should do. Poor, poor little Lucy, how she must miss her father.

Hester sits for some time in silence, mourning Michael and regretting him, and thinking of Eleanor with a kind of admiration. She can't help wondering how much Leila's brother is involved in the move to America. When Blaise finds her still sitting holding the letter, he sits down beside her and takes her hand.

'The thing is,' she tells him, turning the letter over and over, 'I have the feeling that we lost Michael on that awful evening. He looked . . .' She hesitates, searching for a word. 'He looked utterly wretched, rather like Edward looked when he first came home. As if he was in some foreign place where nobody understood him any longer and where he'd utterly lost his bearings. Edward was astounded by the amount of food we had, even though we're still rationed, and the fact that he had clean clothes and sheets. Things like that. Those three years in the camp had completely disorientated him. Well, Michael looked like that on the last night. I shall never forget the way he went rushing out over the bridge to get help and, when we brought him back, it was as if something had broken.'

Blaise holds her hand tightly. 'It would be the worst kind of thing for someone of Michael's temperament. To be deceiving his closest friend. I can imagine how easy it would be to believe that Edward was dead, and submit to the temptation of making love to his widow, but when Edward came back it must have been hell on earth for a man like Mike. To be torn between two people or two different kinds of love. Poor devil.'

'Shall we tell Edward?'

Blaise thinks about this and then shakes his head. 'I think not. He seems to have put them out of his mind. Let's not reopen old wounds. If he asks about him then we shall have to tell him the truth, of course, but he's got quite enough to handle with his memories of what he's been through.'

Hester knows that Edward talks to Blaise about the camp, though he always falls silent when she comes in, but she catches odd fragments that allow her a tiny glimpse of the hell he has survived: the beatings and the torture and the starvation.

'Men bartered food in exchange for tobacco,' he says one afternoon when he and Blaise are having an after-lunch smoke. 'They knew they would die of starvation but the habit had such a hold that they didn't care. When we got tobacco the problem was what to roll it in. We started to use the leaves out of books and we got to the stage where men were wanting to using their bibles. It made a good smoke because the paper was so thin and fine. The padre agreed that bibles could be used so long as each man read the page he was about to smoke.' Hester hears him chuckle. 'It gave a very fragmented picture of the good book. I remember Habakkuk and Micah. He was an amazing man, the padre. He used to refuse to allow those who were sick to be forced out to work. The guards would knock him senseless and then drag the poor devils out anyway. He never gave in, though. He fought for us and was beaten up for us and showed what Christianity really meant by living it. He kept our faith alive even in the most degrading circumstances when it seemed impossible to believe in anything except evil.'

When she comes back with the coffee they are talking about religion more generally.

'I think the only true, honest revolution is the one that takes place within a man's soul,' Blaise is saying. 'Any other kind simply means the destruction of one set of people by another so as to set up a new regime, which in time produces exactly the same kind of misuse of power and privilege. But if a man dies to himself so that Christ begins to live in him that can only be good, surely?'

Later that evening, sitting by the fire, Hester tells him that she and Edward have been reading John Clare's poetry again and Blaise talks to them about their father's work at Cambridge.

'Have you thought about going to Cambridge?' Blaise asks Hester. 'It's what your father would have wanted for you. Edward and I could prepare you for the entrance exam, couldn't we, Edward?'

Edward agrees at once, delighted by the idea, and they immediately set about drawing up a reading programme, joking about how hard she'll have to work. Hester goes along with it readily, though she can't imagine how Edward would cope without her and clearly Blaise can't remain with them for ever. The thought of his leaving them fills her with an unfamiliar misery.

For now, though, Hester is happy: she has Blaise. She accepts that she is in love with him and, to begin with, the joy of having him here at Bridge House is enough. Each morning, when she wakes, her heart beats with excitement rather than with dread. As the spring approaches, however, Hester notices another change in Edward.

'Edward is so much better,' she tells Blaise. 'He doesn't seem mad any more. But have you noticed that there's a kind of resignation about him?'

Blaise looks at her, an odd look. 'The poor fellow. The trouble with these things, Hes, is that you can't have it both ways. From what he's told me I know that it was the thought of Eleanor that kept him going through those appalling times. Coming home to her was what gave him the will to survive. And what happens? He finds her again and then discovers that she doesn't want him any more. Worse, she's in love with his closest friend. Eleanor was the wire in his blood that first of all kept him alive and then drove him mad. He's accepted that he's lost her but he's also lost the thing that made life worth living. Now he's simply existing.'

Hester is horrified. 'Is he really so unhappy?'

'That's the whole point. He doesn't feel unhappy because he doesn't feel anything much. In the camp the prisoners were systematically humiliated and degraded. One of the things that sustained them was the thought of someone somewhere to whom they were important and it was for their sakes they endured and survived when it might have been easier to give up. Edward came back to rejection and betrayal and it's knocked the stuffing out of him.'

'He's got us,' says Hester sadly. 'But I can see that it isn't the same.'

'Not quite.' Blaise smiles at her. 'But it's ever so

much better than nothing. That's why this idea of getting you ready for Cambridge is a good one. It gives him a goal to work for; something worth doing.'

Hester looks at him directly. 'But how could I leave him? You won't stay for ever, will you, Blaise, and then what does Edward do while I'm at Cambridge?'

'We have to think about it. To tell you the truth, Hes, I'm thinking of taking Holy Orders. Oh, I know,' he grins at her expression, 'it is pretty amazing, isn't it? But I feel very strongly drawn to it. This is giving me time to discern; to see if I really have a vocation. Perhaps we might all go to Cambridge and get a house together there. Oh, I don't know! Let's just give ourselves time to think and work and get Edward properly fit.'

And she is too grateful to know that he will be with them for a while longer to make any kind of protest.

Hester's coaching programme continues and Edward chooses *Twelfth Night* as part of her studies. To help her, they read it aloud at night around the fire, discussing the structure and the plot and Shakespeare's characters. They share out the parts, Hester playing Viola to Blaise's Duke Orsino, and although he doesn't suspect it, Edward's choice of play is particularly and poignantly apt for, all through the cold, blowy, green and golden days of early spring, Blaise and Hester are falling in love.

Oh, neither of them knows of the other's feelings – they are both too cautious to let their love show – but each of them grows more and more aware. It is as if their nerve-endings have become abnormally alert to each touch, however casual; their ears attuned to any observation, however familiar. They watch and listen hopefully, almost desperately, but the family trait of detachment runs strong in these two and in this instance it serves them both ill: instead of trusting to intuition they stand off, weighing up their emotions, dissecting and analysing them until their true instincts are weakened by lack of nourishment and smothered by denial.

To Blaise, the eldest of them all, the one who tried to take their father's place when he died, this love he is beginning to feel for Hester feels perilously akin to incest. He has been a big brother to her – he is thirty years old to her eighteen – and it seems impossible, almost wrong that he should have such feelings for her. Even though he tells himself that they are cousins, not siblings, and watches her hopefully to see if there is any sign that she might be feeling the same way towards him, nevertheless he is convinced that it would be quite wrong to frighten or embarrass her with a declaration of love; she depends on him and nothing must be done to destroy her trust in him.

At the same time he is trying to discern whether or not he has a vocation or whether it is some trick of the imagination that gives him a sense of Presence: as if someone is watching him, standing just out of his own line of vision. His heart beats hard, as if it might be some lover who is waiting for him, and he tries to laugh off this new, strange desire. After all, why should he be called?

There's nothing special about you, he tells himself, half-mocking, half-longing for the slowly growing awareness to be a true sign.

He tries to see himself as a priest, thinking carefully about the dedication required, and once again comes up against his love for Hester. He knows very well that the majority of Anglican priests are married yet he wonders how he would manage if his loyalty were to be put to the test.

If I give myself wholly to God, he asks himself, how would I react if something were to be required of me that meant that my wife or children might suffer? Or, put it the other way round: if I have a wife and children will I be able to dedicate myself wholly to God's will?

Yet each time he looks at Hester, his heart turns over with tenderness for her and he longs to reach out and gather her tightly in his arms; and each time he resists lest he should frighten her. He feels certain about one thing: if it is not to be Hester then it will be nobody. He will remain free for God's work . . . if that is what he is called to do. And then it all starts up again: the uncertainty, the lack of confidence in his calling, the longing for some sign.

Hester too is guarding herself from any display of affection that might be misconstrued. She knows that to Blaise she is the youngest, little Hes, and she fears that he might be shocked or even disappointed to think that she feels such strong love for him that it makes her tremble and burn. These overwhelming physical emotions remind her of Eleanor and she is afraid that there might be something shameful about it all. She couldn't bear to disgust Blaise, to have him turn from her in disappointment, and she takes care to give no sign of the heart-aching love that she bears him.

It doesn't help that Edward, who sees nothing of this, has his own strong views on Blaise's future.

'He'll make a first-class priest,' he says to Hester one morning as they walk beside the river. 'He'll be completely dedicated. He's in love with God and with God's creation and he will spend his life trying to minister to it. I had a padre like Blaise, utterly committed to service. He had no idea, of course, the effect that he had on us. He'd achieved that true humility that ceases to be self-aware, but I imagine that none of us who survived will ever forget him.'

The dim, winding path through the damp wood seems to be lit by the golden flowers of the kingcups that grow luxuriantly amongst the trees; the yaffle's laughing call rings out, clear and high above the river's crooning, watery chuckle. As they walk on a little further, Hester screws up her courage to ask Edward a question.

'So you can't imagine Blaise with a wife and children?' she asks at last.

His derisive snort of laughter hurts her more than he will ever know. 'Absolutely not. Or, if he does marry then he'll never be happy. He'll be constantly torn between his duty to his wife and family and his duty to God. It would be hell for a chap like Blaise. He's so whole-hearted, isn't he? It would make him utterly miserable.'

This reminds her of what Blaise said about Michael, being torn between two people and two different kinds of love, and she sees with a devastating clarity that she must never be responsible for ruining Blaise's life.

'Some priests manage it,' she says lightly – almost as if she is making one last desperate throw for happiness.

'Some priests,' Edward agrees, 'but not Blaise. Anyway, I'm not sure we make good marriage material. We think too much. The passionate side of it can make us obsessive and drive us mad, and once that fades we're too detached to make good spouses or parents. Yet at the same time we feel guilty about it.'

Hester is taken aback by this declaration, anxious lest the conversation might edge into dangerous territory, yet fascinated by this view on their shared characteristics.

'Patricia manages very well,' she ventures at last.

'Yes,' he agrees readily, 'Patricia manages. She's very maternal, of course. I just think that the men of our family aren't very satisfactory marriage material, that's all. Maybe I'm biased. Father was always very wrapped up in his work, wasn't he, though Mother encouraged him. She was very like him, actually, and I think we were lucky to have Nanny. Father always tried terribly hard during the holidays to make up for it, poor fellow, as if he felt guilty for all the times we never saw him and

Mother was left alone. He drove himself too hard in all directions and I often wonder if that's why he had a heart attack whilst still quite young. He wasn't much more than forty. Blaise is very like him – well, that's not surprising, our father and his were very much alike – but for a priest I should think that kind of pressure would be frightful. That's another thing about us. We don't seem to cope very well with emotional pressure. Look at Mother when the boys died and I was taken prisoner; you told me she simply couldn't face it.'

His expression has become brooding and Hester hastens to distract him.

'Can you reach those catkins?' she asks. 'Cut them long enough. Thanks. It must be nearly lunch-time. Shall we go back?'

As they retrace their steps, scrunching over the beech mast and dead leaves, Hester knows that at some level a decision has been made and, ever afterwards, when she sees the kingcups blooming along the riverbank and hears the yaffle calling in the wood, she is filled with a strange sense of melancholy and loss.

Duke Orsino: 'And what's her history?'
Viola: 'A blank, my lord. She never told her love . . .'

313

PART THREE

PART THREE

CHAPTER TWENTY-ONE

Lizzie Blake came into the kitchen and paused for a moment in appreciation. The big room with its two windows, one looking west towards Dunkery hill and the other into the sheltered garth, never failed to give her a little thrill of pleasure. A slanting beam of spring sunshine glanced off the toast rack on the large square table and touched the old Welsh dresser that held china belonging to four generations of women – an eclectic display that included Wedgwood and Clarice Cliff; art deco and Royal Doulton. Lizzie had brought one or two pieces of her own from her small house in Bristol to add to the collection and she surveyed the effect with satisfaction.

Lion rose from his bean bag near the Aga and came to meet her, tail waving, and she bent to kiss his silky head before slipping into her chair. She smiled a greeting to Piers, slit open the envelope that he'd put beside her plate and read the enclosed letter with a growing impatience.

'Honestly,' she muttered. 'For goodness' sake!' and, folding the paper, she put it on one side with a smack.

Piers raised his eyebrows but remained silent whilst Lizzie reached for some toast and buttered it with irritated swipes of her knife.

'I'm beginning to lose patience with Jonah,' she announced. 'You know how keen he was about the film event with the sixth-formers? Well, first of all he wrote to say that he couldn't get down for our next meeting at the end of the month and now he's saying that he might not be able to take any part in it at all. His father is very ill so he's been trying to spend time with his mother and now the work's building up; unexpected rewrites and stuff.'

Piers put his own letters to one side, poured coffee for her and refilled his large breakfast cup. 'Do I take it that you don't absolutely believe his reasons?'

'Excuses,' said Lizzie crossly, 'not reasons. There's something going on. Clio was saying the same thing.'

'Clio?'

'Do you remember that she took him to meet Hester last autumn? Well, they got on swimmingly together. Jonah's mother stayed with Hester and her family during the war and it turns out that Hester knew Jonah's grandfather terribly well. Something happened, apparently, some war-time romance or whatever, and Jonah was fascinated by it all and went down again to see Hester after Clio had gone back to London. So, everything's going fine, Jonah's even thinking of dramatizing the story and then, suddenly, with no warning, silence. Hester had a Christmas card from him and then a little note saying his father was ill and something had cropped up with his work – he script-edits on one of the soaps – and that he'd be very tied up for a while. Clio says Hester's really sad and worried. She thinks she must have upset him but can't think how. It was all so curt. You know, a kind of "Good-bye and thanks for all the fish" kind of thing. And now he's telling me much the same thing.'

Moodily she tore off a piece of toast crust and passed it to Lion, who was sitting hopefully by her chair.

'I *wish* you wouldn't do that,' said Piers, distracted momentarily from her recital. 'I hate a dog who begs at the table and salivates all over people's shoes.'

'Oh, sweetie, I'm sorry.' Lizzie made a penitent face, rolling her eyes guiltily at Lion, who crunched appreciatively. 'I wasn't thinking. I'm just so upset about Jonah. I mean, he's usually such a darling and I can't think why he's behaving like this. Apart from anything else, I *need* him. He's a rising star and he'll draw the punters.'

'Well, why don't you ring him up and ask him what he's playing at? Or why doesn't Clio?'

'That's what I said to her. She hasn't got a telephone number or an address, apparently. *She* gave *him* her mobile number but that doesn't help much.'

'Well, *you've* got his number and his address. Ring him up and tell him everyone is worried. Tell him he's vital to your event. You don't have to submit to a secrecy and silence conspiracy.'

'That's very true.' Lizzie appeared to be much struck by this approach. 'We won't let him get away with it. I did telephone his flat actually after his last letter but I just got his answerphone. That's the snag, of course: we can hold people at bay indefinitely these days with our voice mails and answerphones.'

'Hound him,' said Piers brutally. 'You and Clio take turns to telephone. Leave desperate messages. Got his mobile number? Well, phone that too. Text him.'

'I might just do that.' Lizzie finished her toast

thoughtfully. 'But I just wonder why he's taken such a scunner to us all. He was so keen about it. What could it be?'

Piers raised his eyebrows, his mouth turning down at the corners, in a kind of facial shrug. 'Ask him,' he said. 'We don't want him upsetting Hester. I'm very fond of old Hes. They've got the fishing rights along the river there and we used to look after the letting of it all those years she was away. I only really know Hester and Blaise, though I've met Jack and Robin once or twice. Father knew the family much better than I did.' He stood up. 'By the way, has he had his breakfast yet?'

'Oh, yes. He was down early. He said you were taking him to see a client today.'

'That's right. I'm going over to a farm near Simonsbath and thought he might like the drive. Old Hartley has been on our books for years. He and father are old friends.'

'Felix will enjoy that,' agreed Lizzie. 'And I might go and see Clio and Hester. Hatch a plot to deal with young Jonah. Shall I take Lion or will you?'

Piers hesitated, looking at Lion who sat up, ears flattened, tail beating expectantly on the flagged floor. 'Could you manage? Hartley's collies are a tad touchy. I know he likes to come with me as a rule but he'll enjoy a walk by the river.'

'He likes to see St Francis,' said Lizzie. 'He's such an enormous cat that Lion looks upon him as an honorary dog. They go for walks together; it's bizarre. He'll be fine once you've gone. Shut the door as you go out and then he can't follow you and I'll telephone Bridge House and see if they can cope with us.'

Clio was almost as upset as Lizzie. The thing was, as she'd said to Hester several times, it seemed so out of keeping with Jonah's character. If he'd telephoned, disappointed at not being able to go on with his exploration of the past, they could have understood it better. As it was, one Christmas card and a short, unsatisfactory letter didn't offer any kind of explanation.

'I don't think it was anything I told him,' Hester had said anxiously. 'He went off perfectly happily and planning to come down again soon.'

As much as anything else, as far as Clio was concerned, it was seeing Hester upset that was so distressing; she looked frailer, as if she'd been diminished by Jonah's brush-off. Clio was cross with Jonah, miserable by the break-up of her affair with Peter, and anxious about the future.

Waiting for Lizzie – Hester had gone to Dunster – Clio tried to recreate the peace and deep-down

322

joy she'd felt at the convent during Christmas, especially in the chapel. At first it had taken some adjustment: the general atmosphere of quiet, the reflective silences between prayers and psalms during the offices, the sense of reverence and awe. She'd loved the chapel with its plain stone walls and high, over-arching ceiling and the strong, simple shape of the wooden altar table. A carved statue of Mary, serene and patient, stood in an alcove, a wide, shallow bowl at her feet filled with sand and stuck about with votive candles that flickered and streamed in the dusk-light when the office of vespers was sung.

On the morning of Christmas Eve the chapel was decorated: tall silver vases of evergreen and holly were placed on the altar steps, and a sweet-scented fir tree, dressed in silver and gold, twinkled in a shadowy corner. At the midnight Eucharist as Clio sat in her corner next to Hester, watching the faces of the nuns in their stalls, she suddenly noticed the crib and the Holy Family. The small figures were placed on a low table, hardly distinguishable at a distance; yet a hidden light shone upon them in such a way that their huge shadows rose, clear and dramatic, against the ancient stone wall beyond them. It seemed to Clio that this was a paradox: this small, homely event, hardly noticed by anybody apart from a few shepherds, yet foreshadowing something that would shake the world's foundations.

Celebrating with the community, sharing in their joy at the birth of the Christ Child, being with Blaise and Hester – all these things had distracted her from her own desolation and she'd confidently believed that she had found the strength to go forward without fear. Each evening, sitting in chapel during the hour of silent prayer before compline, as the sanctuary light flickered in the darkness and showed the dim, immobile shapes of the nuns, her unhappy heart had been miraculously filled with peace. This wordless sweet communion, which exalted and expanded her heart with love, drew her back to her corner time and again.

Once or twice she'd felt Blaise's eyes upon her, calm and reflective, and she'd wondered if he'd guessed. She was very slightly in awe of him here, as she never was when he came on holiday to Bridge House. There, his resemblance to Hester endeared him to her at once, however long it was since she'd seen him last. His self-contained quietness, his easy-going readiness to fit in and accept anything that might be going on, his way of looking at her intently as if he truly wished to know who she was but without any sense of intrusiveness on his part:

all these things allowed her to treat him as a brother or some very special friend. She never thought of Blaise in terms of age.

One morning after terce, finding him alone in the flat, all her old affection for him had driven out this sense of awe and she'd spoken impulsively.

'If someone had told me that I could spend an hour sitting in silence in a chapel and loving every minute of it, I'd have laughed,' she said. 'I've tried meditation before but it's never really worked. I can't clear my head properly and I get frustrated. It's the same with prayer; you go rabbiting on but it's as if you're talking to yourself. There's nothing coming back. But these last few evenings it's as if I've connected with something. Oh, I don't know how to describe it but it's great!'

He'd probed her with his lancing look: not judgemental, not tolerant, but looking right into her as though he was greeting her from some place deep inside himself. When he smiled she felt as if he'd given her a present but he didn't speak, simply touched her shoulder as Hester did.

Later she'd found a piece of paper on her bed: a photocopy of a page from a book with some lines underlined. She picked it up and read them with curiosity.

Prayers like gravel
        Flung at the sky's
window, hoping to attract
        the loved one's
attention . . .
        . . . I would
have refrained long since
        but that peering once
through my locked fingers
I thought that I detected
        the movement of a curtain.

'Something like this?' was written at the bottom in Blaise's hand.

Finding him sitting at the table, drinking coffee, she'd put her arm round his shoulder and kissed his cheek.

'Just like that,' she'd murmured in his ear – and he'd chuckled with the pleasure of sharing.

As the week passed, Clio felt that she'd discovered a spiritual secret that would sustain her for ever. She'd said as much to Blaise on the journey back from Hexham where she'd driven him to do some shopping.

'It won't last,' Blaise had answered.

So sure had Clio been of Blaise's approval and delight that this display of pragmatism caused her to swivel her eyes from the road to stare at him with dismay.

'What do you mean?'

'I'm just warning you,' replied Blaise, 'because after such an experience it can be terribly disappointing when you find that these feelings can't be enjoyed at will. You might feel that you're not praying hard enough or in the right way and then you might be so disillusioned that you give up any attempt to pray or to listen, that's all. It's grace, something freely given, not deserved or worked for; it's a Gift. Never forget what you've experienced but don't come to rely on it.'

They'd driven in silence for a moment then Clio had begun to laugh.

'Thanks, Blaise,' she'd said wryly.

Blaise had smiled too, rather ruefully. 'I thought it was best that you should be prepared,' he'd said.

And now, Clio told herself, she was glad that Blaise had warned her, because once back at Bridge House, aching for Peter, her future a blank, she'd fallen prey once more to fear and misery. She remembered what Blaise had said and tried to persist with meditation, setting aside a short time every day just to sit quietly in her room with the candles lit, trying to recreate the atmosphere of the chapel. Here, however, she found her concentration wandering, and memories pressing more closely upon her: Peter pleading with her to give him time, telling her how essential she was to him.

'But is this how you see the rest of our lives?' she'd asked him angrily. 'Me just sitting here waiting? All those weekends when I stay in, hoping that you might manage a phone call; and outings together that you've promised, cancelled at the last moment because of some more important family event? Can you imagine how awful Christmas is? And bank holidays? Let's face it, Peter, you're never going to leave Louise and I don't think I want you to, not any more. I'd feel too guilty. Oh, I fantasized about you splitting up, in a very amicable way that didn't hurt the children, but it was complete crap. It was never going to happen. And now that Louise has been so ill, it's shown you very clearly where your heart really is. Hasn't it?'

He hadn't looked at her; he'd stood with his back to her, staring out of the window and jingling the loose change in his pockets. Then, just briefly, she'd relaxed her guard and allowed herself to look at him – his fair crisp hair, the length of his back in the well-cut jacket, his long straight legs – and had felt the utter anguish of love and longing. If he'd turned at that moment and seen her face, she'd have been lost.

Instead, still looking out of the window, he'd said: 'What happened down there on Exmoor? Did you meet someone else?'

She'd almost smiled. How much easier for both of them if she could use such a reason but, 'No,' she'd answered. 'There is no-one else. It simply removed me from your magnetic field, that's all. I realized that I've been in thrall, Peter.'

'And you're not now?'

He'd turned to look at her, then, and it had required an enormous effort to stare at him coolly and reply, 'No, not now.'

'Damn all godmothers,' he'd said, characteristically and matter-of-factly, and when she'd laughed he'd sent her a quick, sly glance, wondering if he'd detected a slight weakening.

She'd continued to watch him steadily but her heart had ached: at no time had he suggested any changes for the future. He'd pleaded for her to be patient while Louise was still ill, told her that he needed her, but he'd made no promises of more time together or hinted that he might one day leave Louise, and, in playing it brutally straight, he'd given her the courage to stand firm.

Back at Bridge House it was easier to bear the

pain, and there was the prospect of the future to distract her, but it was Jonah's defection, she told herself, that was really upsetting her; though sometimes she wondered if she were simply projecting all her own troubles onto him.

She nearly said as much to Lizzie when she arrived with Lion, but Lizzie was chuckling at the sight of St Francis and Lion greeting one another. Lion bowed down before St Francis, large and peaceful in his basket chair, as if at first honouring him and then inviting him to play. He gave one or two tentative barks, and his plumy tail wagged encouragingly, but St Francis simply stared at him imperturbably, showing a benign and friendly indifference to his antics before embarking on a long, thorough wash.

'I know that people talk about growing like their dogs,' Lizzie said, 'but doesn't St Francis remind you of Hester? There's that same delightful detachment. I just love it.'

'She's not feeling very detached about Jonah,' said Clio crossly. 'She'd grown really fond of him and now he's made her miserable, Lizzie. She seems anxious in case she told him something that might have upset him. About his grandfather or his mother or something. I can't believe she has but it's really eating her up.'

'That's why I've come, sweetie.' Lizzie gave Clio her attention at once. 'Piers says we simply mustn't let Jonah get away with it. We mustn't let him impose his will on us. He says that we must hound him.'

Clio frowned, puzzled. 'But how do we do that?'

'I've got his telephone numbers, you see, and we must take it in turns to ring him up and leave messages. You must say that Hester is pining away and I shall say that he's letting me down over the film event. We can text him too. What do you think?'

Clio nodded cautiously. 'It might work. Sorry, Lizzie, I wasn't thinking. Would you like some coffee?'

'Do you mind if we give Lion a walk first? He hasn't had a run yet and I promised Piers.'

'OK. We'll go along the river. It looks wonderful in the woods at the moment. The marsh marigolds are out and the ground is positively golden with them. Hester calls them kingcups and says that they make her feel melancholy.'

'Oh, poor Hester,' said Lizzie. 'I hate her to be miserable. Honestly, I could *murder* Jonah.'

CHAPTER TWENTY-TWO

Hester was sitting in Cobblestones café, staring out at the early March sunshine, thinking about Jonah. Although she was aware of a sense of loss – of missing him – her concern was not simply connected with the fact that she might never see him again. What primarily concerned her was the fear that, at some point in her recounting of the past, she'd touched upon some aspect that had caused Lucy so much pain that further contact was now impossible. Hester was convinced that it was during Jonah's reporting back to Lucy that the trouble had arisen and she cast her mind back again and again over the conversations she'd had with him.

Blaise's warning that it should be a truthful history haunted her, though she could think of no point where she'd dissimulated. Perhaps, in trying to defend Michael from his grandson's judgement she'd made an error in playing down the after-effects of the fight, yet she'd hated the thought of Jonah seeing his grandfather as vacillating and weak: forced to flee the house with his mistress and child. Had the very thing that she and Blaise feared actually happened? Had the heroic figure that Jonah had built up over the years crumbled to dust in the light of reality? As Blaise had observed: 'The young can be so puritanical.' Perhaps it was this aspect from which Lucy had never been able to recover: seeing her father with Eleanor in London. Away from the family, Eleanor would have made her relationship with Lucy's father brutally clear and Hester wondered how the sudden flight had been explained to the child.

At Christmas, with Blaise, Hester had not yet been aware of Jonah's reaction. She'd received a postcard just after his visit, thanking her and telling her that he'd gone straight to Chichester because his father was ill; nothing more except a Christmas card. It wasn't until they'd returned from the North that she'd begun to expect another visit. As the weeks passed she'd grown concerned – perhaps his father's health had deteriorated – yet both she and Clio were surprised at Jonah's silence: it wasn't in character. Then they'd heard through Lizzie that Jonah was back in London, his father was much better, but he was too busy to make the journey to Exmoor.

Hester was glad now that Clio was with her. She'd begun to suffer from anxiety attacks that she seemed unable to control; first thing on waking, or if she was disturbed in the early hours, her gut would churn and her heart would pound with un-named fear. She tried to rationalize these attacks by reminding herself that added to her anxiety about Jonah was the pressing question as to whether she should sell Bridge House. It gradually occurred to her that she was waiting for some move from Jonah before she committed herself: that, in some way, Jonah – and Lucy – were involved in this decision. She told herself that such an idea was foolish yet she couldn't dismiss it from her mind. There was something more to be resolved at Bridge House.

At Christmas, Blaise had asked her if she'd decided what to do and she'd admitted that she had no idea.

How good it had been to see him, to spend such a special time with him! Even Clio, usually so busy and vital and restless, had been calm and quietly happy.

'This reminds me of that year we spent together after the war,' he'd said one evening as the three of them had eaten supper together, discussing the poetry of R. S. Thomas. 'D'you remember, Hes? You, me and Edward.' He'd smiled at Clio, including her. 'We were preparing Hester for Cambridge,' he told her. 'Edward was a very hard taskmaster and we didn't stop for a second, even when we were eating. There were books everywhere.'

'Rather like here,' Clio had said, nodding towards the shelves and piles of books, and they'd all laughed.

'That was a good time, wasn't it?' he'd asked Hester when Clio went to make coffee and they were alone together.

'The best,' she'd answered simply.

He'd stared at her, his eyes seeming to question her, as if surprised at the speed and directness of her reply.

'What was the play we were reading at nights round the fire?' he asked. '*Twelfth Night*, wasn't it?'

She'd allowed a tiny pause. 'That's right. You were Orsino and I was Viola, amongst other characters. Edward was Malvolio with his yellow stockings.' Then Clio had come back in and she'd changed the subject.

'Clio's been happy here,' he'd said on the eve of their departure. 'I feel confident that she's taken the right path. It's good to think of you together just at the moment.'

Now, Hester sipped at her coffee and thought about Clio. On their return to Bridge House, Lizzie had greeted the news of Clio's decision to stay for a while with delight.

'You shall plan the nuts and bolts of the film event,' she'd cried. 'Where the tutors and the students stay and how they get here and all that nightmare. Oh, what a relief. You must be paid the proper rate, of course, just as anybody else would have been. You will do it, won't you? Wonderful! This is brilliant.'

It was evident that Clio was thrilled to be asked – and very grateful to be paid – and was now busy organizing the event. She was extremely business-like and very efficient, and Hester was relieved to see that some of Clio's pain and fear was alleviated by this distraction. This was another reason for staying at Bridge House for the present: she wanted to be able to give Clio space to find her feet again. She could see how much Clio was missing Peter and how hard she was trying to come to terms with a huge loss: Peter and her work had been nearly all of her life and now she had lost both. Hester knew the overwhelming attraction and the danger of being involved with someone who understood your work. Twice she'd had affairs with men with whom she could share mentally as well as physically, a delightful combination – until the relationships fractured and there had been nowhere to go to recover.

She knew that Clio was in that position now and she wondered what the future held for her god-daughter. Hester hoped that Clio wasn't programmed to be attracted only to older, successful men. This had been her own downfall: her upbringing, influenced first by her father and then by Edward, Michael and Blaise, had made the men of her own age seem rather callow. She'd been drawn to mentor-figures, imagining that by drawing them into her life, even physically into herself, she would be imbued with some measure of their wisdom and wit and knowledge, much as Nimue had sucked out the essence of Merlin's magical secrets drop by drop with her kisses.

The detached part of her character had saved her, enabled her to survive the break-ups and betrayals, and watching her friends' relationships had strengthened her growing belief that marriage was not necessarily the answer to loneliness or hurt: often quite the contrary. For herself she'd deemed it wisest to stay unattached, remembering Edward's warning words: 'We don't make very good marriage material.' Reflecting again on Clio, wondering how best to assist her, Hester was suddenly distracted by a child's voice raised in frustration and a scene unfolding beyond the window.

A young man pushing a double baby-buggy had paused outside the toyshop on the far side of the road. The older child was gesticulating, demanding to be taken into the shop, struggling in his seat whilst his father remonstrated firmly.

'Not now,' he was saying. 'We're waiting for Mummy. Perhaps later.'

The child's voice rose even higher in protest. 'Now,' he cried. 'I want to go *in*.'

One or two passers-by glanced at the father sympathetically but others shook their heads disapprovingly. He was clearly discomfited and spoke to his son more sharply, putting him back into his seat very firmly. This caused a further uproar, the child wept as if he'd been badly hurt and the baby began to whimper. Hester felt a pang of compassion for the young father, who now crouched down beside the buggy in an attempt to calm his children. Sensing a weakening of resolve, the older boy sobbed harder, begging to be released, and the man reluctantly began to undo the straps, enabling the boy to climb out. At this point the whole episode might have been resolved except that the mother now appeared around the corner and, seeing her, the boy began to cry hysterically and run towards her. As Hester finished her coffee and went to pay, she saw the boy's mother drop rather theatrically to one knee, taking him to her bosom, ostentatiously comforting him.

'See,' she seemed to be saying. 'I am only away for a few minutes and harmony disintegrates.'

Hester was interested to see that the young man's face grew dark with various emotions: annoyance that he'd been disobeyed; embarrassment that his failure had been witnessed so publicly; and indignation at the child's defection – after all, he had been neither harsh nor cruel. The mother's face wore a different aspect: a faint air of triumph that the child had run to *her*; it was *she* who had comforted and quieted him. The father turned abruptly and began to push the buggy across the road, mother and son following. Their car was parked outside the café and now, as Hester came out on to the pavement, she could hear them arguing, quietly but bitterly, as they folded the buggy and put the children into their seats.

'You always give in to him.'

'I do not. You're just too stern with him, that's all. He's not three yet.'

'I thought we'd agreed that when either of us

made a stand we'd support each other. We agreed that discipline is important.'

'You're just a control freak. He's always OK with me.'

'Only because you're so scared of losing his affection that you give him what he wants . . .'

What a pity it was, Hester reflected, that two people who had presumably once been lovers should descend to this level of bickering and fighting over their child. At what point did gentle, kind, loving conversation morph into tiny bitter remarks, deadly verbal battles for control, insults disguised by forced laughter bandied publicly across dinner tables? How soon did the language of lovers become an ongoing slanging match where it seemed that one or other must be defeated, controlled by jibes and cruel asides?

Saddened by these reflections, she crossed the road, heading for Shakespeare and Hall, the bookshop at the top of the street, where Dawn had several books and some CDs that Hester had ordered.

Books and music, thought Hester with relief, her spirits rising as she waved cheerfully to Dawn through the window. So much more reliable than people.

CHAPTER TWENTY-THREE

It was Lucy who persuaded Jonah to reconsider his decision about Lizzie's film event.

'You can't let Lizzie down,' she said firmly, when he mentioned it on the telephone one evening. 'You simply can't, Jonah. I had no idea you were contemplating it. It isn't fair to her.'

At the other end of the telephone Jonah sat slumped on his old sofa, surrounded by sheets of typescript, newspapers and a plate of half-eaten pasta.

'It's not just a question of the event,' he said half irritably. 'It will be very difficult to be at Michaelgarth without the problem of Hester coming up.'

'I've been thinking about that,' his mother said. 'I think that you'll have to go and see her.'

Jonah was silent. The prospect of seeing Hester filled him with fearfulness. He'd imagined the

341

scene already – after all, he *was* a scriptwriter – and had heard her say lightly, 'Well, yes, I suppose Michael did kill Edward but it was unintentional and it was all such a long time ago.'

He was appalled by the possibility of having to witness a detached indifference to his grandfather's crimes: adultery, murder, cowardice. His mother's outburst that evening had horrified him, especially when reviewed in the light of Hester's description of the fight, and he'd been unable to see any way forward. He felt that Hester had let him down, that she wasn't the person he'd grown so fond of, and the fact that Lucy seemed to be managing better than he was only made him more wretched. He had brought this upon her, forced her to open the terrible wounds and revisit the past, and now he was ashamed that she was more able to come to terms with it than he was.

'Jonah?' His mother's voice in his ear was warm and understanding. 'The point is that we can't just leave it here. I know how you're feeling but it wasn't your fault that we started this. I felt the time was right somehow; the past was forcing itself back into my consciousness. Oh, I know that I was very upset that evening when you came here straight from Hester but some of that was to do with Jerry being ill and going into hospital. Now that he's back

342

home and we're coping again I see things slightly differently.'

'How?' he asked bleakly.

'Well, at the very least we can't pretend that it hasn't happened. You've been to Bridge House and met Hester and she's told you stories about your grandfather and her family. The big stumbling block is Hester herself. We both feel the same about her, don't we? We loved her and trusted her, she got right under our skins, and now we feel that she betrayed us. Well, OK. Perhaps it's time she knew how we both feel. I couldn't do much about it sixty years ago but we can now. I really thought that I couldn't bear it when you arrived that night and we talked. And then Jerry being so ill has put doing anything about it right out of court.' A little pause. 'I know it sounds odd, Jonah, but that original feeling has come back a bit. The conviction that if I could only sort out how I feel about the past then I might have a chance to deal with what Jerry and I have to face in the future. Poor old Jerry. He's got excruciating joint and muscle pains and he's suffering withdrawal symptoms from the extra steroid treatment but he's being so brave about it. God, I hate this bloody disease.'

'I'm sorry, Mum. It's hell, isn't it? OK. I'll phone Lizzie and tell her that I'll do the event. She's got one of her get-togethers coming up soon; you know the sort of thing I went to before? All the tutors are going to Michaelgarth to discuss the shape of the film event and what they'd like to contribute. I'll go down and take it from there.'

'Don't think I'm avoiding my own responsibility here, Jonah.' Lucy's voice was firm. 'The odd thing was that while Jerry was in such a bad way I was seized with a terrible anger, a kind of absolute determination not to give in – or let him give in either. And, when he was getting better, that anger remained but it was deflected back towards the past and I decided then that as soon as Jerry can be left I shall go down and see Hester.'

Jonah was taken aback. 'Well, if you think you can handle it . . .'

'I think I have to. If I don't it will haunt me for ever. Worse than that, it's had such a crippling effect in certain areas of my life that I'm tired of it. I can't afford it any more. That anger I felt, watching Jerry suffering so much, seemed to burn away all my fear and helplessness. I just want to deal with it. I can't leave him yet and he's got follow-up appointments for a few weeks but I don't believe I shall feel differently when the time comes.'

'And if I should see Hester while I'm at Michaelgarth?'

'Then you must tell her the truth. It won't deflect me from what I have to do. Put it this way, Jonah: I feel strongly that this will work out as it should. I told you I just have some kind of premonition that it'll be OK. I lost my confidence in it for a while when things were very black but now I believe that it's the right thing to do. I know that sounds fey and weird but I hope you can accept it.'

Jonah was silent, remembering his arrival at Bridge House and the vision of his grandfather rushing out into the wild night.

'Yes,' he said, 'yes, I can go with that.'

'Thanks,' she said gratefully. 'And thanks for being around so much for the last few months. You've been such a comfort and a help, and we both truly appreciate it. I'm sorry you've got a lot of work to catch up on but you mustn't abandon Lizzie.'

'I know. I was just being cowardly, really, suspecting that the whole thing might flare up again and not knowing how to handle it. It's OK now you've told me how you're feeling about it and I think you're right. We need to lay a few ghosts. I'll telephone her now.'

Despite this new confidence he was glad to hear Piers' voice answering the telephone and saying that Lizzie was in the shower.

'Could you give her a message? Tell her I'll be able to manage that meeting after all. I'll phone later to confirm travel details.'

'She'll be very pleased to hear that.'

Jonah thought he could detect a note of amusement in Piers' voice but, manlike, neither of them found it necessary to prolong the conversation.

Jonah went to the fridge and opened a can of beer. Relieved that the right decision had been taken, putting aside the prospect of actually seeing Hester again, he settled back on the sofa, pulled the pages of script towards him and began to work.

'But what did he *say*?' cried Lizzie. She'd come downstairs from her shower, her hair bundled into a towel, and now stood beside the Aga, holding a glass of Cabernet Sauvignon. Lying on his back in the old dog basket, all four paws in the air, Lion stirred at the sound of her voice. She stretched out her foot, poking his tummy with her toes, and his tail beat once or twice before he subsided back into a deep sleep.

'I've told you what he said. That he'd be coming down to your meeting and that he'd phone nearer the time to confirm travel details.'

Piers, who was cooking a risotto, stirred the

contents of the pan and then sat down at the table and picked up his own glass.

'But you could have asked him,' said Lizzie discontentedly. 'You know, why he's changed his mind and things like that.'

'I thought that you'd probably question him in due course; give him the third degree. Anyway, I imagine that it was one of your messages that did the trick.'

'But I'd hardly started, sweetie.' Lizzie sounded almost regretful. 'I'd left a message on his answerphone telling him that I thought he was a miserable bastard for letting me down, something like that. And I'd texted something short but to the point. "Ring me, you rat," I think it was. But the campaign was hardly under way.'

'Well, he obviously didn't need too much coercion.'

'Mmm. I'd thought up one or two rather stinging and offensive remarks,' Lizzie said thoughtfully. 'I rehearsed them to Clio but she was a bit shocked, I could tell.'

'She doesn't work in the theatre,' observed Piers. 'The poor girl simply doesn't have the same gift for invective. She hasn't had your opportunities.'

Lizzie grinned at him. 'True. I'm thrilled really. I do love Jonah, you know. And now Clio will be able to find out why he's avoiding Hester. I can't tell you how glad I am that I've got hold of Clio. There's more to this film weekend than I'd imagined. She's fantastic! She thinks of every tiny detail.' She gave a little sigh. 'I wonder what she'll do, Piers? D'you think she'll go back to London?'

Piers hesitated for a moment. 'It's odd you should ask that. I was thinking about her today at the Rotary lunch. Do you remember Mark Allen, the lawyer? He was talking about some clients of his. They're an elderly couple from Norfolk who've won the lottery and bought a big house in the Brendon Hills and they're rather out of their depth. As far as I can gather they're the "if you've got it flaunt it" sort, but haven't quite got the confidence to go about fitting out this rather grand house. What they really need is someone who could organize decorators and curtains and all those things but also generally keep an eye on things until they've sold their bungalow and can move down. Mark said that they want to give a big house-warming party and I remember thinking, They need our Clio. They've asked him if he can recommend someone who isn't too intimidating to help them out and I was wondering if it's an area she ought to explore. After all, there are loads of people out there who don't have time for the things they need to get done: organizing events, sourcing furnishings for hotels, walking dogs, fetching people from trains, buying presents. You'd think that Clio would be run off her feet if she just let it be known that she could provide services like that.'

'But that's an amazing idea.' Lizzie was gazing at him, her eyes wide with visions. 'Clio could run her own business – she'd be brilliant at it. But how do you start that kind of thing? How does it actually work? You can't just go round asking people in the supermarket if they need help.'

Piers sat for a moment, thinking about it. 'She could advertise, though in my experience that's not always very successful, and she could put flyers in the local shops – if she intends to stay around here – and she'd probably need a website so that anyone looking for help on the Internet would be directed to it. Anyway, Clio would be much more clued up about it than I am; after all, she's been doing this kind of thing in London, hasn't she? I remember her telling me about a corporate skiing holiday she organized and she planned all the hospitality events for their clients. She's probably got lots of good contacts if she were to think about going for it, and I suppose she could use what she's doing for you as part of her portfolio. Your name recommending her would certainly attract some attention.'

'Oh, I see what you mean.' Lizzie was getting the idea of it now. 'You mean she could talk our event up a bit? Make it sound quite a big thing?'

'Exactly. But she'd need to find other things or people to recommend her. Something she's organized in the past. A party? The skiing holiday?'

He got up to give the risotto another stir while Lizzie sipped her wine thoughtfully.

'It sounds perfect,' she said. 'How clever of you.'

Piers shrugged. 'Not particularly. It was talking to Mark that made me think about Clio. It's her thing, isn't it? The difficulty might be supporting herself while she gets it up and running. Anyway, there's no point getting carried away just yet. She might have something else in mind.'

'I don't think she has. Shall I suggest it to her or will you?'

'I wouldn't dream of it,' he answered, looking slightly alarmed. 'I told you, it was just talking to Mark that gave me the idea. It's a bit much, telling Clio that I've got her future planned out for her. You can't go about deciding on how other people should run their lives.'

'I can. It's brilliant. It would be a terrible waste not to mention it to her and it's so right for Clio.'

Lizzie put down her glass and went to him, slipping her arms round him. 'I must go and dry my hair. How long until we eat?'

He kissed her. 'Ten minutes. Can you warn Father? He's sitting by the fire in the study reading the paper. Last time I looked in he was asleep.'

She went away and Piers poured some more wine. Perhaps he would have another word with Mark, sound him out a bit more about this couple, just in case Clio were to be attracted by the idea.

351

CHAPTER TWENTY-FOUR

Sitting on the sofa, with Tess curled up beside her, Lucy stared into the dying fire and wondered if it had been right to talk Jonah into changing his mind. She'd been too absorbed in looking after Jerry to think much about the on-going effect her reaction had had on Jonah, that night back in early December, and it hadn't occurred to her that it would impinge on his work with Lizzie. Lucy could see the difficulties here but felt very strongly that it would be wrong for him to back out, not only because it was unprofessional, but also because some instinct warned her that both she and Jonah would be damaged if they continued to allow the past to remain unchallenged.

A tiny picture formed in Lucy's head: Hester, down on one knee, stretching out a hand to the uncertain child who stood clutching her father's hand and a grey plush rabbit. Now, as she sat stroking Tess's silky, high-domed head that lay heavily against her knee, Lucy knew that it was Hester who remained to be challenged. The more she considered it, the more it became clear that only Hester could explain why the four of them – Hester, Edward, Michael and Eleanor – had behaved in such a way. Only she was left to direct some light into that dark corner of the past.

Lucy remembered that sometimes, when she'd been growing up, she'd had an impulse to say to a friend's parent or a teacher, 'My father killed someone and it was all my fault.' The impulse was often very strong, though she'd never succumbed to it, and she wondered now if it had been a desire to see if the other person's reaction would be as shocked as she'd imagined. She'd seen herself as a fraud, deceiving her friends and teachers, because they didn't know the truth about her; wondering if they'd be so friendly, or if they'd continue to trust her, if she were to speak out. All the while, the memory of Eleanor's whispered words – 'Your father has killed Edward' – and the expression of shame and defeat on her father's face had continued to weigh on her mind and her heart, heavy and dark, along with the terrible guilt that it had been her fault for breaking the Midsummer Cushion.

When she'd heard the casual words with which Hester had explained the accident to the tapestry, Lucy had felt an instant easing of mind but also she'd been gripped with anger: anger with herself for giving in to the foolish superstition inherited from her mother. To carry that burden for so many years and then have it described as a simple piece of misfortune was almost more than she could bear. Yet she could see now that it could be true, that the string had worn thin and it had required only a touch to send the whole thing down; anyone dusting it might have done it. At the time it had seemed cataclysmic: she'd touched the Midsummer Cushion and broken it and something terrible had happened that had affected them all. The two events had been welded irrevocably together in her mind: the breaking of the precious, magical heirloom had foreshadowed the disintegration of the family. Even when she was old enough to reason with herself, to rationalize the events of that night, at some deeper level the superstitious fear and guilt remained: by disobeying the rules and destroying the heirloom she'd been responsible for the tragedy. This had been her interpretation. Clearly the tapestry had had no such connotation for Hester. That much, at least, was a relief.

Pulling Tess's long silky ears, Lucy considered

how she might approach Hester. An invitation had been issued; it would be simple enough to accept it – but what then? How should she express her feelings, how ask the crucial questions? In her mind's eye Hester was still young; how would she cope with meeting the elderly woman that Jonah had described? Lucy shook her head, shifting forward in her seat so that Tess stirred and looked at her enquiringly.

'Time to go out,' said Lucy. 'Come on, wake up.'

She let Tess out into the garden and stood at the back door, shivering a little and thinking about Jonah. Since that moment in the attic, when he'd first seen the photograph of Bridge House, he'd been driven by a fascination to find out more. He'd longed to know about his grandfather and it was evident that he'd connected with him very deeply after that first visit to Hester. Lucy regretted her outburst – it was cruel that he should be so brutally disillusioned – yet she simply hadn't been able to continue to hide the truth, especially when it was proposed that some kind of screenplay should be made out of the story. The prospect of it still had the power to shock Lucy; again and again she sought for some clue to the way Hester must be thinking about it all that she should even consider the idea, let alone encourage Jonah in it.

A thought occurred to her: in dismissing the breaking of the Midsummer Cushion so lightly, Hester had actually offered some kind of consolation and lifted the burden of guilt. Perhaps she might also be able to shed light on the events that had followed, making some sense of it all and so easing some of the pain.

Peering into the darkness for Tess, Lucy wondered what Hester might possibly say that could bring comfort. It was easy enough to account for the affair between Eleanor and Michael: he, grieving, missing his wife; she, lonely, convinced her husband was dead. That wasn't the problem. It was the way they'd behaved that night on the sofa before Edward had come in, and the way they'd run out on Hester, leaving her to face the music, even though she'd encouraged them to go, that was hard to understand and forgive.

'Why did they behave like that?' she wanted to ask Hester. 'As if they didn't care if he discovered them though they must have known it would send him over the edge into madness. What did Eleanor mean when she said that something terrible would happen and it would be my fault? If it hadn't been for me would they have left Bridge House once they knew Edward was alive and coming home? Why did you stop my father going for help and why did you make him run away once you'd found out Edward was dead? *Why didn't you write to me?*'

Lucy caught herself up, surprised by this final question that had come from nowhere. Just briefly she suffered again the anguish of pain, the sense of abandonment by the family. Even after her father had died not one letter or card had come for her, although they must have guessed where she'd been sent. No word from Hester or Nanny or Jack. Oh, how lonely she'd been then. Not until she'd met Jerry had her sense of rejection and loneliness been eased. He'd cherished and valued her and now she had every intention of making herself strong, casting off fear and guilt, in order to care for him. If this meant confronting Hester then she would do it if she could only find the courage. It was one thing speaking of the intention to Jonah; another thing to carry it out.

Tess appeared out of the darkness and barged past her into the kitchen, looking eagerly for her bedtime biscuit, and Lucy followed her inside and shut and locked the door behind her.

Jerry was awake, propped up by pillows, reading as usual; the bed was strewn with newspapers and books were piled on his bedside table. He smiled at Lucy, taking off his reading spectacles, glad to see her. Somehow he derived comfort simply from her presence.

'I've got a pot of mint tea,' she told him cheerfully, 'and some of those biscuits that you like from Marks and Spencer.'

She set the tray down on a small wooden table on castors, putting out mugs and little plates and making a picnic of it, and he pulled himself higher up on his pillows with a sense of anticipation. By rearranging the room, putting a chest of drawers in the spare bedroom which they now used as a dressing room, she'd contrived a space where he could sit comfortably at the table so making a welcome change from being in bed.

'Did you sleep at all?' she asked, holding his stick in readiness as he pulled on his dressing-gown and swung his feet to the floor. She noticed that his pyjama jacket had the usual patches of dampness and saw how the rash across his face formed a butterfly formation over his nose and cheekbones – and she was seized with fear and compassion. 'I hope the telephone bell didn't wake you?'

'I was awake,' he admitted, 'but I've had a good rest. Who was it?'

'It was Jonah.' She pretended not to see the effort it was for him to walk to the little table, knowing how he hated to have his pain made a subject of preoccupation. 'He was talking about going down to Exmoor to see Lizzie again. He's one of the tutors at her film event. D'you remember I told you about it? It sounds such fun. Twenty sixth-formers are to be selected from schools all over the West Country to write and act out a half-hour piece of television, which they have to film and produce themselves. Lizzie's got a team of professionals to show them how it's done and the local television has agreed to show it, if it's up to scratch. Jonah's getting a script worked out in case they don't have any ideas to begin with. He sent his love to you.'

'He's been spending too much time down here.' Jerry's tone implied that he thought Jonah was making a fuss, though Lucy knew just how much his son's visits had meant to him. 'I'm glad he's back in the swing of it.'

'We're lucky that he can be flexible,' she said as she poured the mint tea from a little flowered pot. 'It's been good that he could come down so often this last couple of months but you're much better now, aren't you? I was wondering if we might go out tomorrow. I could drive us over to Stansted House for coffee or to Bosham; not too far but just to make a change. The weather forecast is good and Tess could have a run somewhere. Do you think you'd manage it?'

'I'm sure I could.' Jerry took his mug and sipped gratefully at the clean, sharp-tasting liquid; the concoction of medication he took each evening always left a disgusting coating in his mouth and ruined the flavour of his after-dinner coffee. He ate some biscuit and watched Lucy's down-turned face; she looked thoughtful but not overly anxious, so that was good. He'd always been aware of the shadow that edged her happiness. He'd been told by Aunt Mary that it was to do with losing both her parents in quick succession when she was small. He'd hoped that it was something she might be able to cast off as they grew up together but it had remained present if not visible, rather like something glimpsed from the corner of your eye, but which disappeared if you turned to look at it directly. He wondered if she'd ever actually been able to do that: to look it in the eye, as it were. Not that he could ask her. He'd feel a fool and, anyway, she'd withdraw a bit and pretend that he was imagining things. But sometimes he'd wanted to – to ask her if she'd ever tried it because he had the feeling that if she did then it might prove that the shadow was simply that: something that would evaporate if her bright gaze was turned upon it. Well, something like that. Not that he knew anything about it except that he wished she'd try it.

Because it held her back, he knew that much. Oh, she'd struggled with it, he could see that; wrestled with it, refused to go under with it, but it was as if she was wrestling with something she couldn't quite see or understand and so she and the shadow were unequally matched and she couldn't ever quite cast it off. It had clipped her wings and stopped her from flying free – if a shadow could do that. He wanted her to be free of it – oh, not for himself, though he knew how much harder she was trying to overcome the shadow now, ever since he'd been diagnosed with this filthy disease. He knew she wanted to be strong and positive, to take the weight. But it wasn't because of that he wanted it. It was simply because he'd like to see her flying free, really free, just once.

She glanced up at him, as if aware of a new quality in the silence, and briefly, as they stared at each other, some deep exchange was made. He smiled at her.

'OK, Luce?' he asked. He'd been asking it at intervals through the years and it meant variously: 'Are you happy?', 'Just saying hello', 'Is anything worrying you?', 'I'm sorry about the way things are at the moment.' He was incapable of speaking aloud his true feelings but the question symbolized his love for her.

She decoded it correctly. 'Of course I am. I was thinking about Jonah going to Exmoor again, and about Hester.' She straightened her back, as if she'd made a decision, smiled at him and stood up. 'And I'm looking forward to tomorrow. I'm going to have a shower. Shan't be long. There's another cup, if you want it.'

He sat alone, listening to the familiar sounds and drinking his tea, and for some reason he could not understand, his heart felt lighter. It was as though his very real longing for the shadow to be lifted had communicated itself to her and strengthened her resolve.

CHAPTER TWENTY-FIVE

Some days later, driving into Dulverton, Clio was finding it difficult to concentrate. Piers' idea, conveyed to her by Lizzie, seemed to expand in her head and crowd out all other thoughts. Once or twice in the past she'd considered setting up on her own but she'd never taken it very seriously. However, listening to Lizzie explaining about the couple from Norfolk had sparked her imagination and she'd begun to feel alert and interested, her thoughts already darting ahead, thinking how such an undertaking might be achieved. Hester was quite as positive as Lizzie, both of them convinced that she could make a go of it.

'And what a great time to start,' Lizzie had said enthusiastically, 'whilst you're here with Hester. You could work from here and keep your costs down until you've got it going a bit.'

It was only after Lizzie had gone back to

Michaelgarth, whilst they were sitting in the book-room after supper, that Clio had raised the subject of Hester's selling Bridge House.

'There's no immediate rush,' Hester assured her at once. 'Robin has already raised his loan against his share of the house and Amy can wait a little longer. Anyway, wherever I go I'm sure there will be room for you until you're ready to branch out on your own.'

'I suppose all I'd need is my laptop and a tele-phone,' said Clio thoughtfully. 'I'd go to the clients, they wouldn't come to me, so I wouldn't need an office as such. But could I make a living out of it?'

'Perhaps the bank could give you some advice about that?' suggested Hester. 'You said you'd got some savings so they would tide you over to begin with, and Lizzie is going to pay you, isn't she?'

'As soon as I've got a business account sorted out. I have to keep things separate to make the tax man happy, you see.'

'Well, then. Perhaps this is the moment to do that and discuss this new idea with someone at the bank at the same time.'

Clio fiddled about restlessly, getting up to throw a log on the fire, kneeling down on the rug to stroke St Francis who slept on regardless.

'You have nothing to lose,' Hester said after a

moment, 'by asking questions. Talk to your bank and talk to this couple. Why not?'

'Do you think I'd manage? Organizing a whole house?'

'Do *you* think you'd manage?' Hester smiled at her encouragingly. 'You've organized events in London and you're doing a pretty good job for Lizzie, by the sounds of things. What's the difference?'

Clio shook her head. 'I suppose there isn't any, not really. It's just the thought of actually going it alone; it's a lot of responsibility.'

'But you like responsibility.'

'Well, I do actually. I enjoy a challenge. It's just all the details you don't have to think about when you're employed. Like what do I charge?'

'I think you simply have to apply your common sense to that. If you decide to stay in this part of the country then you must work out how much you'd need to live on per annum. It would be rather less down here, for instance, than if you want to live in London. Divide it by fifty-two and you've got a rough idea of where to start.'

'I suppose I ought to check out the competition. I could have a look on the Internet and see if there's anyone around here.' Suddenly she'd been seized by excitement. 'It would be rather fun, wouldn't it? Doing my own thing?'

Hester had nodded. 'Great fun.'

And now, as she drove along Lady Street, under the churchyard wall and into Fore Street, she was gripped again by that same sense of excitement. As she waited for someone to back their car out of a space outside the butcher's shop she began to concentrate on her shopping list. Most important was Hester's birthday present. Clio had already decided to visit Julia Maxwell's delightful shop, Eastern Importers, and look at the wonderful Paisley shawls. Hester's ancient shawl was thread-bare, to say the least, and one of Julia's shawls might be just the answer. Anyway, Clio enjoyed browsing, looking at the jewellery and the leather bags, talking to Julia. She might even have some tips on starting a business. Clio parked the car and got out. She felt happy, alive, and, as she crossed the street, it occurred to her that she hadn't thought about Peter since early that morning. She checked her watch: there was nearly an hour before her hair appointment with Ruth at Bodmins House so there would be plenty of time for coffee in Woods after she'd bought Hester's present. She paused in the sunshine to look at the display of beautiful rugs in Julia's window and then went inside.

*   *   *

At the same moment, Hester was writing to Blaise:

So you see that it's come rather out of the blue
and taken Clio by surprise but it seems such a
good idea and she's already begun to explore the
possibilities of earning a living in what is rather
grandly called 'lifestyle management'. Piers is
speaking with the couple's lawyer to see if a
meeting can be arranged and poor Clio is now
in a state of terror mixed with bursts of real
excitement. But that's such a nice state to be in,
isn't it, especially when one is young? Rather
exhausting later in life! I can't say that I feel in
the least like that about leaving Bridge House. I
suppose I could take the option of remaining
here but I can only say that something has
changed and the prospect of staying on doesn't
quite feel the same any longer. That sounds
rather foolish but you might understand. It's as if
Robin has triggered off a different way of my
looking at the future. I suddenly don't feel up
to the responsibility of this big old house without Robin and Amy as co-owners. This might be
irrational but I can't quite get back to feeling how
I did before he telephoned.

As to Clio: at least being here will give her a
breathing space but she'll have to look for her

own place soon. She's been searching the Internet for other lifestyle management businesses and it looks as if being centred around here might be quite sensible, not too much competition but a good balance of town and country – and she loves Dulverton so she might look for a small cottage to rent there. Of course, if I were to move into the town then we could go on sharing for a while. To be truthful, Blaise, it's a rather tempting idea but also a selfish one from my point of view. I'm finding Clio's young, lively company very comforting. However, neither of us could live with the other indefinitely and I can't decide whether an early break would be best all round. When we sell, I *do* hope to make enough money to be able to give her a little bit of a buffer to help her with this new project. We shall see.

We've heard that Jonah will be coming down soon to see Lizzie again so we're hoping that we might find out a bit more about his unexpected silence. It's still a puzzle to me that he should have been quite so non-communicative. I try to persuade myself that it is simply pressure of work combined with his own commitments in London and with his family that have distracted him from his discoveries about the past, but there was so much more to it than that. I think you will agree,

Blaise, that I am not someone who is given to wild flights of fancy, yet I felt that Jonah was not simply looking up an old family friend. I described to you at Christmas – because I couldn't do it justice in a letter – how he reacted on his arrival here and we agreed that, in some curious way, Jonah connected with Michael. It was another wild, elemental night and it was clear that some vibration from that other emotionally charged evening touched him. Ever since then he has been utterly involved in Michael's story – and in us too. I can completely understand that he hasn't had *time* to come back to see us; what I can't understand is his *silence*. Jonah doesn't, in modern parlance, 'do' silence. He is by nature a communicator and I know that Lizzie, who is an old friend of his, is just as puzzled.

By this time you will have guessed that I am fearful that I have told him something that, having now been related to Lucy, has struck some tender point or been misunderstood by her. I have sometimes been accused of being too detached, even cold-hearted, but with Jonah this has not been so. I feel sad, as if I have inadvertently damaged something very dear to me, but, more importantly, I fear that some opportunity might have been lost here, though I don't know what it is. Anyway, he is coming down soon and I hope we shall see him or have a message from him.

Oh goodness, Blaise! What a screed! On a happier note, St Francis sends greeting to Jeoffrey. What a delightful person he is, and when I saw him curled up in the sunshine on a chair in the chapel I thought of Christopher Smart's lines 'For there is nothing sweeter than his peace when at rest'. I hope that the usual winter convent bug, which has been afflicting you all, has abated now that the spring is here again.

I know I don't need to ask but I shall anyway – prayers, please, for guidance at this particular time.

With my love,
Hester

St Francis came sidling and winding round her ankles, and Hester put the top on her pen, pushed back her chair and reached for her shawl.

'Quite right, old friend,' she murmured. 'We need some exercise. Let's go and pick some catkins. Does that sound appropriate?'

As they crossed the lawn together and entered the wood, Hester realized that, in seeking his own history, Jonah had reminded her of things she thought she'd forgotten long since. In recreating the past so vividly for him, and searching her own memory so ruthlessly, she'd become vulnerable again. As she passed between the dazzling gold of the kingcups with their brightly glossed leaves, her usually undefined melancholy became focused and she seemed to hear voices in the river's whisper.

'*And what's her history?*'

'*A blank, my lord. She never told her love . . .*'

She remembered Blaise's question at Christmas: 'That was a good time, wasn't it?' and her own, swift reply: 'The best.'

Well, it was true; there have been many good times since but that brief time with the three of them together was the best. Hester wrapped the shawl more closely around her, as if to ward off loss and loneliness and the terrors of old age, whilst St Francis stalked ahead, tail held high, and down in the woods the yaffle laughed.

CHAPTER TWENTY-SIX

As Jonah travelled down to Michaelgarth he was filled with trepidation. Even though it had been agreed that he should tell the truth, the prospect of facing Hester was a daunting one. He guessed that both Lizzie and Clio now knew part of the story and he wondered how he would deal with their questions. Lizzie, he had no doubt, would be quite open and direct – as she had been with her text messages – but ready to understand his dilemma. Anyway, he had little doubt that just at present she was concentrating so much on the success of her film event that she wouldn't demand a post mortem: Lizzie would simply be relieved that he'd turned up. She would rely on Clio to deal with anything concerning Hester.

As the train slowed down for Tiverton Parkway, however, Jonah's anxiety increased. He suspected that Clio might be more difficult to deal with, protective of Hester, puzzled by his silence; Clio would require some kind of explanation – and here she was now, waiting on the platform, watching him walk towards her. He could see at once that her expression was wary and his heart sank, although part of him was ready to be defensive: he felt rather as if he had been caught between Hester and his mother. He had no desire to criticize Hester to her god-daughter yet he needed to defend his mother's reaction to Hester's version of their shared past, should the question arise.

They stood looking at one another: she with her hands in her jacket pockets, her eyes cool; he holding his overnight bag, his expression neutral. However, she said none of the things for which he'd braced himself: no recriminations, no sarcastic observations. Instead she simply looked at him intently, as if reminding herself about him, and suddenly she smiled.

'Hello, Jonah,' she said. 'Can we go somewhere to talk?'

His relief was overwhelming. 'Hello, Clio. Why not? If there's time. I'm not sure what Lizzie's got planned.'

'There's plenty of time,' she answered, as they walked out to the car. 'You'll probably think I'm being pushy and that it's none of my business but I just hoped that we could get a few things straight between us before I see Hester.'

'Does that mean that I shan't be seeing her?' he asked, cautiously.

She looked at him quickly, hopefully. 'Will you want to? We didn't know, you see, whether you planned a visit to Bridge House, and Hester didn't want to press you.'

He heaved a sigh, a great gasp of frustration, and she watched him anxiously across the roof of the car as she unlocked the doors and he threw his bag onto the back seat.

'This isn't simple,' he said almost angrily, climbing in beside her. 'It isn't just a misunderstanding or a cooling-off on my part. If you think Hester won't object I'm very willing to explain the complexities of all this to you but I don't want to put you in a difficult position.'

'I think I understand a bit of it.' Clio pulled out of the car park and they drove away. 'I know it's to do with your mother staying at Bridge House during the war. Hester thinks she's told you something that's upset your mother and she can't think what it is.'

A rather bitter smile touched Jonah's lips. 'It's rather what she didn't say that's causing the problems.'

'That's why I hoped we could have a talk. Unless you'd rather simply explain it all to Hester and leave me out of it. It's just that she's really upset, Jonah, and that's why I'm interfering. I hate muddles.'

His smile this time was a genuine one. 'I can believe that. And anyway, I think I'd like to talk it through to someone who isn't tied up in it.' Suddenly this was true. 'I've thought about it all so much that I wonder if I'm going crazy. You can give me an unbiased view.'

'I can try to.'

They drove a little way in silence before Clio swung the car left over an iron bridge into a twisting lane and presently pulled into a small lay-by beside a little stone bridge. Still without speaking, they got out and stood together, staring down at the water. The river glittered, shining in the sunshine, sweeping between miniature cliffs of red earth; willows leaned from the banks, their slender branches dipping and trembling in the clear rush of water. A grey wagtail flitted to and fro, darting from the bank out onto the rounded river stones, and making sudden swoops upstream where a shimmer of midges hung in an ever-shifting cloud beneath the branches of a great beech.

When Jonah began to speak, his arms resting on

the stone, Clio leaned nearer so as to hear him more clearly. He told the story very well, as if he'd gone over it time and again, sorting it out in his mind so that now it flowed chronologically, building the whole picture as it grew. He began by describing Michael's arrival at Bridge House with Lucy, of Eleanor's growing passion for him and his more reluctant return of love; he told of Edward's return from the Far East and of Lucy's fears of him and Eleanor, and of her love for Hester. All the while Clio listened, fascinated, her eyes on his face; though when he spoke about the fight, and Lucy's departure from Bridge House, she opened her lips as if she might interrupt – but changed her mind, waiting until he'd finished.

'So that's what happened.' He looked at her at last. 'And the terrible thing is that my mother has lived with this knowledge – that her father killed his best friend and then ran away. Or that's how it looks to her. She's seen him as a murderer and a coward and, until I first met Hester, she's refused to talk about it. Then, when I go crashing in all these years later, Hester doesn't even mention it when she tells me the story, and, to add insult to injury as far as my mother is concerned, agrees that it would make a great television play. When I told my mother in all ignorance that we were thinking about it she was utterly horrified. That's when she told me the truth at last: that Michael killed Edward and was persuaded to run away. She simply can't understand this detached outlook – and neither can I, now I know the whole truth. Of course, Hester has no idea that Mum saw it all. Well, you must be able to imagine now how impossible it would have been for me simply to carry on as if nothing had happened. I simply didn't know what to do for a while, so I did nothing. As it is, having dragged it all into the open, Mum agrees that the best thing is to face it out with Hester.'

He fell silent while Clio continued to watch him with compassion and a kind of horror.

'But, Jonah,' she said when he'd finished his recital. 'Jonah, you've got it wrong. Edward didn't die that night. I don't know why Eleanor should have told your mother that he was dead. Listen to me, Jonah. Edward didn't die.'

He stared at her, his brows drawn together. 'What do you mean?'

'He didn't die.' She put her hand on his arm and shook him slightly. 'I know he didn't. He and Blaise and Hester lived together after the war. Hester's often mentioned that time the three of them were together at Bridge House. In fact, we were talking about it at Christmas with Blaise. Edward prepared

Hester for her Oxbridge exam. He *didn't die*, Jonah.'

His eyes slid away from her urgent gaze, staring at nothing but as though he could see some other scene playing itself out in the middle distance. His face was immobile, grim.

'What happened, then?' He sounded angry, as if defying her to make sense of the story. 'She saw him go into the water . . .' He hesitated, thinking it through, suddenly seeing the weaknesses in Lucy's account. 'But . . . why should Eleanor tell my mother such a terrible lie?'

'I don't know. I'd need to think about it. But that's why Hester didn't make anything of it. Why should she? She insisted that Michael and Eleanor should go simply because it was impossible for them to stay any longer, and they agreed with her. It would have driven Edward raving mad to see them together after that. Look, Hester's told me a bit about all this in the last few weeks, mainly because she was trying to see what aspect of what she told you might have upset your mother, and although I don't know all the ins and outs of it I do know that Edward didn't die.'

'But Michael knocked him into the river, and Hester wouldn't let him go for help.'

'There must be some other explanation about

that. You must ask her. But surely this explains everything else? Obviously your mother must have been terrified and, having seen the fight, there's no reason why she shouldn't have believed Eleanor, but at least it makes sense now. Not why Eleanor should tell such a terrible lie but it makes sense about Hester.'

Jonah raised his head. On either bank of the river the combes rose high and steep, covered with larch; above the tallest of them, black against the pale blue sky, a raven flapped his slow, calm way.

Jonah took a breath, allowing his mind to experiment with this new information: Edward had not died. He longed to believe it. His heart was beginning to fill with a tremulous joy. Clio watched him anxiously, willing him to accept the truth. He turned to look at her and, quite instinctively, she opened her arms to him and they embraced.

'Sorry.' He let her go, feeling a fool. 'It's just a bit overwhelming. I'd convinced myself, you see, and yet I didn't want to think about Michael like that. The way Hester talked about him, I'd begun to love him.'

'I can see that.' She was remembering that first arrival at Bridge House and Jonah plunging out into the rain. 'Oh God! And your poor mother. Living with it all these years.'

'I'd like to speak to Hester,' he said urgently, catching her arm. 'It's not that I don't believe you, Clio, but I want her to describe it to me exactly as it happened and then I can explain it to my mother. Can you phone her?'

'There's no signal here but we'll just go straight there. Come on.'

'We need to warn her.' He hung back anxiously. 'It's not fair to arrive unexpectedly.'

'Don't be a twit.' Clio reached into her pocket for the car keys. 'Hester will be only too pleased to tell you the truth and get things sorted out. Trust me. Get in the car, Jonah. We're going to Bridge House.'

CHAPTER TWENTY-SEVEN

All day she'd been waiting. Ever since Clio had gone off to Michaelgarth, knowing that she was to pick Jonah up later that afternoon, Hester had been waiting. She'd guessed that Clio would broach the subject of his silence and all day she'd been wondering how he would react, what he might say. She'd been unable to settle to any work but had roamed through the house, into the garden and the wood, and then back again, stalked by a puzzled St Francis. Picking things up and putting them down again, unable to eat or concentrate, she'd stared out of windows, smoothed cushions, her mind distracted.

She was standing on the terrace when the car drove over the bridge and pulled up. Jonah climbed out and stood for a moment, looking at her. She instinctively raised her hand in greeting and then let it drop, her heart hammering painfully in her side, unable to move forward. It was Clio who came round the car and led Jonah in through the little gate on to the terrace. Hester could only gaze anxiously at him, trying to read his face, puzzled by the almost elated expression she saw there. He came to her and took her hand in his, and she grasped it eagerly, gratefully, still staring up at him.

'Jonah.' She spoke his name tentatively – and then Clio was there, taking her other arm and leading her into the house, through the drawing-room and on into the book-room where the fire burned, comforting and steady. Hester and Jonah stood facing each other on the hearthrug whilst Clio remained near the door, watching.

'Clio told me something amazing.' He was still holding Hester's hand. 'She told me that Edward didn't die.'

Hester frowned, puzzled. 'Didn't die?'

By the door Clio shifted, ready to put in a word of clarification, but Jonah spoke again.

'Not then. Not when they fought. She says that Michael didn't kill Edward.'

'*Kill* him?' Hester was surprised into an expression that was almost amusement. 'Of course he didn't kill him. Edward died over two years later from pneumonia. Who said Michael killed him?'

Jonah heaved a great breath. 'Mother did. She believed that Michael killed Edward and then ran away.'

'*Lucy* said that?' Hester stared at him. 'But why on earth should she imagine such a thing? She didn't even know about the fight. She was in bed.'

'No,' said Jonah. He let go of Hester's hand and gently pushed her into the armchair beside the fire. He sat opposite, leaning forward, arms on his knees, hands lightly linked together. 'No, she wasn't in bed. She couldn't sleep that night because of the storm, so she got up and went into your bedroom. She said the light was on and that she hoped you might be persuaded to read her a story. You weren't there but she got up on the little stool to look at the Midsummer Cushion.' He paused. 'Can you guess what happened next?'

Hester, sitting forward, studied him through half-closed eyes, her face strained and anxious, as if she believed this might be a test question that it was crucial she should answer correctly. Suddenly her face relaxed and she smiled sadly.

'Ah, poor Lucy. She reached up to touch the Midsummer Cushion and the string broke and it fell to the ground. Poor little girl, poor Lucy. What a shock that must have been. She loved it so much. And so that's why she asked you to ask me the question? "What happened to the Midsummer Cushion?" '

Jonah nodded. 'It haunted her, you see. She lost her balance and reached out to clutch at something to save her. It crashed down to the floor and immediately afterwards there was the fight and she thought that it was all her fault. She'd been told that if it broke something terrible would happen.'

'That was simply a family superstition.' Hester dismissed the notion. 'Nanny cashed in on it when we were little, to stop us from touching it when my mother had it reframed, and the story grew in the telling. But wait a moment, Jonah. I still don't quite see where this is leading us. So Lucy got up and went into my room and the Midsummer Cushion was broken . . . What happened after that?'

'She came downstairs, looking for you, and went into the drawing-room. She says that Michael and Eleanor were sitting on the sofa together, talking, and suddenly Edward burst in from the terrace and she hid behind the sofa . . .'

'That's it.' Hester struck her hands together lightly, almost triumphantly, her eyes closed as she recalled the scene: the shadowy fire-lit room, the drawn curtains, the newspaper sliding to the floor and the unexpected flash of colour behind the sofa.

384

'So it was Lucy,' she said softly. 'I could always imagine that scene, you know. I remember it clearly, the room as I saw it that evening as I came in from the hall and switched on the light, and yet I could never quite pin down the patch of colour behind the sofa. It shouldn't have been there and I could never place it. Oh, now I see!' She stared at him in sudden realization. 'So she saw it all.'

Jonah nodded. 'She saw the fight, saw Michael knock Edward into the river, but what then, Hester?'

She nodded, her hands clasped tremulously, reliving that evening in her mind's eye.

'Wait a moment. Yes, we were all out on the terrace. I looked down into the river and saw Edward struggling in the water. Eleanor seized me as if she thought I might plunge in after him. Michael ran out towards the road to get help but I called him back. I knew there would be no traffic at that time of night and, anyway, Edward was being dragged downstream. I knew exactly where he'd try to get ashore. He'd been familiar with the river since childhood and I guessed he'd strike out for the little beach where we used to paddle. Even on a night like that he'd have a chance there but I needed Michael to help me, you see. We all agreed that he'd have to leave Bridge House, he and

Eleanor and Lucy, but I needed his help first. We ran through the house leaving Eleanor to get Lucy up – there was no sign of her then – and when we reached the little beach Edward was there, clinging to an overhanging branch. He screamed with rage when he saw Michael but he was too weak to resist his help. Between us we dragged him up the bank and over the lawn and he fought like a child might fight an older, stronger brother. It was pitiful. We got him into the kitchen and I told Michael to bring towels and dry clothes and Edward's medicine before he went. Even when Michael had disappeared Edward continued to struggle with me but he'd been hurt and he was exhausted, and in his condition it was all too much for him. Presently, Michael just pushed in the things through the half-open door and went away. The sight of either of them would have driven Edward right over the top. It was only later that I realized that I never said goodbye to Lucy.'

Hester sat back in her chair, exhausted by her recital, her eyes closed, but she was frowning as she continued to think things through. Jonah watched her silently, and Clio, knowing now that the mis-understandings were cleared up, slipped away to the kitchen to make some tea.

'But why?' asked Hester at last. 'I still can't quite

see why Lucy jumped to the conclusion that Edward was dead.'

'Because Eleanor told her that he was. She told her that Michael had killed him and that she must never breathe a word to anyone or he would be taken away to prison. She saw Edward go into the river, and Michael run out over the bridge for help, and heard you call him back. Then she ran back upstairs as the three of you came back indoors. She didn't know you'd pulled Edward out. She has believed all these years that Michael was a murderer and a coward. That, having killed Edward, you and Eleanor persuaded him to run away.'

Hester sat in silence, her face sad. 'Poor little Lucy,' she said at last. 'How very terrible. How she must have hated us! No wonder she didn't want to talk about it. And now?' Her face altered as she looked at him. 'And you, Jonah? You believed it too?'

He opened his hands in a gesture of despair. 'What else could I do? I went straight from you to Chichester and told Mum what you'd told me. You never mentioned pulling Edward from the river and so she thought you were still covering up. I told her that we were thinking of making a play of the story and it was then that she told me what she thought was the truth. I admit I was horrified and neither of us knew what to do next.'

'How she must have hated us,' repeated Hester quietly. 'How very terrible. Why should Eleanor have done such a thing?'

Jonah shrugged. 'I can't imagine. What motive could Eleanor have had to lie? That's why Mum believed her, I suppose. There was no reason not to, and she'd seen Edward go into the river.'

Clio came in with the tray and put it on the revolving table. 'I've been thinking about that too,' she said. 'Ever since you told me, Jonah, I've been trying to think why Eleanor should do such a thing. The only reason for that kind of lie to a child is to make her behave; to do what you want her to. It was a threat to make Lucy behave. Could that be it?'

'She said she didn't want to go,' Jonah remembered. 'She got back into bed and curled up small and when Eleanor came in she pretended to be asleep. Eleanor told her they were going to London but Mum refused to get up. She struggled with Eleanor and that's when she told Mum that her father had killed Edward and if she didn't do as she was told he would go to prison. Something like that.'

'There you are then.' Clio was triumphant.

'That's the sort of thing I meant. She wanted Lucy to get up and do as she was told, double-quick. She was determined to get her own way and used the means at hand to force Lucy into action. I doubt she gave it a thought afterwards.'

'I suspect that Eleanor saw her chance and seized it.' Hester was thinking back into the past. 'She might well have even set the scene in the first place, hoping that Edward would see her and Michael together. I know that she'd had enough of pretending and I suspect that Michael had put her off for too long, using the excuse of keeping Lucy here as a shield. When Eleanor saw the opportunity she made the most of it and she certainly wouldn't have allowed Lucy to get in the way after that. It didn't do her much good. Michael was dead within a few months. But Lucy . . .' Hester shook her head sadly. 'To think of her living with such memories for all these years.'

'But not for much longer.' Jonah put his cup and saucer down. 'Do you think I could make a telephone call, Hester?'

'Of course you can.' Hester hesitated. 'Should I . . . ?'

He shook his head, smiling at her. 'Not just yet. I think she'll need time to adjust to it.'

He went out. Hester looked at Clio, dazed.

'It was a wicked thing to do,' said Clio. 'Eleanor must have been a monster.'

'I never liked her,' admitted Hester. 'But even so, I can hardly believe it of her. I suppose she had no idea of the damage. Oh, poor Lucy. She adored her father. What a terrible burden she's carried. Thank God Jonah came here, Clio. She might never have known the truth.'

'And nor might he. Is he like Michael, Hester?'

'Very like him physically, as you saw from the photograph. And he's inherited his creative instinct but I would guess that he's probably tougher emotionally. Why do you ask?'

'Oh, no reason,' answered Clio lightly. 'Just interested to know what Michael was like. I'm really hooked now, you know.'

Hester smiled. 'Yes,' she said. 'I can see that.'

CHAPTER TWENTY-EIGHT

For Jonah, there was a sense of *déjà vu* as Clio drove him to Michaelgarth. This time he was less aware of the countryside through which they drove, though he still had the impression of light and water; yet his mind ran continually on the joyful knowledge that he could think well of his grandfather again and that he could allow his natural feelings for him full rein. At the same time he was conscious of a sense of frustration. His mother's reaction had not been the unrestrained joy he'd wished for her and he was disappointed; almost cross.

'What do you mean?' she'd asked him sharply. 'What has Hester said? I was there, remember. Did you tell her that?'

It was almost as if she hadn't wanted to believe the truth; as if she saw this new explanation as some kind of trick or deception.

'But Edward didn't die, Mum,' he'd repeated.

'He didn't die until over two years later. Clio told me that before I even saw Hester. Clio is Hester's god-daughter and she told me how Edward and Hester lived together after the war. Hester and Michael pulled Edward out of the river after you'd gone back to bed, that's why you didn't know anything about it, and they all agreed that it was right that the three of you should go. He didn't run away, Mum, and he didn't kill Edward. Aren't you pleased? I am. I feel as if someone's taken a millstone off my back.'

'But why should Eleanor lie?' she'd asked indignantly, rather as if she actually thought it more likely that Eleanor was being wrongly accused than that Michael was what she'd always believed him to be.

Now, as he and Clio drove up the steep road that led onto Winsford Common, Jonah experienced again the flash of irritation with which he'd responded to this question.

'I don't know why,' he'd cried. 'You can probably answer that better than I can. The point is that Michael wasn't a murderer or a coward. That's got to be good news, hasn't it? Isn't that what's been eating you up all these years?'

'Yes,' she'd said, after a short silence. 'Yes, of course.' Her voice had been subdued. 'It's just such a shock. I simply can't believe that Eleanor should have been so wicked.'

'Sorry, Mum,' he'd said penitently. 'I didn't mean to shout at you. I just thought you'd be so pleased. It's a bit of a shock, I can see that. Would you like to speak to Hester?'

'No,' she'd answered quickly. 'No, I need to think about it, Jonah. Try to understand. Tell her . . . oh, I don't know. Tell her I'm glad and that we'll speak soon.'

He'd been disappointed, hoping perhaps that she and Hester might have had a moment of reconciliation, and he'd had the feeling that Hester had hoped for it too, though she'd managed to cover her disappointment quickly.

'There will be time for that later,' she'd said. 'The important thing is that the truth has been discovered.' She'd kissed him goodbye; the first time he'd ever seen her display any great emotion. 'I'm so glad you came back, Jonah,' she'd said.

Clio was aware of him beside her, shifting in his seat, staring out unseeingly over the common, and she guessed at the reason for his dissatisfaction. She'd seen his expression when he returned from making the phone call and wondered what Lucy had said.

'It must have been a great shock for your mum,'

she hazarded. 'After all these years. I think I'd want to search Eleanor down and kill her if it were me. I'd like to slap her about a bit and watch her suffer.'

He grimaced wryly. 'I suppose it was a bit optimistic to think that she'd feel like I do. She couldn't quite take it in.'

'Well, that's natural, isn't it? It's different for you. Correct me if I've got it wrong but you've only just got to know Michael, haven't you? I mean you've known he was a soldier and that he was blown up and things like that, but it's Hester who's made him come alive for you. You've believed he killed Edward for how long? Two months? OK. Now you know the truth and it's not too much of an adjustment. You'd begun to love him, you said, and now you can go right on with that. But your mum has lived with it for nearly sixty years. Remember how you felt for two months and you never even met him? Well, this was sixty years, Jonah! Most of her life. She's had to think about it, deal with it, all that time – and now, suddenly, it's all changed. It's not true. I don't think it would be too easy just to say, "Wow! Great! So that's that then!" I'd be bloody angry, like I said. Someone else has spoiled her life, like they've stained it or something, or irreparably damaged it. You don't wipe that kind of pain out with one telephone call.'

Jonah looked at her with relief and affection. He thought: I really like her. She's so easy to be with. I don't have that feeling I usually have with women, that if I make a particular move or say a certain thing I'm liable to transgress some unwritten rule that I should have had the sensitivity to know about without being told.

'I didn't quite see it that way,' he admitted. 'I was too busy being thankful that I could just go on feeling good about him.'

Clio thought: I really like him. I feel I've known him for ever. I suppose that could be a problem. I don't want to start feeling sisterly . . .

'And now you can go on and write your screenplay,' she said, grinning. 'That's what it's all about really. I know you creative types. You're quite ruthless.'

He laughed. 'I must admit that I've never allowed the truth to spoil a good story,' he chuckled, 'but this was just a tad different. Oh God, and now I've got to face Lizzie.'

'Lizzie's fine,' she reassured him. 'She just wants her event to work well.'

'And you've been helping her.' He glanced sideways at her. 'I've been too preoccupied to ask how you are. I gather you've quit London.'

'That's right. It wasn't going anywhere so I've

started up my own business in lifestyle management, seeing that I'm such a bossy-boots.'

He settled in his seat, relaxing. 'Far be it from me to contradict a lady. So how did you start? What gave you the idea for it?'

As they drove through Winsford and out towards the valley road, Clio told him about Piers' contact and how, through him, she'd met her first clients.

'They're quite sweet really,' she said. 'Rather insecure with all this new dosh but definitely "if you've got it flaunt it" types and they clearly feel they can trust me. Probably because I have no difficulty at all in telling them how they ought to be doing things. They like my confident approach. She told me that I'm what they describe as a "class act". I'm organizing decorators and plumbers and masses of other stuff. They found the house rather more quickly than they bargained for and they'd already got a cruise booked so I'm looking after it all for them while they're away. They want to give a party when they get back so plenty more work there. I couldn't have found a better way to start. Only time will tell whether I can actually make a living like this. If not I'll pack it all in and go back to London.'

He watched her admiringly. 'I admire your courage,' he said. 'It must be scary to go it alone.'

'It is a bit. But being with Hester has given me the space to try it. I can't rely on her much longer – she's moving, as you know – but it's giving me enough time to find my feet. These clients are taking up nearly all of my time, and I've got Lizzie as well, of course, but I might have to get a part-time job in due course to help pay the bills until I'm properly up and running.'

Watching her, he had the unsettling, almost painful, sensation of knowing exactly where his heart was located, and he folded his arms lest he should be tempted to reach out and touch her arm.

'So what is your business called?' he asked. 'The Angel in the House? Fairy Godmothers, Inc.?'

She chuckled. 'You can mock but it was really difficult to come up with anything remotely reasonable. The first thing I had to do was to open a bank account for the company so I had to think of something quickly. It kept me awake at nights, racking my brains for ideas. I kept a pad and pencil beside the bed ready to jot down names. And then I suddenly had this thought that when we were all talking about it we kept saying 'It's all about making time for people to do things; to get on with their lives. Giving them time for other more important things than waiting in for the plumber or planning a party. Giving them *time for* . . . See? So that's what

I called it, Time For, except I use the figure 4 instead of the word. I checked the Internet to see if anyone was using it as a web address and nobody was so that was that.'

'Time 4,' he repeated, trying it out. 'Very neat.'

'A friend of mine in London is working on the website for me,' she said enthusiastically. 'She's starting a web design company so we agreed that she'd design my website for a nominal fee if I would be her first client and reference. I'm writing my own copy for the website and I've got a contact who's designing the logo for me. It's terrific fun, actually, and Piers put me in touch with his accountant to explain about submitting a business plan to the bank and being self-employed. That side of it's a bit mind-blowing, I have to admit.'

'But you're enjoying it?'

She nodded. 'I am. The next thing is to look for something to rent ready for when Hester sells Bridge House. It'll have to be very small, that's all I can say!'

'Hester must be really gutted about moving.' He suddenly remembered her expression when he'd come back from the telephone call. 'I hope Mum will feel that she can talk to her soon.'

'Hester will understand,' Clio told him. 'Really she will. Just relax, Jonah.'

'I will,' he said. 'Honestly, I will. I'm going to concentrate on all the ways I can use this new business Time 4. Picking me up from railway stations, getting scripts sorted out, choosing presents . . . Are you staying at Michaelgarth for dinner this evening?'

'Yes,' she answered, slightly surprised by the change of direction. 'Why?'

'Oh, nothing,' he said lightly, concealing his pleasure. 'I just wondered.'

After they'd gone, Hester found that she was as unsettled as she'd been before they'd arrived. She could hardly believe that Lucy had been labouring under such an appalling misapprehension for the greater part of her life, and again and again she remonstrated with herself for neglecting her after Michael's death and Eleanor's departure for America.

'I should have written again,' she murmured. 'I shouldn't have left it to a child of four or five to decide whether she wanted to be reminded of the past. I shouldn't have simply assumed that she was happy with Michael's aunt.'

She piled more logs onto the fire, made more tea, and then wandered about aimlessly, wondering exactly how Lucy had reacted to the unexpected telephone call. It had been clear from Jonah's expression that she'd received the news with mixed emotions; clear too that she was not ready to talk.

'And I can't blame her,' muttered Hester, pausing to stroke St Francis, gaining a small measure of comfort from the mechanical, smoothing action. 'What a shock it must have been. Oh, how she must have hated us all.'

Presently she sat down at the table in the breakfast-room and began a letter to Blaise, explaining the terrible misunderstanding and Jonah's reaction to the truth.

You came closest to it when you suggested that Eleanor might have turned Lucy against us once they were all in London, though it never occurred to me for a single second that she might believe such a terrible thing. Why should it? I didn't even know that Lucy had witnessed the fight. Jonah is clearly relieved that he can continue in his good opinion of his grandfather but I gather that Lucy isn't yet ready to rejoice. And who shall blame her! I wish I knew what to do but I am afraid to interfere and feel that the ball should be left in her court to respond to when she thinks the time is right. Yet that was the attitude I took all those years ago, and see where it got us all. Perhaps I should write to her.

Oh, it was so good to see Jonah again, Blaise. I thank God he came back. To think that he too might have carried that terrible burden all his life. I can only imagine that Eleanor saw her opportunity and was determined that Lucy wasn't going to stand in her way of getting Michael to herself at last. She probably had no real idea of the damage she was doing; Eleanor was always a very self-centred woman – tunnel vision, they'd call it now – and she had no imagination. Jonah told us that Lucy didn't want to leave Bridge House that night, and that she defied Eleanor and said she wouldn't go. I suspect that Eleanor just said the first thing she could think of that would make Lucy obey her.

I am in an odd state of shock, though it is a relief to have Jonah's silence explained. What a comfort Clio has been to both of us. She and Jonah are becoming attached to one another but it is too early to be sure how they truly feel. She's looking for some small flat or cottage to rent in Dulverton and I've decided to put Bridge House on the market at last. Perhaps that will galvanize me into taking positive action as to what to do next. Yet I still feel that there is something else to do before I leave: it's a strong feeling that Bridge House has some final part to play in this small drama. I should like to think that Lucy might come to see me, just once before I go, but it is probably asking far too much. I must be glad that Jonah has come back.

With love,

Hester

PS. I can't get over the horror of Lucy living with this ghastly thing for all these years.

CHAPTER TWENTY-NINE

In the cathedral, outside the chapel of St John the Baptist, Lucy stood staring up at the Chagall window with its vivid jewel colours and strange animals and the winged people playing all kinds of instruments. She glanced at the plaque below the window which proclaims, 'O praise God in his holiness . . . let everything that has breath praise the Lord', and indeed it looked as if all the odd-looking creatures were rejoicing in some way. She wished that she too could rejoice: she knew that it was incumbent upon her to rejoice, to be grateful and happy now that she knew that a lifetime's truth had all been a terrible mistake and that Eleanor had lied.

Staring up at the window, Lucy steadily swallowed down the bitter-tasting bile of resentment and anger – and guilt. Why, she asked herself, why was it not possible simply to accept the truth and be glad? After all, she *was* glad – of *course* she was glad to know that her father was not guilty of killing his friend and running away. Here was the relief for which she'd longed; that she could think about him again, freely and lovingly. And she wanted to – oh, how she wanted to – and yet, following fast on the heels of the shame and misery she'd nursed in secret for so long, had come a huge wave of bitterness and terrible rage that was steadily filling the great space where once the secret horror had greenly flourished, and was cramming itself into every little corner so that there was no room left for joy.

Fiercely Lucy stared away the tears that brimmed in her eyes, blurring the glorious colours and the happy, dancing creatures. Her tears of bitterness distorted the joyful scene and she blinked them away, touching the back of her hand to her eyes, setting her lips more tightly together.

'Why didn't you tell me before?' Jerry had asked, shocked. She'd seen at once that he was terribly hurt to know that she had never shared with him something that had been such an integral part of her. She could almost see him thinking: What else might she be hiding? and she'd been filled with new anxiety and despair. To damage Jerry's trust was unthinkable.

'Listen,' she'd said urgently, kneeling beside his chair, holding his hands, 'just listen for a minute . . .' and she'd told him the whole story properly, trying to show that, even by the time they'd met, she'd buried her knowledge so deeply that it was impossible to disinter it. Even as she talked she could see the pitfalls looming ahead of her: if she'd buried it so deeply then why had it continued to affect her so much? If she hadn't needed to confide because it wasn't important then why was she now so adversely affected by this new discovery?

She'd thought: I can't win with this one. He's simply got to trust me. He must understand that this doesn't reflect on him in any way.

'I knew there was something,' he'd said at last, 'but I always put it down to the fact that you'd lost both your parents so traumatically.'

'And part of it was,' she'd cried, hoping to lessen the importance of the other thing in his eyes and so preserve his confidence in her need of him. 'And you helped me to deal with it, Jerry. You know you did.'

They'd talked for hours, until they were both exhausted, and Jerry – true to form – was already beginning to think less about his own shock at her secrecy and more about her reaction to Jonah's discovery.

'But you can be happy now?' he'd said hopefully, making it more a statement than a question – almost willing her to accept the joy – and she'd responded quickly that she could, of *course* she could, relieved that he seemed to be ready to accept that no harm to their relationship had been done.

'Poor old Luce,' he'd said. 'Poor Luce. What a terrible thing to live with. But now you'll be free of it. Thank goodness Jonah got to the truth of it.'

She longed to repay this generosity, to be happy simply because it would delight him to see her step free. Consciously she concentrated on the wonderful news – Edward had not died – reliving the nightmare scene in the light of this information, seeing how everything fell into place. There *was* joy here, and relief, but at the same time it seemed that some great emotion against which she'd pitted herself for so long had been unexpectedly removed; as if she'd leaned all her life against a restricting wall that had been suddenly toppled, and now she was kneeling helplessly amongst the rubble rather than standing upright, gazing out at a new and glorious view. This was crazy, she told herself anxiously. Surely she hadn't been actually *dependent* on the fear and horror and guilt? Yet it felt as if she had been; as if, in some macabre way, it had sustained her, and now that it was gone she felt exposed and confused amongst the ruins of the carefully constructed lie.

Occasionally, her hatred of Eleanor threatened to overwhelm her and she prayed for deliverance from such a destructive emotion. Yet it seemed unbearably cruel that those few words should have had the ability to poison her life: to make her unable to think happily of her father whom she'd loved so much. And then there was Hester . . .

'She'd love to see you,' Jonah had said, 'only she thinks you might need time to adjust. She sends her love.'

That had been several weeks ago and still Lucy was unable to make the necessary gesture of friend-liness.

After all, she never wrote to me: the thought rose childishly in her mind and Lucy dismissed it with an impatient exclamation of self-contempt. Hester's behaviour too must be seen in the brighter light of the truth. Here was the chance to make all things new, the real opportunity to change for which she'd strived, and she seemed incapable of taking it. Turning from the window she made her way through the cathedral, back to Jerry; past the Lambert Barnard paintings of the Bishops of Chichester where they'd first met, and back home to his hopeful, watchful gaze that longed to see her set free at last.

Coming out of All Saints' church, Clio paused for a moment to look out over the trees and roofs of Dulverton with a sense of pleasure. She loved this little town, and the prospect of living in it excited her. In her bag were the details of a flat for rent: a small piece of an old house, high on an attic floor, from which she would have a view much like this one.

Clio was seized with a tremor of excitement and apprehension at the prospect of this further step towards complete independence. She'd driven Hester into Dulverton this morning, to do some shopping and go to the library, whilst she collected the details of the flat from the estate agent's office. Having made an appointment to view she'd come out into the street, passing around the double flight of steps outside the town hall, still clutching the details in her hand and glancing at it now and then as if she could hardly believe her luck. Collecting her chaotic thoughts, she'd folded up the paper and pushed it into her bag, determined not to allow herself to become too hopeful. That's when she'd decided to spend a few minutes in the church.

Ever since Christmas she'd fallen into a habit of taking a few moments out of the rush of her newly expanding life; going into All Saints' to sit in the corner of a pew, to spend time in meditation. Very occasionally she recaptured a fleeting sense of the peace and joy she'd experienced at the convent, though most of the time she'd find that she was simply allowing plans and anxieties to crowd out any quietness of mind.

Nevertheless, she clung firmly to Blaise's advice: 'Never forget what you've experienced but don't come to rely on it.' She didn't rely on it but gradually she was coming to value these moments, and now, standing below the medieval tower that watched over the town, she felt a tiny echo of that peaceful detachment from stress bringing her strength. She took in a deep breath, noticing the daffodils fluttering in the sharp, cold April breeze, listening to the bustle of the town drifting upwards, before she set off down the path. Passing under the lich-gate, through Bank Square and into Fore Street, she saw Hester emerging from the library and hailed her.

'I've got an appointment for tomorrow afternoon,' she told her triumphantly. 'It looks good, Hes. It's very small but it's all newly done up. Three flights of stairs, though! I'll be thin as a rake. I was hoping you'd come with me to view it. Will you be able to manage them, d'you think?'

'As long as I'm allowed a breather on the way up,' said Hester cheerfully. 'Of course I shall come. Time to go home?'

'I'm afraid so,' answered Clio regretfully. 'I wish we could stop for coffee but I've got to dash over to the Coles to meet someone delivering furniture. We'll stop off and have tea and delicious cake in Lewis's tomorrow after we've viewed the flat. I asked the agents if they had anything new that might interest you but nothing has come in that you haven't already seen. I wish you could find something, Hes.'

'So do I,' said Hester, waiting for Clio to unlock the car doors. 'The difficulty is that I don't know quite what it is that I want, which makes it rather complicated.'

As they drove out of the town Hester quelled a twinge of uneasiness, determined to trust this sense of waiting that had grown so strong: it was a gift, knowing how to wait, and she was trying to accept it patiently.

'Something will turn up,' Clio said confidently, buoyed up by her own good fortune. 'I just know it will. I'm sorry I can't stop, Hes. I should be back about four o'clock if all goes well but I'll phone you if I get held up.'

They crossed the little bridge and then Clio reversed the car, turning so as to be ready to drive out again. Hester climbed out, clutching her library books and her shopping, and waved her off. It was only after she'd found her key and unlocked the door that she saw the parcel leaning in the corner of the porch. Clearly the postman had been unable to fit it through the letter-box earlier and she hadn't heard him ring the bell.

She carried her things in and then returned for the parcel, a medium-sized Jiffy bag, reused and with Blaise's familiar writing. It was with a sense of anticipation that Hester went through to the kitchen, pushed the kettle onto the hotplate and then hurried back into the breakfast-room to open the parcel. St Francis came pacing to meet her, jumping up onto the table and pressing himself beneath her arm, purring a welcome. She stroked him with one hand, holding the letter with the other, waiting for the kettle to boil.

Darling Hes,

I'm sorry it's taken a little while to answer your letter. There was so much in it to think about and I've spent a great deal of time trying to take it all in. Yes, I did suspect that Eleanor might be at the root of the problem but I had no idea of the

411

extent to which she might have harmed Lucy. No wonder that she didn't want to talk about the past to Jonah or that she had tried to wipe us all from her memory. At one point, in a previous letter, you wrote that Jonah said she had decided that the time had come to confront the past in order to deal with new difficulties in her life; she needed to change in order to cope. Well, we can only be grateful that she was courageous enough to go through with it. I fully agree with you that the thought of her carrying this weight for so long is appalling but what worries me now is that she might buckle under new pressures. To keep this secret hidden for so long will have required energy and determination, and their sudden removal might allow other adverse feelings to flourish in their place. Imagine the temptation she's under now to put all that energy into hating Eleanor and feeling bitter about the damage she's suffered! I'm sure that she will want to embrace this opportunity for change but it might prove surprisingly difficult. I remember writing to you about something like this back last autumn and reminding you about the enclosed book on the teachings of St John of the Cross, which I know you've read. It just might help if you read it again in regard to Lucy. I admit to feeling fearful for her, Hes. She'll need help, and who better to give it than St John of the Cross? Of course I might be quite wrong but I send it because it feels right of this moment when you are both very vivid with me. I've marked some pages relating to the *desire* for change and the importance of *remembering* that desire when one feels incapable of any effort and overwhelmed by failure. I wish you could get her to Bridge House – I feel that it's important.

Anyway, enough of this for the present. There is something else I want to 'talk' to you about, Hes. I've been feeling for a while now that I should retire from the chaplaincy at St Bede's although I hope to remain available for the sisters and the Abbey, should they require my assistance at any time. A younger man, just retiring from parish life but looking for a house for duty, is very willing to take my place at St Bede's and I've decided to move into Hexham. Would you consider joining me, Hes? Do you think we could share a house together as we once did all those years ago? I have some savings and you should get a reasonable share when you sell. Shall we buy a small cottage or a flat together? I know how much you love this part of the world and how attached you are to the sisters. I think we could be happy, Hes. Let me know what you think.

The rest of his writing blurred and swam as she stared down at the page and she was conscious of a high whistling noise that had been going on for some time in the background. The kettle was boiling. Hester put the letter down and briefly buried her face in St Francis' warm fur before hurrying through to the kitchen. Happy, grateful tears poured down her small face as she made coffee and took it back with her to the table, settling down to read part of the letter again and again.

It was much later, when she'd just begun to accustom herself to the joy, that she saw a line scribbled on the back of the sheet.

PS. It has just occurred to me, Hes. Have you thought of inviting Lucy to see your latter-day version of the Midsummer Cushion? A very healing prospect if you think about it?

Hester laid the letter down thoughtfully and took up the Jiffy bag. The book was familiar to her: *The Impact of God* written by the Carmelite Father Iain Matthew. She sat for a while, the book lying beside her on the table whilst she drank some coffee, momentarily distracted from her new-found joy. Blaise had an inner wisdom she'd never attained and she was fearful now that she might misinterpret him. She wondered how the book might help: should she read it, hoping that if she and Lucy were to meet it might give her some insight into Lucy's pain? Or should she simply give the book to Jonah to pass on – and, if she were to do that, how would Lucy receive it? How would it assist her to step free from the past? Blaise's warning about Lucy's inability to accept the truth filled her with fear and she prayed silently for guidance.

Presently she opened the book, so as to refresh her memory, and the opening line struck her forcibly with its relevance to Lucy's need. 'St John of the Cross speaks to people who feel unable to change.'

At once the words filled her with an amazing confidence. Putting the book back into the bag, Hester seized a felt pen from the jar of pencils and biros on the table and wrote across the label in large black letters: 'THIS IS FOR LUCY'. With a sigh of relief, as if something vital had already been accomplished, she put the bag aside and once again picked up Blaise's letter.

'Do you think we could share a house together as we did all those years ago?'

'Yes,' she answered him silently, and happy tears flowed again. 'Oh, yes, Blaise, I think we could.'

CHAPTER THIRTY

April continued a capricious, teasing month, offering the benison of unexpectedly warm spells that gave way to cruel hail storms, and with a heavy fall of snow on St George's Day that weighted the crimson flowers of the azalea and laid a dazzling carpet for the bluebells in the wood. Wrapped in her warm new shawl, Hester paced the terrace in the sunshine and withdrew into the house when the black clouds gathered; and each day she waited for a message from Lucy.

When the heavy downpours of freezing rain fell high up on the Chains, the level of the river rose at an alarming rate. The great tide of icy water roared and raced, foaming whitely over the rounded stones, battering broken branches against the stone piers of the bridge, rising rapidly even as she watched, first from the terrace, exhilarated as usual by this dramatic event, and then from the shelter of the drawing-room as the rain drove down in chill, soaking spikes and the thundering of the Barle in flood obliterated any other sound.

One cold evening in early May, when the river was running slow and quiet in its bed and a thrush was singing at the end of the garden, the telephone rang. Hester shifted St Francis' warm weight from her side and got up from the sofa to answer it.

'Hester,' said Jonah. 'Great news. Mum says she'd like to come and see you and she says that the last week in May will be fine. She's arranging for someone to stay with Dad. I didn't tell her why you wanted it to be later rather than earlier, I just said that you were going up to Hexham for a week and that there were things happening to do with selling the house. Anyway, it'll give her a bit more time to adjust.'

'That's wonderful news.' Hester could barely control the swift uprush of spirits. 'I am so pleased. Will you tell her so?'

'Of course I will.'

'And you'll let me know the dates once she's fixed with whoever it is who will stay with your father? Any time after the twenty-first will be fine. She'll stay here, of course? For as long as she likes.'

'I've made a note of the date. I'll tell her.'

Clio emerged from the study and Hester said,

'Oh, here's Clio. I expect you'd like a word?' and held out the phone to her.

Clio took it, only very slightly embarrassed at the assumption that they would want to speak to each other, and Hester went back into the drawing-room. She was too deeply moved by grateful joy to be able to continue the conversation; all she wished to do was to sit for a moment and think about Lucy, returning at last to Bridge House.

'Hi, Jonah,' Clio was saying brightly. 'How are you?'

'Bored, frustrated, driving myself mad. In other words, I'm writing. How about you?'

'It's going fairly well. I've got Lizzie's event up to speed. She's away working for most of July and August, some TV sitcom thing, and so she wants everything ready to go before she starts. I've designed the leaflets and we've decided to target sixth-form colleges and libraries.' She'd relaxed now, perching on a chair at the table, and hunched slightly over the telephone as if creating an intimate place for them both. 'The Coles are an ongoing job, which is really great from my point of view. We're working on the dining-room. So when are you coming down to see my new place before I move into it next month?'

'Soon. Is this a formal invitation?'

'Well, I mentioned it to Hester, who said that she'd be away next week if you'd like to keep me company for a few days.'

Jonah gave a crack of laughter. 'Good old Hes. Not quite your stereotypical godmother, is she? Nothing remotely protective or motherly about Hes.'

'Hester doesn't do maternal. I remember she said that to me once. She thought it would be a relief for us to be on our own for a change. Well? It would be nice to have some company . . .'

'You've got it. Just let me know the dates. Does that mean I shan't see Hester, though?'

'I think you've got a thing about my godmother,' Clio said lightly. 'You could come at either week-end; before she goes or when she comes back. I can't take her this time but she's determined to drive herself. I feel worried but at the same time I think she needs to have a go. She's so thrilled at the thought of being with Blaise again that I think it will give her all the energy she needs.'

'That's what I wanted to talk to her about, you see. We never got as far as what happened after the war, with Hes and Blaise and Edward all together, and it might be important. I'm trying to see the shape of this play; where to begin, where to end. Mum seems a bit more relaxed about it now. She's coming down to Bridge House, by the way, in a couple of weeks' time.'

'But that's fantastic. Hester must be really pleased.'

'She sounded it. I am too. I think none of us can really move forward until Mum's been back to Bridge House. I know Hester feels the same.'

'And was it Hester's message that made her change her mind?'

'Yes, it was. It was the thing needed to sort of jolt her out of her shock. It made her curious, you see. Hester simply said, "Tell Lucy that I'd love to show her the Midsummer Cushion once more before I leave Bridge House." She was horrified to hear that poor old Hes was having to go and I think that that was part of her decision too. It would be terrible to think that she'd left it too late ever to see Bridge House again.'

'Good for Lucy,' Clio said. 'I'm looking forward to meeting her . . . for all sorts of reasons.'

He chuckled. 'She wants to meet you too. Don't know why. Just something I mentioned in passing, I think.'

'What?' asked Clio immediately. 'What did you say?'

'Can't remember now,' he said maddeningly. 'So what are these dates then?'

She told him and waited while he muttered and checked through a diary and muttered some more and then told her which days he could manage.

'Can you meet me from the station?'

'I suppose so,' she said with exaggerated patience. 'Are you ever going to be able to drive again?'

'I have a confession,' he said. 'I might as well make it at once. I've never passed a test. I have an antipathy to driving. I am clumsy, get distracted easily, crash into unsuspecting cyclists, and anyway I don't need to – at the moment.' A silence. 'Does that mean it's all off?' he asked anxiously.

'No,' she said, after a moment. 'No, of course not. I'm just . . . well, surprised, that's all.'

'But not horrified and repulsed?'

She laughed. 'You're an idiot, Jonah. Of course I'll pick you up. Let me know when you can get down and I'll tell Hester that you're coming for the weekend before she goes to Hexham, and staying on for a few days. We could go to Woods one evening . . .'

Later, she put her head round the door and grinned at Hester.

'Great news about Lucy, isn't it?'

'It's wonderful news. I can hardly take it in.' Hester removed her reading spectacles and looked at Clio with a kind of happy disbelief. 'I've imagined it so often, you know; going through it in my head, and trying to picture exactly how it would be, but none of the scenarios quite fit satisfactorily. I shall have to ask Jonah to write the script for us.'

'It's rather scary,' agreed Clio. 'It'll be best for you and Lucy to do this one alone, I imagine? I shall be around, of course. In case you need me.'

Hester nodded. 'Quite alone,' she agreed. 'I think that Lucy and I will have much to say to each other. But I hope that she'll stay for at least one night and anyway, you'll want to meet her, won't you?'

The question sounded innocent enough but Clio coloured a little.

'Of course I will, after all you've told me about her. Oh, by the way, Jonah can manage the first part of next week when you're away in Hexham.' She spoke quite casually, though unable to repress a little smile at the thought of it. 'But he'd like to come earlier, for the weekend, so as to see you before you go. I've said that's OK.'

'Good.' Hester replaced her reading spectacles and smiled back at Clio. 'You'll have fun.'

Clio's smile grew wider: she beamed. 'I know,' she said happily.

*   *   *

So it was in late May that Lucy came again to Bridge House. Horrified at the prospect of such a crucial meeting taking place on a railway platform – a feeling that Hester had readily understood – she'd insisted on taking a taxi from the station. Hester was waiting for her on the terrace when the car drove in over the bridge and turned again to go back out. When the sound of the engine had died away, Lucy passed through the little gate. The two women stood staring at one another, each seeking some sign of recognition in the other's face, while the river murmured in the hot sunshine and down in the wood the cuckoo called.

This time it was Lucy who looked down, just a little, at the older woman, but it was Hester who spoke first.

'No grey rabbit this time?'

Lucy smiled involuntarily and Hester reached out for her hand, holding it tightly for a brief moment.

'Not this time.' Lucy returned the pressure readily. 'Though I still have him. He was a great favourite with Jonah.' She set down her case and looked about her curiously. 'I've thought and thought about how this would be,' she said. 'How much I'd remember and whether I'd think that everything had shrunk. You know how people say that, when they go back years later to places they've known as children? The odd thing is that I don't really remember any of it at all. Just the atmosphere and odd flashes of things.' She grimaced a little. 'You'd think I'd remember this place particularly, wouldn't you?'

'Not necessarily. You children spent much more time in the garden and the wood than on the terrace. If you were inside the drawing-room looking out on a dark wild night you might have a different experience, of course.'

Lucy looked at her again, a long, searching look. 'What a mess,' she said bitterly. 'Wasn't it, Hester? I can't get over the waste. All those years of thinking that it was all my fault.'

Hester was silent for a few seconds, watching her compassionately. She gave a tiny sigh. 'I only hope you can forgive us, otherwise nothing can be salvaged. You being here is . . . it's a miracle. Thank you for coming, Lucy.'

Lucy leaned on the wall, staring down into the water, and when she spoke again, Hester came close to her so as to hear her voice above the sound of the river.

'Why didn't you write to me, Hester?'

The older woman felt unexpected tears pricking and stinging her eyes. 'Probably because you didn't answer my letter,' she said remorsefully. 'I thought you might not want to resurrect the past, you see. Eleanor told me that you'd said you'd settled in with your aunt and that you'd soon be starting school . . .'

'*Eleanor* told you?'

'She wrote to tell us that Michael had been killed and that she was going to America but that letters and cards would be forwarded to you from the London flat. We all sent Christmas cards and letters: me and Nanny and Jack. I remember he was very particular about me sending his card. And then we heard from Eleanor just after I'd sent the package to you.'

'Jack sent me a card?' Her face crumpled, her lips trembled. 'Oh, how much that would have meant, back then.'

'You never got them.' It was a statement, not a question. 'So that explains it. I never thought of that, you see. I just assumed that you were busy with a new life, after all, you were only four or five – and you must take into account that I had no idea that you'd seen the fight and that Eleanor had lied to you. Even so,' Hester shook her head, 'it doesn't excuse the fact that I should have stayed in touch. Made sure. I was taken up with Edward, and with Blaise. I didn't think clearly. That was unforgivable.'

426

Lucy covered Hester's hand with her own where it lay clenched on the stone wall. 'I keep going over it until I think I shall go mad, you see,' she said. 'I don't want to but I can't seem to help myself. I can't step free of it. And then Jonah gave me your message about the Midsummer Cushion and it was like a kind of trigger. I always feel that it all started with the Midsummer Cushion and that, if I saw it again, I might be able to put everything into perspective. You said that I should see it before you leave Bridge House – we'll talk about that later, Hester, if we may – and I wondered if you meant that I ought to see it on your wall, where I first saw it.'

'That's not quite the way of it,' answered Hester carefully. 'I have a different reason although I hope that the outcome will be the same. Are you ready to see it now or would you like to see your room or have some coffee or something?'

Lucy shook her head. 'I'd like to see the Midsummer Cushion first,' she said. 'I feel that it's terribly important somehow.'

The two women stared at each other, each one's heart was beating fast: Lucy's with a fearful anticipation; Hester's with terror that she might have misjudged the situation.

Hester swallowed down her fear resolutely and

turned towards the house. 'Come, then,' she said. 'Come and see.'

Lucy went with her into the house, staring round as they passed through the drawing-room, trying to fit the shape of it into the memories that had haunted her for so long, and Hester hesitated, eyebrows raised, as if suggesting that Lucy might like to take time to look around her or ask a question, but Lucy instinctively shook her head – all that must come later – and followed her out into the passage. On the hall table a Jiffy bag with the words 'THIS IS FOR LUCY' written across it in black ink was propped against a jar, and she glanced at it curiously before going on again – not up the stairs as she had imagined but through the kitchen and so into the garden. Hester crossed the lawn, walking quickly as if to ward off questions, and Lucy hurried to keep up with her, growing more and more puzzled. As they approached the gate in the hawthorn hedge Hester paused, turning to Lucy.

'Remember the vegetable garden? And the chickens?' she asked. 'Yes? Well, it wasn't always a vegetable patch. It's just that we needed to grow our own food during the war. It used to be a little meadow, you see, and afterwards, when I moved back after I'd retired, I had an idea.'

She stood aside and Lucy went up to the field

gate, still frowning with puzzlement, and then caught her breath in a tiny gasp of amazement. The small square hayfield, some three-quarters of an acre, was a patch of vivid colour. Bounded by flowering hawthorn hedges, the sweet feathery grasses were thickly sown with wild flowers. Blue cornflowers, scarlet field poppies, butter-yellow buttercups, rich pink clover and delicate lilac-coloured lady's-smocks all bloomed in abundance. The rosy haze of sorrel clouded the edges of the hayfield and the scent of bluebells drifted in the warm air.

'"It is a very old custom among villagers in summer time to stick a piece of greensward full of field flowers and place it in their cottages, which ornaments are called Midsummer Cushions,"' quoted Hester softly. 'I decided that, rather than try to mend and patch the tapestry, or to grieve over its loss, I would try to make something new. I wanted to create a living reminder of the Midsummer Cushion. What do you think, Lucy?'

Lucy bit her lips. 'I think you were right,' she said at last. 'Can we . . . go in?'

Hester lifted the latch and swung the gate open. Lucy passed through into the hayfield, advanced a few steps, and then turned to look back at Hester with an expression of wonder.

'It's quite beautiful,' she said. 'All the flowers, just as I remember them.'

She extended her arms, as if she would embrace them, and Hester smiled, remembering the small Lucy stretching out her eager hands to the silken flowers in the frame.

'Rather better like this,' suggested Hester, 'than imprisoned under glass? And we can pick some for you to take home as a keepsake. You could press them into a book, if you would like it?'

She saw that Lucy was near to tears and she put out a hand to her, just as she had reached out to her all those years before, and they went together into the hayfield, becoming a part of the small tapestry of living colour that rippled and danced in the warm west wind.

THE END

ACKNOWLEDGEMENTS

Extract from 'Folk Tale' by R. S. Thomas, from *Experimenting with an Amen*, Macmillan, London, 1986: © Kunjana Thomas, 2001.

Extracts from the poems of John Clare are taken from *John Clare – Selected Poems*, edited by Jonathan Bate, Faber and Faber, London, 2004.

My thanks to Sarah Jordon of Time 2 (www.time-2.com) for introducing me to Lifestyle Management.

My thanks also to Caroline Day of the Devon Lupus Group (www.lupusuk.com).

THE WAY WE WERE
Marcia Willett

It was in the middle of a snowstorm when Tiggy
arrived at the remote house on Bodmin Moor. She
was alone, her partner tragically dead in an accident,
and Julia, her dearest friend, welcomed her into
her warm and chaotic family. Tiggy started to
live again and await the birth of her child,
temporarily secure in the supportive
love which surrounded her.

But Tiggy's happiness is destined to be short-lived,
and nearly thirty years later, when her son is about
to become a father himself, the next generation
discovers that there are secrets from the past
which must be uncovered . . .

A wonderfully engrossing new novel from
this well-loved author.

9780593057735

AVAILABLE NOW FROM BANTAM PRESS

BANTAM PRESS